H

T

Retribution

Published by The Creative Peak(TCP)

Book Design: T M Goble
Cover Image: Copyright Shutterstock

Newsletter

Receive T M Goble's Occasional Newsletter
containing
Information future publications
Insights ino the writing process
Full details at the end of the book

01

Alex shivered. Today would be a challenge. The fond images that had been snatched away from her would return. They would be traumatic. She needed to be brave. No one else on the trip to Brighton knew of her secret as she had never shared details of her former life with her new colleagues.

She and Jack, her police partner, strolled through the bustling holidaymakers along West Street. The visitors' exuberance and excitement were in sharp contrast to the dark thoughts which filled her mind making her stomach roll with tension. He touched her arm, 'You are thoughtful today. Less chatty than normal.'

With no sensible reply, she shrugged and turned her face away in case he noticed the moistening of her eyes, 'No issue, feeling quiet today.' They had left their police motorbikes at the Conference Centre and with time to spare wandered to find coffee. Their services would not be required for the diplomatic escort for another hour. The ozone filled her nostrils as they progressed towards the seaside at the end of the street. As her heartbeat quickened, she gulped to avoid the nausea which rose in her throat. It would be the beach that would force the images from the past to invade her mind. Keeping her emotion hidden from Jack would be difficult, as he always managed to spot her mood.

The early chill wind had kept them in their motorbike leathers, but they now unzipped their jackets as the sun punched through the clouds. Trying to avoid being melancholy about her recurring thoughts she forced a grin onto her reluctant lips, 'You are not chatty.'

He grinned, 'You do enough talking for both of us.'

'Untrue.' She chuckled as there was an element of truth in his words.

Glancing in the shop windows they drifted further along the street in amiable silence. The cafes and pubs were busy and the laughter and high spirits of the crowd helped to lighten her mood for a short while. She liked Jack, who had been her mentor since she had joined Scotland Yard's Diplomatic Protection Group. A tall, muscular man with dark hair greying at the temples and a handsome face. He kept calm and advised without bossing her. Having passed her probation in the unit, he had requested that she became his partner. Whether he had any other than professional motives, she had never discovered. That suited her as a new man in her life held no appeal. Her current outlook wasn't conducive to a serious relationship. As a partner he was perfect, steady in his outlook, professional and he always followed the rules.

Finally, they reached the end of the street and the wide promenade which bordered the seafront stretched out before them. As they waited to cross the busy road, she struggled to keep her emotions under control. Had Jack noticed? Attempting to control herself she allowed her eyes to sweep across the wide walkway while she studiously avoided the vista of the coastline. Would the haunting images ever leave her? The vibrant handsome face with the striking blue eyes that sparkled with mischief filled her mind. Images of him rolled through her thoughts like a photograph album. Each led her towards the major disaster in her life. Could she ever forget the death and destruction? In the early days of her grief an idea had formed. Holding on to it gave her a reason to reshape her life. It wouldn't bring him back, but it focused her thoughts during the long grey days and the endless lonely nights. It had grown as she had schemed and plotted, and then with hope and determination she had initiated the first steps of her plan. It had become her life's mission. It was her secret. Not even her family had any idea of what she intended to achieve.

Jack turned towards the Conference Centre, 'Enjoy yourself, I'll go and check on the bikes.'

Nodding, he quickened his pace and strode along the service road behind the Centre.

She didn't need to reply which would have been difficult as the sight of the promenade caused another gulp to clog her throat and words were impossible. She lowered her head and walked away, grateful to be alone.

With tears in her eyes, she rested against the blue promenade rail. The salty tang of the seaside assailed her nostrils. The holidaymakers on the beach, intent on enjoying themselves were loud and excitable. The wind blew in gusts causing the beach umbrellas to twist and flap while seagulls soared overhead screeching as they dived to snatch food from unsuspecting hands. The clouds raced across the sky and there were intermittent blasts of bright vivid sunshine making the sea sparkle. The waves dragged the shingle as the tide changed. Despair gripped her. The last visit had been so different. Full of fun, activity and glamour. Returning to this location had been difficult. The Sergeant who allocated the duties didn't know the memories it would invoke as keeping her past a secret was an integral part of her plan. No one must find out. Waiting was an endless component of the job in the Diplomatic Protection Team. Exact timings were tricky. Today it allowed her too much unoccupied time and forced her to remember the joyous occasions when she had been here with her husband. A scene from his last action blockbuster had been filmed on Brighton beach. That day she had stood on the promenade watching the action and the endless retakes. Afterwards they'd had a romantic candlelit dinner at an exclusive restaurant overlooking the beach. It had been a perfect day.

Screwing up her eyes, she prevented the tears from forming although a sob caught in her throat. A few weeks later he had been killed. His life terminated in a hail of bullets. The scene was ingrained on her memory. The blood, the screaming and the barrel of the gun. Three years had passed but no closure had been secured. The terrorists were still at large. The authorities, despite early action, had made it a pending file awaiting further information. They had failed. Despite her protests, nothing had happened. Three armed men had carried out the merciless attack in the heart of London, but the police had not captured them. She, Matthew and her best friend Mariam had received invitations to the Odeon, Leicester Square for a film premiere and had arrived early. Stepping from the taxi the area was quiet and even the red carpet was still rolled up at the entrance waiting to be placed in its final position.

Mariam had looked stunning in a midnight blue and silver sari, whilst she'd opted for a turquoise satin flowing gown with a plunging neckline. Matthew in his tuxedo looked suave and handsome. As they stood chatting together on the pavement, with no warning, three men opened fire.

Despite the warmth of her motorbike leathers she shivered. Why had she been spared? Luck? There would never be an answer, but her husband and best friend had died. Guilt of survival had overtaken her dragging her down into the depths of depression and despair. With the help and comfort of her family she had somehow struggled back to face the world once more.

The radio earpiece crackled forcing away the sad memories. Why had her name been mentioned? The Sergeant standing outside the Brighton Conference Centre caught her eye. Holding the microphone close to her mouth to blot out the noise from the beach. 'Yes, Sarge.'

'One of our homeless friends, complete with shopping trolley and cardboard, is about to set up for a sleep in the promenade shelter.' Alex scanned the shelters and nodded, 'Can you move him on.'

Not a normal job for a member of an elite police division, but she would do it in good spirits to help her colleagues. 'Yes, Sarge.'

Alex strolled along the promenade. Visitors had been encouraged to move to Marine Parade on the other side of the Palace Pier until the International Conference had finished and the delegates had dispersed. The public were kept moving outside the Centre. With many international VIPS in the audience, security levels were high.

The man, scruffy in several layers of ragged and dirty clothing, snarled as she approached. 'I'm a British citizen, with a shopping trolley and a few bits of cardboard and I'm entitled to sit on a public bench. Alex nodded but kept her expression neutral; within a few minutes he would have the cardboard wrapped around him and be fast asleep. His smell reached her. Beneath the whiff of cheap cider lay the more ominous stench of body odour mingled with urine. She took a step back in an attempt distance herself from the unpleasant aroma. 'You cannot stay here, it's a major police operation. People can pass along the prom, but no one can stop.'

He waved a dismissive hand though his hands trembled as he clutched the trolley's handle; his eyes were not glazed, and his voice hadn't slurred. The cider which would send him into a drunken stupor would be hidden in the trolley. Despite his ramshackle appearance he was in his mid-forties but living on the streets with dodgy alcohol and drugs had taken its toll. His hair hung in a tangled mess of straggly grey strands and his face was haggard and grimy.

Alex nodded towards the Sergeant who had given her the instruction to move him on. 'Come back later when we have gone.'

Eyeing her up and down, he ignored her comment, 'You are too pretty to be a copper and one that has a gun.'

Was the vague look managed? She suspected that his eyes would be sufficiently alert to nick anything that came into his path. Another glance to the Sergeant to check he wasn't watching before she stuffed her hand in her pocket, 'Here's a fiver, there's a cheap café under the prom, buy yourself a meal and a cup of tea.' She doubted he would, as alcohol would be more tempting, but she had tried to help. With a grunt he snatched the money and shuffled away.

When the conference reached its mid-morning break her escort duties would begin. It had been a forlorn expectation that joining the police after Matthew had died would allow her a chance to discover information about his death. At the time it had seemed the perfect way forward, but disillusionment had gripped her in recent months. It had been a naive assumption that she might solve the deaths of her husband and best friend while the combined efforts of the police had failed.

Alex pushed thoughts of Matthew aside otherwise she would plunge into a low mood for days, so with a resigned sigh she crossed to join her colleagues outside the Conference Centre. Many police officers were standing and waiting. A few nodded. The street sleeper had taken her money and disappeared.

Bored, she searched for something to attract her attention as she waited. A young boy and girl meandered their way along the pavement clutching their brand new buckets and spades. Their eyes gleamed with excitement. As they drew near, they hesitated. Their wide eyes looked at her and their parents noticed. Smiling at the adults, she crouched and gave them a small wave, 'Hello. Are you on your way to the beach?' Grinning, the little boy about five years old caught the hand of his younger sister and approached. 'What are your names?'

The little girl stepped forward to take charge; Alex giggled. 'I'm Emma and this is my big brother Liam. Are you a lady policeman?'

She giggled again, 'Yes, I am.'

Liam put his head on one side, 'The police have guns. Are you going to shoot anyone today?'

Alex held her breath, 'No one is shooting today as

most English police do not have guns.' She ignored the holster at her side. 'We are here to make sure everyone stays safe.'

He studied the other police nearby then with a wave of their hands they scampered back to their parents, who mouthed, 'Thank you.'

Her earpiece sprung into life, 'Officers for the Egyptian escort to appointed stations.'

Alex strode to her police motorbike. Jack, already astride of his bike, waved a greeting. Removing her general purpose earpiece, she put on her helmet and switched on the built in police radio and waited. The clouds scudded away and the sun shone brightly. They started the engines and at walking pace drifted the bikes to the front of the Centre to await the VIP.

She had calmed from her internal trauma of viewing the beach. During her last visit to Brighton it had been filled with extravagance, in true Hollywood style. It had been day upon day of the high gushing life of the film industry. The chats with Matthew's fans had become her highlight as she had been swept into the euphoria.

Checking her bike and the road ahead, she would take commands through her headset. Tears ran down her cheeks, but no one would see as she closed her visor and waited. The return to the holiday rendezvous had brought the memories flooding back. It reinforced her resolve to bring the killers to justice in whichever way possible. It would be an uphill task, as she had only one clue.

02

Alex's helmet isolated her from the world as she manoeuvered her bike into the starting position. Gulping away the tears, she resolved that after finishing her shift she would spend the evening alone in her flat planning her way forward. The lack of progress would make her sad, but she would not allow the killers to avoid justice. It was her only chance of ever regaining a normal life. She had been spared from the carnage and it had become imperative to have closure for her husband and best friend.

Forcing her mind back to her police duties she must wait until the VIP delegate had entered the car she had been assigned to escort. Jack had joked he wanted a peaceful time today so she was assigned to lead the diplomatic convoy. Reality hit her. How would a single police constable be able to track down terrorists when the combined forces of the police and Secret Services had failed? Would she never reach her goal? A deep breath didn't stem the flow of hidden tears within the helmet.

'I'll pull out to stop the traffic, you lead the Bentley.' Her focus returned. Jack's calm voice had detailed her operational duties. She forced herself to concentrate as her mind tended to drift. A quick flash of blue lights from Jack stopped the seafront traffic. She responded with a flash and pulled out into the road. The Bentley slid out behind her. Regretting she hadn't checked the route, she would follow her satnav which had already been programmed. With busy traffic and early season holidaymakers, she proceeded at a slow pace along the coast road towards the Palace Pier.

With a simple day planned to escort a minor diplomat, an early finish beckoned and then she would concentrate on her plans. Flashing her eyes wide open, the satnav indicated to take Madeira Drive and not the main coast road. There would be reasons, but as it wouldn't be what she expected, she needed to focus.

Alex grimaced and wiped the visor of her helmet. The dust from the hot road swirled, covering her and the Honda police motorbike. Her hopes of early success in her quest to find the killers of her husband had failed miserably, leaving her with a sense of frustration. It hadn't been as straightforward as she'd expected. Increasingly in the front line, she might lose her life in pointless action. Her plan had failed, but she didn't have another one, even though she'd filled sleepless nights with grandiose and impractical schemes.

The past few duties had been mundane and had given her time to deliberate, but no obvious strategy had emerged. Escorting VIPs, she had never heard of, had become the low point.

With a struggle, she kept her focus on the task. Blowing her whistle, she manoeuvred close to the early season holiday crowds lining Madeira Drive. The sun beat down as the morning developed, ozone filled her nostrils.

An elderly couple waited to cross the busy road. Alex

slowed her convoy to a stop, flashed blue lights to warn oncoming traffic and opened her hand for them to cross. Once safely across they acknowledged with a wave and beaming smiles.

Hot inside her police leathers from the late spring sunshine, her concentration wandered. Images of her past life flitted through her mind. With an impatient shake of her head, she pushed them away, trying to suppress the pain they brought. A lump formed in her throat and she wanted to scream out loud at the injustice that life had thrown at her.

Drifting forward, she used her whistle to warn a careless man, who had stepped into the road twenty metres ahead. She kept a careful eye on the crowds who would wander between the slow moving traffic. The errant holidaymaker peered through his overlarge sunglasses and scampered across with a quizzical glance at the two police outriders and the Bentley with tinted glass. She nodded to a police constable and community support officer who chatted at the roadside.

With practiced precision her eyes scanned the crowd, but the tourists, intent on enjoying the sunshine, had little interest in the slow-moving car and motor bikes as they passed. She slowed to a walking pace at a zebra crossing. The following Bentley and the police bike at the rear would reduce their speed in unison. Her mind drifted. What could she do to resurrect her plan? Nothing else mattered. She had to bring the perpetrators to justice. Initially she had assumed that the task she had set herself was achievable, but as the days drifted past and the months dragged by, she'd had doubts, although giving up was not an option.

The scream penetrated her helmet and dragged her

back from daydreaming. She hadn't been concentrating. It would be the reason for her death; complacency and failing to focus. She tensed and her eyes scanned the crowd. Although late morning, she expected the noise to be high spirits from a drunken tourist, but she had to be prepared for action. Voices filled the police radio in her ear. Control attempted to identify the source of the noise. A second scream.

Should she stop the bike, and the car, or take off at high-speed with siren blaring and blue lights flashing? She edged her bike forward, hand gripping the throttle, her body tensed, ready to respond. With precision, her eyes automatically searched through the holiday crowds with no need for dramatic action unless she identified the danger.

The scream and increased focus would be a false alarm, but why put herself into this danger. A transfer to the investigations department within the Intelligence community would help her cause. After today, she would attempt to investigate a job that had the potential to give her the information she needed. It might be dangerous, but diplomatic protection could also threaten her life. The crowd quietened, another false alarm, but the voices on the radio were still agitated. They would calm when no activity apart from an early drunk had been detected.

03

Mustafa Mohamed completed the preparation for the evening meals at his restaurant. After wiping his hands on a cloth, he patted his ample girth and a satisfied sigh escaped his lips. Picking up the large knife he returned it to its block. The strong smell of garlic wafted in the air mingling with the spices he'd used to create the marinade. An excellent start to the day. A few more chores and he would have completed his morning's work. Picking up a mop he swished it across the tiled floor then ensured that all the surfaces were clean and tidy. He flicked the switch on the dishwasher, the lights flashed and it rumbled into action. His north London restaurant would only have a few regular lunchtime diners, which would be easily accommodated. Whistling to himself he crossed his arms and leaned on the counter. With luck, if Fatema wanted to shop in Oxford Street this afternoon, he would have an hour in the betting shop.

The door into the kitchen from the restaurant burst open bouncing back on its hinges with a resounding thud. He jumped. 'Doha, do not bang the door.' His daughter would ignore his remarks about her ebullience as she had done throughout her adolescence.

She grinned at him and her eyes lit up with a twinkle of mischief. The face of his beloved daughter melted his little resolve. 'Can I make myself a sandwich for lunch?'

Shaking his head, he blew out a long breath and answered with a soft laugh, 'What do you want? Remember, I am the chef.'

Skipping across the room, she threw her arms around his neck and kissed him on the cheek, 'Grape leaves with meat and rice, please.'

Taking the ingredients from the fridge, he studied his daughter as she filled a water bottle. A bright, intelligent and lively young woman with a beautiful delicate face. His heart sank. The devastating memories flooded back. She was now the same age as her elder sister before Satan took her life. Above all else he wanted Doha, who was now his only daughter, to have a carefree existence. As he lived a peaceful life, he had no reason to be concerned. Doha hovered as he completed the vine leaf sandwich. Kissing him on the cheek, she gathered her belongings and lunch then skipped out the door. He sighed, but he had no reason to worry about his sensible daughter.

His eyes brightened and he rubbed his hands in anticipation. The yard would be the last of chores, then checking Fatema would be content, he would wait for her to leave the restaurant. He had studied the newspapers and a horse at Kempton Park sounded interesting. He anticipated it would bring him a significant return. The yard needed clearing, he couldn't ignore it but it was the most despicable job of the day.

As he crossed the small, cobbled yard, the air reeked of diesel fumes from the traffic as it wound its way up the Edgeware Road attempting to leave the centre of London. It crawled at snail's pace through the busy stretch of road. The motors rumbled and whined with the occasional screech of a tyre on the tarmac.

He screwed up his face at the nagging pain in his knees as he crossed the uneven ground of the yard behind his restaurant. Although only fifty years old, cooking every evening for six days a week, gave him stiff legs in the morning. He gave a resigned shrug and used his handkerchief to mop his brow. It had come as a blessed relief to enjoy such a peaceful existence after the turmoil and aggression of his youth.

Smoothing his grey, once white top, he pushed at the splodges of Koshari sauce that had bubbled over enthusiastically last night, coating his front. The baggy black and white check chef's trousers bore the same marks. He shuffled his feet in his favourite plastic clogs, which had split but were his most comfortable pair. The used plastic food coverings were heavy, so he rested them on a wheelie bin and wiped his thin, curly, black hair away from his deepset narrow eyes. A smudge of sauce on his hands trailed across his forehead making him swear, but not loudly as Fatema would complain he'd become ungodly. A second swipe removed the sauce from his face, although some clung to his bushy eyebrows.

He shivered as the morning's spring sunshine hadn't penetrated the shadows of the overreaching neighbouring buildings. The cobbled yard spilled obnoxious smells from the wheelie bins. The putrefying smell of the waste food from the end metal bin permeated the yard.

Flexing his shoulders, he tipped the full plastic bags into the waste bin pushing them down to ensure the lid could be closed. Then he stretched his back before dumping the empty crates near the dilapidated wooden gate. A self-satisfied smile creased his features as he had made good progress this morning and the anticipation of an hour's relaxation in the betting shop still filled his mind.

Jumping as the back gate scraped open over the cobbles, the postman handed him three letters. With a perfunctory nod, he dragged the gate closed. The business had declined in recent months. English people were often deterred by a lengthy list of Egyptian dishes. He would need to change the menu, but not too much, as he wanted his Egyptian regulars to stay with him.

He eyed the envelopes, two of which were bills from suppliers. Paperwork bored him. Stuffing them unopened into the pocket of his trousers he closed his eyes to enjoy the sun which had entered the yard. He missed the heat of Cairo although it was a decades old memory as London had become his home. The ever changing London weather brought a scowl, but he relaxed his face and attempted to enjoy the weak morning sun.

The third letter, a cheap brown envelope, bore a poor quality computer printed address. The ink had only managed some letters from the words, Nile Restaurant. He scoffed, not even his name had been written on the envelope, another piece of junk mail. Bureaucracy annoyed him but he had become a meticulous man with his paperwork after a food inspector threatened to close his restaurant because his documents weren't in order. Since then he would never throw away an unopened envelope, but after checking the contents he would bin it. Slitting his finger along the top, the weak paper of the envelope yielded and tore to reveal a single folded sheet of A4. He snatched it out.

It wasn't an advert as it didn't have large hideous letters at the top. There was nothing else in the envelope, so he threw that in the overflowing bin. Unfolding the sheet of paper, his eyes narrowed as the first glance made him curious. A photocopy of a newspaper article. One glance at the headline and his mouth dried and a coldness welled up his back as his body shook.

Gripping the paper, his eyes scanned the Arabic headlines and the faded, grainy black-and-white photo. As his legs turned to jelly, he slumped onto the crates; the wall stopped him falling. He reread the headline to make sure, but his insides told him the truth as they quivered. Resisting the urge to retch he reread the words at the top. 'Fifteen dead in Cairo Souk shootout.'

Transfixed by the thirty-year-old article, images of his nineteenth birthday flooded back. The day before the shooting, but no rejoicing memories surfaced. Why had he received the press cutting? Why now? Why wait thirty years? How had they traced him? What was he going to do? His mind raced as his stomach heaved.

The memory of the cold feel of his hand on the gun had never left him. He shivered to the core as his mind passed in slow motion through the squeezing of the trigger. The horror. The stench of blood had filled the air. The screams of the dying. The vengeance. The passage of years had not erased the gory details. He had killed and someone wished to bring back the memories.

04

Jane Craddock dusted an imaginary fleck of fluff from the epaulet on her shoulder and her fingers smoothed over the pristine white blouse. The reflection of her slim figure in the plate-glass window of the Conference Centre foyer brought a self-congratulatory smirk.

The climb through the ranks of the police hadn't been quick or easy and it had taken time to reach Chief Inspector. She wouldn't dwell on the tough hurdles she'd had to endure to achieve her status. They were in the past and best forgotten. Squinting in the bright sun that poured into the building, she acknowledged a police constable who strode past.

Why her presence had been deemed necessary at the Brighton Conference, she had not understood, but the message had come from senior management that she would be expected to attend. Having studied the intelligence reports, no escalation of security seemed necessary. She sighed; it could only be a political instruction to show the efficient police presence at a major international conference. Not that anyone in the security world expected an incident.

Standing to one side of the smart entrance foyer, she

would be expected to demonstrate the presence of the police. Such political gestures annoyed her and reminded her of being a constable standing at scenes with little information.

Her desk in Scotland Yard held the key to her future. She could control her unit from there and lay the ground for her next promotion. In the past close familiarity with her immediate boss had always worked to her benefit. After taking over her unit, her boss had changed which meant extra work for her as she now had to ingratiate herself with him. A family man, but younger than her, the Superintendent had risen through the ranks at a fast rate. Her face brightened as her anticipation mounted; he could help her up to the next rung of the ladder.

Scanning the foyer for unusual movement or peculiar noises, she shifted from foot to foot in irritation. Would this mundane assignment draw to a rapid close? The patronising International Trade Conference delegates bored her.

Sensing another officer next to her, she glanced and her mouth thinned with displeasure. She would need to resolve the problem with her Sergeant, a lazy, incompetent officer, who blamed others for his failures. She waited for him to speak but gave a sneer towards him as she didn't want to listen to his usual diatribe of mundane words. Perhaps he could be succinct and to the point for a change.

Aware that he towered over her and looked down on her she refused to catch his eye, 'Status?'

'The delegates keep requesting changes to the agreed escort schedule.'

Jane rolled her shoulders as a shiver of exasperation swept through her, 'They always want changed arrangements, it's your job to make sure the protection is in place whatever they request.' The audible sigh from the Sergeant increased her annoyance and she scowled, 'For once, make this operation run smoothly, so we can return to London.'

The grunt as he moved away heightened the tension of the muscles in her shoulders and neck. When she returned to her Scotland Yard desk, she would deal with him. Sergeant Sandy Johnson had become too full of his own importance. He needed to be put in his place and as his boss, she was the one who intended to deal with him. Her mouth formed a hard line, but her back straightened as a thrill of anticipation at his dressing down filled her mind.

He drifted away from her, 'Where are you going?'

He shrugged, 'To rearrange the transport escorts again.'

As she hadn't been convinced by his statement, she followed him to the street. Was he skiving off and leaving the others in the team to check on the delegates? He glanced up and down the escorting police cars and bikes that had assembled, mumbled into his radio about the Egyptian delegation and turned back to the building.

Jane snarled at him, but he grinned. 'Have you been to Swindon recently?'

She shivered as he walked past her. Gulping, she followed him into towards the Conference Hall, 'I don't know what you are talking about.' He grinned again and went in the opposite direction.

Stepping into the back of the hall, she needed a minute to herself. He couldn't possibly know why she went there. Perhaps he was winding her up as he had seen her rail ticket. No matter, he would have to be dealt with sooner rather than later.

Jane swallowed. Perhaps the time had come to give up her nocturnal habits, but she'd always been careful in her planning and execution so no one in the police would find out. Was Sandy Johnson guessing? If not, she could have manifest problems.

05

Returning to Brighton had focused Alex's mind. Would she ever discover the identities of the killers? Hoping wasn't good enough. Alex's gloved hands gripped the handles of her motorbike as she drifted at slow pace at the front of the three vehicle convoy along Madeira Drive. Muscle tension ran through her body as she waited for further information. The second scream from the crowd of holidaymakers had dissipated. The chat on the radio eased. The assumption had been drunken holidaymakers fooling around.

The whine of the bullet through the air snatched her focus. Adrenalin flooded her body. Spinning in her saddle, she concentrated on spotting a gun. The crowd scampered and screamed, colliding in their desire to escape. Alex remained calm, her training coming to the fore. While watching the crowd for sudden movements, her hand moved to the holster and she flicked open the securing Velcro and let her glove fall to the ground. Her long, manicured fingers slipped around the grip of the Glock pistol while her eyes scanned the scampering terrified people.

A hooded figure, clad in black, rushed from the crowd towards the diplomatic car. Screams filled the air as the public scrambled away from the person pointing a gun at the car. She turned her bike and accelerated hard as the alert blared from the radio. Jack, her colleague on the rear bike, yelled into his radio, 'Gun attack on the diplomatic escort group, Madeira Drive.'

Bringing her bike to a halt, she leaped to the ground and drew her gun. Dipping on to one knee, she raised the Glock pistol in a two-handed grip with her arms outstretched and brought the sight in line with the assailant. A shudder ran through her, as she couldn't fire because of the crowd. 'Armed police, lay down your gun!' A cold sweat trickled down her sides. In the distance a car engine roared and a woman screamed.

The tyres of the diplomatic car screeched as the driver stamped on the accelerator to remove the VIP occupant from the danger zone. Alex blocked out the screaming and shouting from the crowd as she concentrated on the gunman twenty metres away. More shots filled the air but not from the approaching figure, the tyres burst in rapid succession stopping the car. Spinning, she scanned the panicking crowd for the source of the gunfire. Three more darkened figures rushed forward, armed with pistols. Alex aimed at each, but with no clear shot, it was impossible to fire. 'Armed police, lay down your guns!'

They rushed towards the car. 'Kidnap attempt!' she screeched into her radio. They aimed at the driver, who raised his hands in the air and slid in his seat. She sprinted to one side for a clean shot with no crowd in the background. A sledgehammer smashed through the windscreen of the car. The screaming crowd panicked to find the safest route, railings on one side and a rock face on the other restricted their options. Alex ignored the crowd as she focused on the assailants.

Reaching the backdoor of the car, the first figure hit the glass with a hammer. It shattered and he thrust a gloved hand inside to open the locked door. Alex sprinted and crashed into the raider before he opened the door. Her momentum bounced the figure into the car and he staggered off balance.

Alex smashed the butt of her gun into his face as he turned to fight her. Reeling from the impact, a straight arm punch with the heel of her hand to the bridge of his nose sent the man sprawling and unconscious with blood streaming down his face. Alex opened the door and jumped in, landing on the legs of the screaming woman. She dragged the young woman down to the floor, 'Wade musatah.' Alex pushed her down, 'Lie flat.' Falling on top of her, she covered her to the best of her ability.

A shadow came onto the back of the car, Alex turned and raised her gun at the assailant outside the rear window. The figure hesitated as Alex's gun pointed at him. Alex held her fire for a split second as two police officers wiped the figure from her eye line. For an agonising few seconds she lay on top of the kidnap target until relief spread over her as the radio reported three figures captured. She had seen four come from the crowd, 'Attention, attention, four black-clad figures emerged from the crowd, one is still free.'

Two loud thuds reverberated in the air. Plumes of smoke belched from the canisters on either side of the car. 'All units, secondary attack!' Alex searched the windows, but little was visible through the billowing smoke. It enveloped the car, entered her lungs and stung her eyes. 'Smoke bombs,' Alex called into her radio as she tensed for the next wave of attack.

06

Fatema sang her favourite song, Tamally Maak, in the restaurant as she cleaned the tables in readiness for the evening customers. She smiled with pride as Doha finished sweeping the floor, tucked away the broom and skipped up the stairs to her room. She had become a laughing and happy young lady who had a dutiful respect for her parents. Fatema was proud of her daughter.

With the cleaning and tidying complete, she would assemble the ingredients for making cold snacks for lunchtime. Entering the storeroom, she glanced through the small window into the yard and stopped. She replaced the tins of tomatoes on the shelf that she had picked up in anticipation of her task. They could wait while she worked out what had made Mustafa so agitated in the yard. Supported by the used plastic food crates, he leaned against the wall. Until the post had arrived, he'd been his normal self. She had ignored his usual swearing and cursing at the mess in the yard as she had tidied the storeroom. What had been delivered in this morning's post to cause the reaction? She would wait for him to tell her. He wasn't a man to be rushed, but the clear weakness in his legs and his expression of despair made a shiver run through her. Untying her apron, she placed it on the hook in the storeroom while her eyes remained fixed on him. The small, grubby window and the darkness of the storeroom would ensure she remained unseen.

'Mum,' the shrill insistent voice shouted as footsteps approached. 'Where are you?'

Fatema twisted her lip as she didn't want Doha to interrupt her observation of Mustafa, so she didn't reply, and expected her daughter wouldn't bother to find her. It wouldn't be an important matter as they had chatted earlier. She narrowed her eyes as Mustafa studied the paper and then the sky. His lips moved. Is he praying? That wouldn't be like him.

The storeroom door opened, Fatema jumped. The light flooded in. She had no option but to twist away from the window and focus on her daughter, whose elegant figure filled the doorway. Doha's face was eager and alive with affection and delight. 'What do you want?' She attempted to look busy by picking up a tin of tomatoes. A quizzical expression passed over Doha's face as she glanced at the apron hung on the hook.

Fatema glanced through the window at Mustafa, who remained slumped on the crates. Doha's inquisitive eyes caught Fatema's glance and she moved to the window. 'Dad! He looks ill, I'll go to him. Come on, mum, he needs help.'

Fatema caught Doha's waving arm, 'No, wait.' Doha tried to wiggle free, but Fatema gripped her hand. 'He's not ill.'

Doha stretched to peer through the window despite Fatema's firm grip. 'Mum, he has slumped on the crates, he must be ill.'

Fatema's mind raced, but she kept her grip firm. The apparent illness had resulted from reading the letter. Anguish covered her daughter's face. She caught the other flailing arm. 'Listen to me.' The intense brown eyes focused on her face. 'Your father has received an unpleasant shock that arrived in the morning post.'

'We must support him.'

'No, Doha, we will leave him to regain his composure. Then perhaps he will explain to me, but it is nothing to concern you.'

'But what has happened? What type of letter has caused such a reaction?'

Fatema screwed up her eyes, 'You are a young woman who will soon leave your sixth form for University.'

'Yes, but what about dad's shock letter?'

Fatema continued the firm grip and closed her eyes, 'You are old enough to understand the truth. A few years ago, your father became heavily involved in gambling and borrowed money at top interest rates. The restaurant only just survived, and we nearly lost our flat.'

Doha's arms flopped to her side as her eyes moved to the window, 'I didn't know.'

Fatema forced a bleak, tight-lipped smile. 'If the letter is from the money lenders again, we need to support your father.'

Doha's head dropped and her face scrunched up with worry, 'Does Dad still gamble?'

'Sadly, yes. When you are at school and I go out, he nips to the betting shop.'

The backdoor into the kitchen opened. Mustafa stood in the doorway clutching the frame for support. His face had paled and sweat beaded his brow. 'I'm going out.'

Grabbing his old anorak from the hook, he twisted away and the kitchen door crashed behind him. Doha went to run after him, but Fatema held firm. They moved to the window as Mustafa scurried across the yard and dragged the gate closed behind him.

Fatema rubbed her hands over her face and prayed that the gambling had not gripped Mustafa again.

07

Alex clutched her gun, searching for movement outside the car windows as she lay on the trembling, sobbing woman. 'Stay there until it's safe to move,' Alex whispered into her ear, 'the danger is passing. Hudu.' Perhaps the familiar language would help. 'My colleagues are taking away the attackers.' The noise level decreased.

The police radio blared in Alex's ear, 'Stay with the target, relief car is coming.'

'You will be protected; I will stay until the car arrives to evacuate you.' The increasing sound of sirens indicated police swarming into the area. Alex pressed her earpiece tight to hear the details of the messages.

'Five armed units deployed around the target.'

Alex rolled from on top of the young woman. 'Are you hurt?'

'No.' Her voice trembled and tears rolled down her cheeks.

With faces only inches apart, Alex flipped up her visor and smiled at the pale face with large brown terrified eyes.

'It's Shani, isn't it?' Alex recalled the person she had been designated to protect.

'I'm not hurt, only frightened,' came a weak, muffled

voice with a strong Egyptian accent.

Alex let out a calming breath. How a mundane and simple escort task with only two outriders had turned into a major kidnap attempt would require high-level investigation. Intelligence reports had failed, otherwise the daughter of Egypt's trade minister would have been identified as a target. 'You can move back to the seat as it is safe now.' Alex laid her gun on the floor to help the shaking woman. 'We will wait for another car to take you away.' As she slumped back onto the seat Alex studied her checking for signs of any injury. Slim and attractive with an intricate lace shawl draped across her shoulders, she was about the same age as herself. Alex tried to keep her voice calm after the surge of adrenalin, which hadn't yet receded after the conflict with the kidnappers, 'You will be fully guarded and removed from the area.'

Shani nodded, 'You spoke Arabic, I have never met an English police officer who can speak our language.'

Alex grinned, 'My mother is Algerian.' Despite the trauma she had suffered, a small shaky grin found its way through Shani's mask of bewilderment.

The reassuring calm voices on the police radio gave Alex confidence that the incident had finished. 'Relief car coming alongside, prepare to transfer.'

'A police car will draw alongside of this car. Armed officers will guard the route between the two cars, which will only be a few steps.'

'Will you come with me?'

'No, I will remain here, but you will be safe.'

'Thank you, but I do not know your name.'

'Police Constable Alex Drummond.'

Three police cars approached. They slowed and

stopped. Alex caught Shani's hand, 'Wait for the call on my radio.' Four armed officers facing outwards took up a position in between the cars.

'Effect transfer; go!' sounded over Alex's radio earpiece.

She patted Shani encouragingly on the arm, 'A few quick steps and you'll be away from this terror.' Alex nodded to a fellow officer outside. The door opened. Alex guided Shani to the door of the Range Rover where another officer waited to whisk her in. Alex slammed the door, 'Go! Go!'

With a squeal of tyres the three car convoy sped away along the road. She breathed a sigh of relief. At least the young woman was safe and three of the kidnappers had been caught. To her knowledge no one on the police team head been injured.

One of her armed colleagues approached, 'Good work, Alex, you saved the day.'

Wanting to come down from the high of adrenalin, she stretched and rolled her shoulders as she strode towards her abandoned motorbike. Her hand checked her holster, but she had placed her gun on the floor of the attacked car when she had helped Shani. With an impatient grimace at her forgetfulness, she turned to retrieve it.

08

Mustafa's thoughts were in turmoil as he lurched away from his backyard. Would his idea work? It was the only solution. He needed help and to talk the matter through with someone who would understand the terror and shock that now enveloped him. After a short but seemingly endless journey, he scampered as fast as his aching knees would allow, from the London underground station. Despite panting, he half trotted, broken by quick strides, only when he could no longer sustain the pace. Desperation forced him on. Gasping for breath he fought his way along the crowded pavement trying to control the panic that threatened to consume him.

The sun shone and he sweated, but he had been transfixed with dread by the single photocopied sheet delivered in the morning's post. Turning into Park Royal, he hobbled along, his overweight body lurching from side to side. His movements were stiff and awkward as he progressed towards the multi-storey building accommodating the head office and food processing factory for Kay Foods. Would Fatema be concerned because he left the restaurant in a rush? Scanning the building, he prayed that the person he wanted would be there, but the reception and security staff might prevent him from entering.

Without hesitation he took the front steps two at a time despite a pain shooting through his leg. At the top, sweating and breathless, the stainless-steel revolving glass door swept him into a white marble reception area, where low-level uncomfortable seats had been marooned in the large expanse. Despite the floor to ceiling windows facing the spring sun, the air conditioning held the temperature at a reduced level. But he found no comfort from the cool air as he was too hot from the rush to reach the building. Only the newspaper article mattered. His hand had never released the tight grip on the single sheet since he'd opened the envelope in his yard.

Scanning the area, he made a beeline for the single reception desk. Half limping, he panted as he crossed to the steel and glass desk with only a computer and phone on the surface. Behind the desk sat a young, dark-haired woman in a neat sky-blue blouse. The colour matched the company logo that filled the wall behind her. To one side, a screen of pot plants separated her desk from the entrance to the major part of the building. The welcoming smile from the receptionist dropped away as Mustafa staggered towards her and she backed into her chair.

A movement from near the open staircase caught his eye. Under the stairs, a half-hidden desk with screens. The security guard manning the surveillance equipment stepped forward with purposeful intent. A bald, angular man, wearing a smart blue uniform, frowned at the unex-pected arrival, dressed in shabby clothes, who now stood at the reception desk. The information Mustafa had received this morning overtook everything in his life. He wouldn't permit anything or anyone to stand in his way. He planted his feet in a wide stance and pressed his lips together in a tight firm line while his narrowed eyes focused on the approaching official.

'Deliveries around the back, old man!' The guard snapped and raised his arm close to Mustafa's face to indicate the direction. Mustafa snarled, showing his yellowing teeth, ignored the guard and stammered to the young receptionist, 'I've come to see Abdul Kadir.' The guard stepped forward to block his progress.

The receptionist shook her head.

'Back door for you!' The guard curled his lip.

'Tell Abdul, it's Mustafa Mohamed from Cairo.'

The guard shook his head and eyed the stained white top partially covered by a torn and dirty anorak. The multiple splodges of colours on the black and white chef's trousers glowed under the harsh halogen spotlights beaming down. Mustafa didn't move, 'Why do you want to meet with Mr. Kadir?' snapped the receptionist, 'he doesn't see anyone without an appointment.' She eyed Mustafa and her lips twisted with scorn.

'It's private!'

'Get out, you fool, he will not want to talk to you.' The security guard flapped his hand in an impatient gesture. 'If you've business with Kay Foods, go to the back door! If you have a complaint to make against the company, that doesn't give you the right to meet the Managing Director.'

'Mind your own business,' Mustafa snarled at the security guard, 'it's nothing to do with you, I want to see Abdul Kadir.' He leaned towards the receptionist who twisted back in her chair, 'Tell him I'm here! It's Mustafa Mohamed from Cairo. If he says no, I'll leave.' He screwed up his eyes so he could read the expression on the young woman's face, 'If you tell me he will not see me, you will be lying. I will contact him then you will be sacked.' The receptionist hesitated, her mouth opening and shutting like a startled fish out of water. A hint of uncertainty marred her pale features, 'Do it!' He slammed his fist on the desk.

09

Jane opened her eyes wide as the call came through of an attack on the diplomatic escort. Screwing up her face, she needed to know the details but the controllers were issuing instructions for the incident. Jane shouted to the local officers, 'Secure the Conference Hall, armed police authorised to draw weapons. No one in or out.'

The call had come for armed personnel to attend the coast road. Many had heard the call and mounted their bikes and dived into the cars as blue lights flashed and sirens screamed. Jane prayed it would be a false alarm, but she feared the worse.

One of her team opened the rear door of a police car, 'Ma'am.' She and Sergeant Johnson jumped into the back. The car sped to the end of the back street. Traffic had halted. The driver waited as a car attempted to back up to allow passage. Weaving through the traffic became a slow process. The progress became agonisingly stop and start. The longer the drama lasted, the less likely the incident would be a false alarm. She urged the controller to announce the incident had been contained. Breathing deeply, as her mind raced through an alarming range of possibilities. If her officers were involved it could be disastrous for her, especially if any were injured.

Her phone buzzed. As it was her Superintendent, she had no option to answer. She flicked it to speaker mode as the driver cut the noise of the police radio.

The clear voice echoed. Jane grimaced as she recognised the Yorkshire accent, 'Chief Superintendent Green here. Where are you, Inspector Craddock? Give me an immediate update!'

Not helpful as usual. Her face distorted with annoyance. A slight smirk tugged at the mouth of Sergeant Johnson next to her in the back of the police patrol car. Despite flashing blue lights and the siren screeching, the car made slow progress along the gridlocked coast road of Brighton. Jane twisted her lip, 'Heading to the scene of the shooting. Initial reports suggest Jack Taylor and Alex Drummond prevented a kidnap.'

'Is Sergeant Johnson with you?'

'Sir!' Sandy leaned close to her phone.

'How many in the escort for the Minister's daughter?'

The Sergeant grimaced, 'Two, sir, low key, no known threats.'

'Then you damn well misjudged the situation. What did the intelligence report say from our own units in the Met or MI6?' The Sergeant twisted around and nodded to the Inspector; intelligence reports were her job.

'No report, sir.'

'Did you damn well ask for one?'

'No, sir.'

'Sort out the incident, close it down with no other trouble. I want full reports from both of you on my desk at the start of business in the morning. Is that understood?'

'Yes, sir.'

Jane flopped back into the seat and closed her eyes with frustration while her thoughts raced. How could she distance herself from the problem? And more importantly how to place the blame onto Sandy Johnson.

10

Alex's adrenalin bubbled. The attack had been thwarted, but a gunman had escaped. She wanted to find him. Could there be another attack? Unlikely with the area swarming with police and the target removed from the scene.

A flash of light reflecting from the crowd caught her attention as she turned to retrieve her gun. Control reported that three attackers had been captured. Officers moved along the busy promenade looking for suspicious behavior which could identify the man who had escaped. The public had been forced back a hundred metres to allow the forensic team space to investigate.

The raiders in the kidnap attempt had been wearing black with their faces covered. Her eyes swept across the crowd alighting on several people who wore black. She dismissed those at the front as they wore only black tops or dark trousers, but not the black lightweight material the attackers had worn.

Despite the bright sun, the wind had a chill so only a few wore shorts. Resolving to pick up her gun, she gave a last glance at the crowd and noticed a man go to the motorbike rank in the shelter against the rock face lining the road. He wore black trousers like those who had completed the raid but his white top contrasted. The standard sports trousers were cheap and plentiful. They had come from a high street shop, so finding men wearing them in the crowd would not be unusual. His face remained hidden because he wore a baseball cap pulled tightly down. He glanced from his bike to the crowd and ran his eyes over the police as he half cowered behind the motorbikes. Why behave in such a nervous manner? What was he trying to hide?

The crowd watched the police with interest, but this man studied them. Alex smirked and guessed the man's bike would be illegal and so he glanced towards the police, hoping to avoid being stopped. Could it be more as he wore black trousers? It would do no harm to speak with him. She walked towards him to provoke a reaction. His eyes never left her.

She took in his full description, but the emblem on his baseball cap stopped her mid-stride. Fifty metres away, the emblem, too difficult to see in detail, caused a shiver to run through her body. Could this be a breakthrough? She had been caught in Leicester Square in a terrorist attack. Today could be another one. Were they linked? She pleaded that the symbol on the baseball cap would be the first link back to the terrifying experience that had changed her life. In one grim moment her flamboyant lifestyle had somersaulted away from her, to be replaced by a bleak nightmare that wouldn't leave her. This man might be a terrorist. Could he be one of those she was searching for? She couldn't ignore the opportunity to investigate. It had become her mission in life to track down those responsible. She slowed her walk so as not to arouse his suspicion and focused on the motorbikes attempting to give the impression that was her interest.

After the initial excitement of seeing the distant symbol, she surmised that disappointment would follow. She had seen many similar shapes before. It had become hard to remember the exact orientation of the interlocking crescents. Most likely another false alarm. Her body quivered. A sweat broke out on her forehead. That night would always be with her. It was ingrained into her memory. The interlocking crescents tattoo had been revealed on the arm of a gunman as he pointed his gun at her. Her nightmares focused on recalling the exact shape of the emblem, convinced that when she found it, she could pursue her purpose. It had to remain a secret. Determination gripped her.

Moving in an agitated manner as she approached, he tugged his cap tighter. Alex focused as he stared at her. A black top lay on the pannier of the bike. At this distance it might have easily been a raider with black trousers and black top, but she suspected another false alarm. An excited buzz echoed through the crowd as she closed to twenty metres. Other police officers moved close to the front of the cordoned crowd, but she strode through the middle of the open space. She flicked at the volume control on her headset and turned down the radio to blot out the background noise from the continual police calls. Her whole being focused on the man that she approached.

One voice blasted through loud and clear, 'Alex, where are you going?'

'Someone is acting suspiciously by a motorbike under the shelter, probably nothing but he appears nervous. He's wearing black trousers with a black top laying over the saddle of the bike.'

The radio controller's voice responded, 'If he's been

there since before the raid, he might be a valuable witness.'

Another voice echoed in her ear from Sergeant Johnson, 'Alex, approach any potential suspects with care. If you believe there is any cause for concern, summon back-up.'

Alex's face was drawn and tense behind the closed visor; the Sergeant had picked up her suspicions. Her eyes hadn't left the man who mounted his bike.

Alex opened her visor, 'Can you wait a minute please, I want to ask you a few questions.'

In a flowing movement, the man opened the side pannier on the bike, pulled a gun and fired at her. Alex responded to the man's sudden movement and dived behind a concrete waste bin. The bullet whistled high above her out to sea. Alex shouted into her radio, 'Armed man firing from the motorbike shelter. Request immediate armed assistance.' What a nuisance she hadn't picked up her gun as she would have a clear shot with no one behind him. Would she have killed him or just injured him? She wasn't sure.

Yanking his motorbike from the confined space he kicked other motorbikes to free a path. He struggled as his bike became entangled as others fell. The crowd screamed as he raised the gun. Panic broke out. Alex's concentration remained entirely on the man. Commands came over the radio. 'Armed officers deployed. All officers to note the position of the crowd.' Alex called into her radio, 'Man, about five feet eight inches, aged about fifty, slim, white T-shirt, black trousers with a Kawasaki track bike.'

Using the bin as a cover, she sprinted away from him as he untangled his bike with one hand while waving the gun with the other. The splutter told her it wouldn't start.

Fellow officers were moving along the edges of the wide road while others tried to keep the public out of a potential firing line.

Keeping low behind several parked cars, she sprinted back to her motorbike, which had remained lying on the ground. Over a hundred metres away. She grabbed the handlebars and was astride the bike in one fluid movement. In the distance the Kawasaki spluttered into life. He fired another two shots, but she couldn't determine his target. The crowd screamed. Officers took cover. An armed and dangerous man, but her mind focused on the emblem on his baseball cap which bought back the horrific memories of the gunman's tattoo that fateful night. The emblem on his baseball cap was fixed in her mind. Had he pulled the trigger that night and was he part of the gang that had committed the horrendous murders? No way would he escape. Her mind was made up. She'd follow him.

It would take too long to fetch her gun, so she fired up her bike and accelerated hard along the open space. The Kawasaki had taken off with the man waving his gun. He remained in sight, but the armed officers couldn't fire. Instead of leaving along the road, the bike mounted the pavement and powered, with high revs, down the pedestrian ramp towards the beach. The crowd screamed and panicked as the best way to avoid the roaring bike. People dived for cover. The Kawasaki disappeared down the slope, Alex lost sight of it.

She turned on her flashing blue lights and siren, hoping they would clear her way. The radio barked, 'Suspect exiting along the beach path. Do not engage in fire, the public is too close. A police helicopter has been summoned and will pick up the pursuit. All units do not pursue, it is too dangerous to the public.'

Alex took a deep breath. Adrenalin surged through her, pushing all sensible thoughts aside. She would disobey orders. Opening the throttle of the powerful police bike, she didn't hesitate. The Kawasaki was no longer in sight but she followed the same route down the pedestrian slope to the beach. The radio blared, 'No pursuit, no pursuit.' Alex ignored the command. They didn't understand. He mustn't escape. The voice from police control came over loud and clear, 'Helicopter deployed and will arrive in the area within minutes.' Another officer came on with an excited voice, 'Suspect moving towards the entrance to the marina.' With lights flashing and siren blaring, she cleared a path through the throngs of people. If she could catch and arrest him, it might be the key to unlock the past and blot out the nightmare of that atrocious night.

On a straight stretch of path, the Kawasaki weaved around obstacles and onto the road by the marina. Cars screeched to a halt. Riding through a pedestrian area, despite her blue lights and siren blaring, she couldn't race at full speed because of the crowds. Cars skidded to a halt at the marina entrance as the Kawasaki cut across them. Drivers used their common sense as they saw the approaching police bike, and remained stationary, allowing her to weave between them and continue the chase along the road towards Peacehaven. Had the man committed an error of judgement by coming onto the open road as he only rode a track bike? The police motorbike had far more power and she would close on him. She had to catch him as she wanted answers. Did he hold the key to the carnage that had altered the course of her life?

Although unsure about how she would deal with him,

keeping him in sight would help until the helicopter took over and the armed units closed in. She would worry about arresting him when she had closed the gap. Alex shouted into her radio, 'Kawasaki taking the coast road along the cliffs.'

He glanced behind. She had closed the gap as her bike flew down the outside of the traffic. He swerved across the oncoming traffic and turned onto the grass above the cliffs. She gritted her teeth. It was essential to follow him although it was risky as her bike wasn't built for cross country and the uneven surface, so she had to slow. His tyres gripped better than hers, but she wouldn't give up the pursuit as she was determined he would be arrested. She skittered the motorbike across the bumpy surface.

11

Mustafa prayed that his idea would work. He moved uncomfortably on the spot as his knees ached from the rush to reach the building. He glowered at the security guard whose eyes never deviated from him. The receptionist shuffled in her chair and edged away. The swish of the automatic doors from the offices opened. The receptionist and security guard glanced towards the sound. The company boss, Abdul Kadir, stood in the centre of the doorway. A six-foot high portrait of him adorned the wall next to where he stood. The immaculate grey suit, company coloured blue tie and white shirt gave a pristine appearance. A look of surprise crossed the security guard's face.

Mustafa focused on the man in the doorway.

Abdul fixed on the three. He rubbed his hands together. The frown on his face melted away. Striding forward, his teeth gleamed white against his dark skin as a smile spread across his face, 'I cannot believe that after all these years you appear from nowhere, my eternal friend, Mustafa.'

The security guard's and receptionist's eyes opened wider; their lips parted in amazement. Abdul, ignoring the scruffy stained clothes, wrapped his arms around

Mustafa and hugged him. 'This is a wonderful day. We must celebrate our meeting. I have prayed that you were granted a new life. It is a blessing of God that you are here today. Come, we will go to my office and talk.' Mustafa's emotionless face stared at him and he shook his head in sorrow. The joy drained from Abdul's face.

'It is good to meet you, Abdul. I've followed your progress from a distance and thank God for your success.' The intense stare from Abdul's face withered. As Mustafa's face remained fixed, his eyes flicked to the two people nearby.

The guard stepped away to return to his screens under the stairs. The receptionist, realising that eavesdropping would be undiplomatic on the boss of the company, busied herself with non-existent jobs.

Abdul screwed his eyes as he studied Mustafa's face. 'What is your concern? Do we need to talk in private?'

Mustafa opened his hand to the far side of reception, a large empty space where they would not be overheard. Abdul nodded but glanced at Mustafa several times as they crossed the foyer.

Mustafa retrieved the crumpled paper from his pocket and checking there was no one nearby, unfolded it and pushed it into Abdul's hands. He took the paper and meticulously unfolded it. At the first sight of the grainy image his eyes widened. A quick glance at Mustafa and he returned his full concentration to the paper held in his now shaking hand. He took a deep breath that he exhaled slowly.

Moving his gaze up, his dark eyes focused as he studied Mustafa's face, who waited for the second of the three gunmen, on that day in the Souk, to speak.

12

The progress of Jane's car along Brighton sea front had been slow despite blue flashing lights and two of her team on motorbikes trying to clear the way. She wiped her sweaty hands down the side of her skirt and glanced at Sandy Johnson, who stared out of the window at the passersby as though he had no concerns. It would be a different story when they returned to London. He would have a major problem as it would be his head on the block for the failure of the operation.

The car passed through the police cordon into the area near the attempted kidnap. The local police appeared a shambles with no clear organisation or method. An established procedure was to set a control point manned by the most senior officer present who would delegate tasks, but a mixture of specials, constables and two sergeants milled all talking and listening to their radio. She shook her head. The Radio Control Unit could not see what was happening on the ground and needed to take instructions from the senior officer present at the incident. Jane assessed the situation and concluded it was a mess. Another problem to sort.

Glancing at Sandy, she would expect her Sergeant to

leap out of the car and take control. Instead, he appeared more interested in a woman in shorts who meandered away from the disturbance.

With no clear central point of command, Jane leaped from the car as it skidded to a halt. She addressed the assembled but disparate officers, 'Report!' She had to settle the incident and ensure the best outcome, although that would be difficult. Bringing her radio mike in front of her face. 'Alex, where the hell have you gone! Report! Report!'

'Instructions are not to pursue,' Sergeant Johnson screeched into his radio.

A local uniformed Sergeant stepped in front of the two special constables that the Inspector had bellowed at.

'One of your constables approached a man in the motorbike shelter at the far end of the road.'

'Why?'

'It's Drummond,' interrupted Johnson.

The local Sergeant ignored the interruption, 'Reason not known, ma'am, she approached him and according to the witnesses the man drew a gun and fired.'

Pressing the microphone close to his mouth, Johnson shouted, 'Where's the bloody helicopter, it should be here by now.'

He spun round, 'You two are armed, why are you here?'

'The order was not to pursue, Sarge.'

'Christ, save me from bloody incompetents, the message stated not to pursue the gunman, but your colleague is out there.'

'Unarmed,' interrupted the local Sergeant.

'Get after her, I want her back here in one piece.' Sandy Johnson gestured towards the promenade with an angry wave of his arm.

Jane's calm but authoritative voice silenced both the men, 'Sergeant, armed units to secure this area and the motorbike shelter. Are roadblocks in place?'

'Struggling to reach the designated points, ma'am. Brighton's in gridlock, the cars cannot get through. More bikes are on the way.'

'Why had the response been so slow? That you will answer in your reports, believe me. High profile visitors are in town and you use specials to line the route.'

The local Sergeant, taller than her, frowned, 'The conduct of all the officers and our reactions will be in my report.'

Opening her eyes wide, she had to look up at him to determine his attitude. But she understood the look. Give me a bunch of inexperienced and part-time staff for a major incident and I do not have time to train them. While she could have sympathy for him, he had let her down and the consequences would fall on her.

Jane wiped her face and mumbled to no one in particular, 'What are you doing, Alex?'

Johnson's face twisted in annoyance, 'Being a bloody pain in the arse as usual. Why can't she follow orders for once? Do not pursue is simple enough for anyone to understand. What a stupid bitch!'

13

Alex closed on the inexperienced rider who struggled to control the sliding bike. The Kawasaki track bike slipped and slid on the thickening grass; a solid wooden fence blocked his way. Suddenly, he appeared to master the technique, allowing a sliding turn and passing between concrete bollards as the cliff narrowed. With a roar of acceleration, he returned to the coast road.

Alex attempted the same but her bike tyres, not made for cross-country, slipped and lost their grip as the bike tipped beyond control. Her body tensed at the potential disaster. The bike would no longer stay upright, and unable to control the sliding motion, she moved ever closer towards the edge of the cliff. Making one last desperate attempt to regain control, her knee skimmed the ground but having no chance of retrieving the bike, she released her grip from the handlebars and jettisoned to the grass. The impact on the soft earth forced the air from her lungs. Rolling to a halt on the lush grass, her bike slithered, with the engine still spluttering, over the edge of the cliff.

Her radio blared in her ear, 'Alex! Report.'

Despite gasping for air, 'Safe and unhurt, I repeat, safe and unhurt on the clifftop.' Laying still to catch her breath, she listened to the approaching sirens. Disappointment swarmed through her. The crescents' man had escaped. She'd had such high hopes of catching him and finding out what he knew of the assassinations in Leicester Square. Tears filled her eyes as with reluctance, she focused her attention back to the present. She had disobeyed orders and crashed an expensive police motor bike. Trouble lay ahead. A police motorbike negotiated the same gap onto the grass and despite the roar of the machine it travelled slower than she had tried in the pursuit and halted next to her. Jack propped it up and dived onto the grass next to her. They flicked up their visors.

'He escaped,' moaned Alex.

'The team will find him.' Despite him enduring the same traumas as her as the rear rider on the escort, he grinned, 'Are you hurt?'

'No, only bumps and bruises.'

A police Range Rover arrived on the grass. Jack helped Alex to her feet and guided her to the waiting car.

It had been the opportunity she'd longed for, but she'd blown it and had to face the consequences. She would never tell them the reason she followed the Kawasaki as it was her secret. She'd disobey orders again if the chance arose.

Jack whispered as he took her to the Range Rover, 'You're a maniac and will be on the carpet this time. Everything you have done today has been against regulations, so prepare yourself.'

Alex grinned at him, 'But we stopped the kidnappers.'

Jack stopped her, 'Stand and check you are okay.' Other officers rushed to her side. An ambulance stopped on the side of the road and the paramedics sprinted towards her.

Her legs had become weak but the adrenalin still flowed. She leaned on Jack's arm and wanted to resist the attention but these were her colleagues in the emergency services and would fuss over her until assured of her health.

'Let's take you to the ambulance to give you a check over.'

'No ambulance, I am fine but reassure yourself by sitting next me as I must now return to face my Sergeant.' She grinned at Jack, who relaxed his shoulders.

The paramedic persisted, 'A fall at speed can be dangerous, please let us examine you.'

She patted her hand, 'From a motorbike onto soft grass isn't an issue.'

The medic grinned and squeezed her hand. Jack announced to the nearby officers, 'Alex is about to be invoiced for the loss of a motorbike that seems to have finished in the sea.' The laughter broke the tension, which Alex appreciated. But she had lost her first known links with the interlocking crescents and would have to explain her actions in deliberately disobeying orders.

Jack, sitting next to her in the back of the Range Rover, touched her hand. 'You are a magnet to aggression when guns are fired. I have been an armed officer for years and have had to draw my gun to protect colleagues, but in the few months you have been with us, major incidents occur.'

Alex grinned, 'My magnetic personality?'

14

Mustafa plodded along the Edgware Road, head down with his hands stuffed into the pocket of his tatty anorak. One hand still gripped the crumpled sheet of paper which had arrived in the morning's post. How would he break the news to Fatema? Who had decided to resurrect that disastrous day in the Souk? Why wait thirty years? It made no sense to him, but the danger would be manifest. He stopped as his eyes scanned the road ahead. Whoever had sent the anonymous note knew his address and could be watching. He pivoted and checked the people walking behind. No obvious person appeared to be following him, but the delivery of the anonymous letter had evoked fear, which would have been the intention.

He eased open the back door of his restaurant, where the spicy aroma of traditional Arabic food lingered in the air. Fatema would have cooked lunch for the few midday customers. He hesitated as, despite the chill wind, sweat poured down his face. With hands clenched into fists, he shuffled through the storeroom and a groan escaped his lips. How would he find the right words to explain the disastrous news to Fatema?

Stopping, he gulped. The old days should have gone.

He enjoyed the peace of the restaurant with his wife. He tried to reason with himself that no attack would come from the perpetrators of the newspaper article as he lived in London in the twenty-first century. Gang ridden Cairo of thirty years ago was a distant memory. In those days, he'd always carried a gun and a sharp-pointed dagger. He'd used both frequently. Fury and hatred had bubbled through the city. Staying alive meant defending yourself. The old images of Cairo spanned before his eyes. The plotting, the fights and the hunger.

Taking a deep breath, he slipped into the restaurant. Fatema, wearing a multicoloured yelek, sat at the table folding serviettes to prepare for the evening customers. This would be a difficult explanation. The usual fleeting smile from Fatema never materialised as her eyes bored into him. Had she guessed? Hesitating, her voice only just reached him, 'The truth, Mustafa. I must have the truth.'

In the past he had tried to lessen unpleasant news for his wife. Although she appeared to be the archetypical Egyptian wife, round, smiling and hardworking, her fragility had grown over the years. He feared for her life and sanity after the death of their oldest daughter, Mariam. With his shoulders slumped, he slid into a chair opposite her while his heart thumped against his ribcage.

Nervousness gripped him and he let out a harsh breath as, touching his wife's hand, he screwed up his eyes to study her. The bright brown eyes bored into him. Her mouth twitched, then her eyelids, but she didn't speak. Withdrawing her hand, she began the slow meticulous folding of a serviette. His mind ran through the words. The silence hung, but he wouldn't be rushed. As he drew in his breath to utter the first words, the back door into the storeroom swung open. He tensed, Fatema's eyes flashed over him.

'Hi, mum, dad, I'm home.' Doha bounced into the restaurant but stopped as she saw her parents sitting at a table and a quizzical expression crossed her face. She slipped out of her jacket and kicked off her shoes, 'Shall I make tea?'

Mustafa shook his head.

Her mother gave a flash of a smile, 'Did you have an enjoyable time?' Doha nodded. 'Leave the tea until later, I want to talk with your father.'

Doha's eyes flicked over her parents and with hands on her hips she gave a weak shake of her head, 'Father, what have you been doing all day, the yard is a mess?' He didn't reply. Doha shrugged, 'I'll change and tidy it for you.'

'Leave it please, Doha. The crates will be too heavy.'

Doha bounced to the table and kissed her parents on the cheek, 'I'm seventeen years old and perfectly capable of lifting them. You carry on with your conversation, I'll do the yard and then make the tea.' With a swoop, she picked up her jacket and shoes, disappeared through a door and clattered her way up the stairs.

The right words remained elusive, so he slipped the newspaper article from his pocket and pushed it across the table. Fatema only read the headline and tears rolled down her cheeks, but she ignored them. 'I've been to see Abdul,' Mustafa's voice had lowered to a whisper. She gave an imperceptible nod. 'With contacts at the Embassy and in our old country, he will try to discover more.'

The strength and calmness of Fatema's voice surprised him, 'He has money and people to protect him, we do not. Husband, we knew the old days would return. You and I will suffer when that evil time comes, but how do we protect Doha? I do not want her tainted by violence and hatred.'

15

The salt air of the seaside reminded Alex of the joyful times of her childhood as she leaned against the promenade railings facing towards the sea. The gentle waves, after the squall had passed, lapped onto the pebbles. The calm grey-blue sea stretched to the horizon. Children paddled and played on the beach. The ozone smell triggered the memories of her honeymoon in Barbados, she shuddered. The rich and opulent life of being in love and married to a film star had gone forever.

Despite the time that had passed, the guilt of survival rendered her sleepless nights unbearable. As the grief of her loss had dissipated, injustice had come to the fore. In those long dark lonely nights, a plan had formed. She would find those gunmen. The first part of her plan had been to become a policewoman. She had not confided the actual reason for enrolling to anyone. Had joining the police been the best way to achieve her aim? A poor decision. It would be a slow process to find the killers when the combined forces of Scotland Yard and MI6 had failed.

She hadn't seen the detail of the emblem on the baseball cap and had lost the man in the pursuit. Her stomach twisted. It had been an opportunity and she had missed it.

Could she rely on her colleagues to affect an arrest? Pressing her earpiece, she sighed as tears welled. The helicopter had lost the man in a wooded area. Patrol cars found the bike, but the man had escaped. While the air and ground searches continued, the man had evaded capture. She blinked away the tears at another false dawn. So far, she had made no progress in her quest, but she wouldn't give up. It had become her mission.

The ebb and flow of the waves on the shingle summed up her life. Progress forward, but then forced back. Shaking her head, she had to concentrate. Jack had been right; she would be on the carpet for not following police procedures. A plan to justify her actions would be helpful, but nothing sprang to mind. She wouldn't reveal the actual reason.

Sergeant Sandy Johnson had made a makeshift office by commandeering a promenade shelter to receive the initial reports from the officers close to the kidnap. She was last to be interviewed. She didn't have a defence. The radio message had been clear.

Jack wandered over to join her as they waited. He had loosened his leathers in the hot sun and as usual appeared casual and relaxed. Although not making a fuss when he arrived on the grass next to her, she'd guessed he had been concerned whether she had been injured.

She liked him, and the way he studied her showed more than a professional interest. Her Mediterranean olive skin, long flowing black hair and her slim, tall figure caught men's eyes. Office rumours suggested Jack's divorce would be imminent. Would he make a play for her?

Did she want a man? It might hinder her quest. Besides, no one could replace Matthew. Tall, handsome and a successful film star. He'd swept her off her feet and had been the love of her life. Shaking her head to blot out the images of Matthew, she gazed out to sea, listening to the squawking of the seagulls. Jack gave her a small nod as he leaned on the railings. She stayed silent, letting the adrenalin rush of the incident drain away.

She dismissed the future attentions of Jack being neither in the mood nor wanting a man. Her mind drifted. Jack left her alone as he strode towards the seaside shelter for his meeting with the Sergeant. The speed of the debrief concerned her. Had Sandy Johnson been informed that there would be a formal investigation. Why had he decided on conducting the closedown meetings in a makeshift seaside shelter?

Alex continued her gaze to the distant horizon. Jack's touch on her arm made her jump, with his face close to hers so no one heard. 'He's in a foul mood and wants to speak with the boss before you. Sorry I did my best for you, but your prospects are gloomy.'

Alex touched his hand and catching his eye gave a nervous grin, 'Thanks, Jack.'

With her back against the railings, Alex focused her attention on the seaside shelter where she would soon have to explain her actions. Chief Inspector Jane Craddock strode briskly along the promenade and with a grim expression joined the Sergeant. She hadn't glanced in Alex's direction. Had she deliberately ignored her? Alex sensed that she would not be impressed with her performance this afternoon. The roar of the sea on the pebbles drowned any chance of listening. They stood and faced each other, so she had no chance to lip read. Would she be suspended for disobeying orders?

16

Jane Craddock stood in the promenade shelter. Heat burned her cheeks and anger spiralled from the pit of her stomach. What a mess! The blame might land on her shoulders, but it had been another mistake by her Sergeant, who had become a serious liability and had the potential to halt the progress of her career. She had been determined from the start that her career in the police force would be successful. Promotion had come her way and she would allow no one to jeopardise her progress through the ranks.

Alex had become a deep mystery. Why blatantly disobey orders and put her life on the line? They had never bonded. Women together in a man's world made sense to her, but no friendship had emerged. It would be a good strategy to leave Alex to the Sergeant until she had spoken with the Superintendent, whose advice would be the key to minimising the mess caused by Sandy Johnson's incompetence.

Sergeant Johnson scrutinised his notebook. Jane tapped her foot in an impatient gesture. From her point of view, it had been a disastrous day. As she had an impending meeting the following day with the Superintendent, she needed answers to clarify the situation and allow her to make sure that Sandy took the blame.

'What do you want?' Her expression was venomous as she spat the words through gritted teeth. Why had he asked her to the shelter? She had better things to do with her time as she needed to calm the senior officers and reduce the damage to her reputation?

'It's not my fault,' he slammed his notebook onto the bench.

Waiting until he lifted his head, she gave him a long sneering glance, 'Face facts, Johnson, you've messed up with the allocations this afternoon.'

'There was no one else spare and you'd given me no intelligence report.'

'Don't blame me.'

'What was I supposed to do if you don't give me enough staff or the relevant information?'

'Christ, I don't believe you.' Anger laced her voice. 'Put several cars together and provide a decent escort. What's so difficult about that?' Snatching up his notebook, he gave a dismissive wave of his hand. Her mouth twitched and tightened as she narrowed her eyes. 'I'm not waiting around arguing with you, now what the hell do you want, I'm busy.'

He huffed, twisted his lips and opened his notebook, 'Constable Alex Drummond disobeyed orders about no pursuit then did her own thing, the same as usual.' Jane didn't reply but gave a cold sneer. 'She took her bike off-road, which is against the rules, but then crashed it and would have killed anyone under the cliffs.' Jane stared intently and rubbed her hand over her face but remained silent. 'I want to suspend her pending a full investigation. We can tell the Superintendent tomorrow.' He slumped back on the wooden bench with a frown and closed his notebook with a sharp click.

Jane's lips curled and she perched on the edge of the bench and leaned forward towards him and waited. With her stare and body posture, he would have to lean forward. She wouldn't speak loudly.

Running his hand over the top of his head, he bent towards her.

'Yep, you're right, she broke the rules and can be reckless but everyone else, including me, thinks she's a bloody hero. By preventing the kidnap, she has saved you, me and the Met Police a great deal of hassle. The newspapers have a hero so will not ask embarrassing questions about the police and your management of the situation.'

Screwing up his face at her words, he leaned away, but a finger beckoned him back. Her expression darkened and a flicker of mocking amusement flashed across her features, 'I understand now, it all comes together.'

'Understand what?'

'When she first arrived in the section, you were all over her like a rash, helping her settle in you called it.' He took a deep breath. 'The other day in the office I watched you.' He didn't respond, his body remained rigid. 'When Alex entered the room and stood with her back to you, your eyes never left her arse. Your face revealed your thoughts. I reckon you've tried it on with her, but she wouldn't let you get your leg over, so now you want her sacked.'

17

Alex lost interest in the clandestine conversation between her two bosses. As they had faces like thunder, her interview would be difficult. The Sergeant, usually a fair and helpful man, was a policeman who followed the rules and had advised Alex to toe the line on every occasion, otherwise she would receive another mixed report at the end of the year. Not that a poor assessment would worry her as her secret assignment surpassed any internal police report.

As the Inspector left the shelter, she didn't glance in her direction. Sergeant Johnson stretched his long legs out in front of him. The dark blue police windcheater and trousers remained in a pristine condition, but her leathers were covered in mud and debris. The conversation would be stressful as she had to defend herself, but no excuse for her behaviour surfaced. He flicked his hair to one side in an irritated manner. Should she be a submissive female with wide eyes never leaving his face? Shaking her head, she dismissed the idea. That approach could wait for another day.

Alex returned her stare to the choppy grey sea and waited. The continual lapping of the sea with the resonating slide of shingles blended with and reinforced her agitated mind. Would dismissal from the police force follow this unfortunate incident? Her quest was important and being a policewoman would help her achieve it.

'Join me.' The Sergeant continued to write in his notebook. Senior officers in the police never liked it when an operation had gone wrong. Initially they wanted someone to blame and she would be in the firing line, although the lack of background intelligence couldn't be ascribed to her. After reflection, they would take a more reasoned view, but that wouldn't be forthcoming today.

Alex unzipped her leather top as she sat on the rough wooden bench opposite the Sergeant, as his piercing brown eyes focused on her. Shaking his head, he turned the page of his notebook and gave an exaggerated sigh, 'I have no option but to make this a formal meeting.' Did he expect her to have an excuse? She remained silent. 'Depending on the conclusion it might lead to disciplinary action.' It would be the outcome that she would expect, but she would wait for the main thrust of the conversation.

'I'll start at the end and work backwards.' Squaring her shoulders, her eyes darkened as she tensed herself for the reprimand. 'Your reckless pursuit of the suspect endangered the public by riding fast through crowded areas. The position of your bike within the crowd made your lights and siren ineffective, as they could not see or hear which way you were approaching. That incident would be enough for disciplinary action, but then you took police equipment, the motorbike off-road, for which it is not designed. In doing so you lost control of the bike which disappeared over the cliff. It could have resulted in serious injury and probably death to anybody on Undercliff Walk, but the bike caught a promontory on the cliff and finished in the sea. There are no other words to describe it, but disobeying clear orders and the wanton destruction of police equipment.'

'I wanted to keep him in sight until the helicopter arrived.'

'It's damn reckless, Alex. You are not a one-person police force, so I cannot understand the logic of pursuing a man who has a gun when you are unarmed. You contravened express orders not to pursue, but what would have happened if you had caught him?' The Sergeant shook his head, 'He had a gun you didn't.'

'Sorry Sarge, I made an error of judgement.'

He rolled his shoulders and faced her, revealing the tension in his face as he frowned, 'Since you've been in the police service you have been a brave officer. We have already had the Egyptian Embassy contacting us to thank the police for saving the life of the daughter of the Minister for Trade.'

'They were trying to kidnap her, not to kill.'

'You and I know it would have ended in her death even if there had been demands for money.' He stopped writing and tucked his notebook into his pocket. 'The senior staff will decide what to do with you. The young lady concerned, who you protected and saved, has asked to speak with you and the Egyptian Ambassador also wishes to meet you. With your breaking of many police procedures today, I would assume you would automatically be suspended from duty.' Alex twisted her face away from him and out to sea. 'But whether the police force can suspend and discipline someone when prestigious political contacts wish to meet her is beyond my reasoning, so I shall leave it to the senior officers.'

She didn't want to pursue the conversation; common sense should prevail. Next time she would act more reasonably at the sight of the emblem, as it would give her the best chance of finding out the people behind it. The Sergeant glared at her, his gaze alarmingly direct, 'Alex, I'm sorry to have to say this but I find it difficult to have you in my command and I shall request that you are moved out of the Special Escort Team.'

Alex's eyes focused on her Sergeant. It wouldn't be worth protesting. The special Escort Team was boring work so she would bide her time. The Sergeant nodded to her, she pushed herself up from the bench and left the shelter without speaking.

18

Alex concentrated in the morning sunshine. Big Ben struck twelve forty-five above her head. The relief cover would arrive within fifteen minutes. It had been an easy few hours watching and listening to the passing London traffic and tourists. How many photos of her had been taken that morning? Following the attack in Brighton, duties had been changed because of the increased terrorist level. After internal arguing within Scotland Yard, she had been allocated to support police officers outside the Houses of Parliament. Keeping the Heckler & Koch MP5 semi-automatic gun pointed towards the ground, she stood at the visitor's entrance to the Houses of Parliament with views to Parliament Square and along the Thames Embankment towards Vauxhall.

The possible disciplinary action had been delayed as the seniors argued about her future. Sergeant Sandy Johnson, her immediate senior officer, wanted her suspended. Although she hadn't spoken with Chief Inspector Jane Craddock, Alex had been allocated a duty and not suspended.

The morning had been quiet with her only activity stopping enthusiastic tourists moving into restricted areas as they endeavoured to take photographs. The mundane duties were wearing thin. Her eagerness to move forward with her quest made her restless. The unsuccessful chase in Brighton had heightened her resolve. Throughout her time in the police she had been patient, but her aim drifted away from her rather than coming closer. The threat of disciplinary proceedings would lesson her chances.

The screech of tyres dominated the London noise and the hubbub of Parliament Square. Her full concentration returned to her job. The car screeched on the far side of the square and skidded around the corner, narrowly missing a bus. Although fifty metres away, the four occupants of the BMW stood out. The driver fishtailed the car as he struggled to control it.

Please, please, no attack. Her breath stalled. She had raised her gun to follow the car. Her eyes narrowed and her finger rested on the trigger. If the car approached the Houses of Parliament entrance, should she shoot? It could be a car bomb, or the terrorists might leap out with guns. Four against one would give her no chance but she wouldn't go down without a fight. How many could she kill before they killed her? She hadn't had time to register whether her armed colleagues had drawn their weapons and whether they had the car in their sights. Checking such matters was out of the question as her sole concentration remained on the approaching vehicle.

The car weaved as the driver battled the slaloming and it turned towards the House. Alex trained the sight on the driver. Her finger remained against the trigger. The car swerved wide as it crossed the front of the House. Other traffic stopped. Her stomach tensed. Twenty metres away, if he twitched the wheel towards the entrance, should she fire? Stepping forward onto the pavement, she showed the occupants that her gun focused on them. The car swung away from her and along the embankment as the driver regained control. Her finger relaxed. Police sirens wailed as two cars sped after the errant driver. Alex relaxed her shoulders, then returned the gun to pointing towards the ground.

The momentum of the crowd returned to normal, but Alex had to wait for the adrenalin to settle. Would she have fired? Uncertainty gripped her. If they had been four terrorists with guns and a booby-trapped car, she would be dead. A futile death without achieving her aim. With knowing nods from her colleagues, she resumed her position and took a deep breath to calm herself following the false alarm.

A smile formed on her lips as she spotted a familiar figure striding along the pavement from Vauxhall. Wearing a deep green wax jacket, thick brown skirt with black tights and block heeled black shoes, she moved with a purpose. Alex waited until the figure came close, 'Are you ignoring your sister?'

Tanya spun around in confusion as the words lifted her from her daydreaming. Tanya's eyes surveyed her, travelling slowly across Alex from head to toe as the colour drained from her face. No doubt it had been a surprise to see her wearing full police equipment, with a pistol, handcuffs, taser and radio while clutching the semi-automatic gun. 'Alex.' Her sister took life in her stride, so losing colour and stammering were uncharacteristic.

Alex nodded towards four police officers walking towards them, 'This is the relief team. Walk back to Scotland Yard with me, I'll dump the weapon, find an inconspicuous jacket and we can have our planned lunch.' The silence from Tanya throughout the brief walk became unnerving as normally she never stopped talking. Alex's eyes scanned the people and traffic, searching for potential threats, but Tanya lowered her head and stared at the pavement ahead.

The distance between them had been increasing in recent months, which saddened Alex. She wanted a return to the fun days with Tanya, but circumstances were forcing them apart.

19

Mustafa mechanically prepared the dishes for the evening's business as his mind searched for the elusive solution. They had no future if they ran away. Where would they go? How would they earn money? They had been traced from the days in Cairo but he and Fatema had agreed to wait and hope that Abdul with his resources and influence could find a solution. But could the future of their daughter be hidden from the perpetrators of the threats. Despite exploring potential solutions, only one had materialised and that was far from ideal.

Mustafa glanced at Doha's back as she washed the plates from the lunchtime diners. As the pungent, sultry air increased, he flicked on the extractor fan.

Fatema entered from the restaurant, 'A new table of four.' She placed their menu choices on a magnetic bar near the door. Mustafa with a deadpan expression examined the list and took ingredients from the fridge.

The back door crashed back; Doha jumped. 'Dad, you still haven't fixed that lock.' Mustafa's legs turned to jelly, he dropped the ingredients, staggered and grabbed the worktop for support. When the door had crashed back, he had envisioned his enemies flooding into the kitchen to snatch or kill Doha. She pushed the door closed.

He rested awkwardly against the worktop with one hand steadying himself, 'Are you ill, dad?'

'No, finish the washing up!' When the kitchen became busy with a full restaurant, he always remained calm and never became irritable, but he had lost his equilibrium as his life had been turned upside down.

Doha looked hurt at his snapping but followed his instruction and washed the dishes, although her singing had stopped. He couldn't carry on living his life under such stress.

Still focusing on the meal preparation and without looking at his daughter, 'We want you to go away.' The words seemed to hang in the air between them. Since receiving the photocopied sheet, he had agonised how to explain the situation to Doha but nothing acceptable had sprung to his mind that Doha would accept as a reason. No way could he tell her the truth. How could he explain his actions?

Doha stopped washing dishes and turned to face him and placed her hands on her hips despite them being covered in washing-up foam.

'Where? Why?'

'To your Aunt in Manchester.'

'I did not know I had an aunt in Manchester. Why have you never mentioned her? If she is a relative, we should have visited?'

'I've been too busy in the restaurant.'

'I don't understand.' She mopped the drips from the floor. 'Why must I go, as my school exams are approaching? I will willingly visit during the summer holidays when I have free time before going to University.'

'I have spoken to Abasi and he is prepared to welcome you into his house.'

'Will you come?'

'No, we are needed to run the restaurant. You will go as soon as I have agreed the exact dates. You do not need an adult chaperone for the train.'

Doha sighed, 'What has happened, dad? Why have you decided I must go away?'

He sliced the meat on the chopping board with extra vigour, 'Please do not argue or question my decision. I have decided and I will arrange it.'

'Why!'

Mustafa stopped cutting the meat and faced Doha, his face a mixture of anger and confusion. 'Do not question my decision. It is final.'

Turning away from him, she finished drying the plates and left the kitchen without another word.

A shiver racked his body despite the heat of the kitchen. Doha had grown to be a sensible young woman and, on any matter, up to the present, either he or Fatema would have taken the time to explain, but he couldn't burden her young life with the knowledge of how her parents had spent their youth. How would she react if she knew of the terrible crimes?

20

Alex passed the landmark revolving sign for Scotland Yard and walked onto the Thames embankment. Tanya had been startled as it had been the first time she had seen Alex in full police operational uniform. Alex must calm Tanya. They were growing apart. Alex accepted that she was to blame. Keeping secrets from such a loving sister was not easy. In the cold dark days following Matthew's murder she had been a tower of strength. Her unwavering support coupled with the tender care and protection from her parents were the reason she had come through the depression which had engulfed her. Tanya was a wonderful sister. Could they return to the lively, teasing atmosphere that they had enjoyed for so many years?

The fleeting images of the screeching car in Parliament Square filled her mind with the consequences of an attack. The scattered thoughts mixed with the repercussions of her out-of-order behaviour in Brighton. The early morning text from her sister with an invitation for a lunchtime sandwich together had come as a surprise. What did her sister want? Tanya avoided London, so why make a special trip to meet for lunch? Alex sauntered across Westminster Bridge trying to relax although it would be an uphill battle to deceive Tanya who stood, face to the sun, with her back to the Thames.

Alex waved and quickened her pace, 'Hi Tanya, lunch is a splendid idea, will you talk to me now?' Tanya always organised, passed her a bag with a sandwich, a packet of crisps and a cold drink. Dropping onto an empty bench facing the London Eye, they opened their sandwiches. An excited group of passing schoolchildren screeched, allowing Alex time to gather her thoughts.

'The sight of you carrying a gun gave me a shock.' Tanya shivered.

Alex didn't want tension between them. She patted Tanya reassuringly on the arm, 'But you understand about firearms as we've trained with guns since we've been adults.'

'That's different, they are for target shooting or for the Modern Pentathlon, not real guns that can kill.'

She touched the back of Tanya's hand, 'Many police officers are trained to carry arms and never fire them on duty.'

Tanya busied herself undoing the packaging on her sandwich and wouldn't look at Alex. Another step had come between them as no words would pacify Tanya. Silence ensued as they ate their New York deli sandwiches and focused their attention on the tourists' boats ploughing their way up the Thames against the outgoing tide. A second raucous school group passed by, adding to the general noise of the centre of London.

Tanya glanced several times but remained silent as she munched slowly on the first half of her sandwich. Then before starting on the rest of her lunch she let out a long slow sigh before speaking, 'You're in a serious mood.'

'I'm on the carpet again after an operation failed.'

'Your fault?'

She could detect no hidden meaning in the question, 'I didn't help the situation, so I'm the one they can blame.'

Once again there was a long silence then giving her a sideways glance, 'It might be a good ending.'

Alex grinned, 'It's not sufficiently serious that they will kick me out of the police force.'

'Tell me what happened?'

'No.'

'Why not? Mum and dad spotted you on the news last night.'

Alex would have preferred her involvement not to have become public. On the news, there had been many comments from the public about the bravery of the police and several mobile phone videos of the police rider chasing the escapee.

'Operational secrecy.' She grinned.

'Mum and dad were terrified. You chased the gunman.'

Alex gazed at a pleasure launch chugging down the Thames. 'You didn't ask me for lunch to talk about mum and dad watching the news.'

'No, I didn't, but we are concerned about you. They asked me to find out whether you would reconsider the career you have chosen.'

Alex gave a silent sigh. They'd had a similar conversation at frequent intervals since Alex decided to join the police force. Why did they keep asking her to leave the police when she'd told them it was out of the question? 'You know the answer, I'm in the police and that's where I'm staying.' Although whether she would be allowed to stay by the senior officers was a different matter.

Tanya wasn't deterred by the usual response, 'You've thrown away a promising career in the United Nations as a translator. If returning to that role doesn't appeal, dad has offered to find you a good job working for his oil company.' Tanya gave a pleading look with her eyes.

Alex's conscience nagged that she couldn't give a positive response. Her family did not know her secret. They would not understand. They had not witnessed the terror. Finding the masked killer was now her mission in life. It gave her a reason for still being alive and helped the guilt that assailed her when she remembered that dreadful night. Taking a deep breath, she concentrated on keeping her voice calm and positive, 'We've been through this before. The police were brave beyond belief when they rescued me after the terrorist attack. The only way I can repay the kindness and bravery has been to join them, which allows me to support my colleagues, which I do to my full ability.'

'Okay, I know why you joined up as we've had this conversation so many times before. I've given up hope of persuading you to leave the police, but mum and dad asked me to try again so I have.'

'I love them to bits the same as you, but I am an independent woman and I take decisions about my life however hard it is for them to accept.' Alex wanted to break the conversation, so she finished her sandwich and crisps, took Tanya's plastic rubbish and crossed to the waste bin and popped them in.

She received a wonderful cheery grin from Tanya as she plonked back down on the bench next to her. 'Are you busy next weekend as I lose track of when you're working.'

'I'm on duty but I am not sure of the details.'

'That's a pity I was hoping you might do me a favour.'

They strolled back across Westminster Bridge, heading towards police headquarters as it was time for Alex to return to work. 'What favour?'

'There's a charity event and the usual groups have entered teams, including mine. Unfortunately, one of my team fell off his hunter yesterday, breaking his arm, so he won't be able to ride. Can you take his place?'

'I've done a lot of extra duties recently so I could ask my Sergeant to swap me on the rota.'

'That would be brill!'

A flicker of grim humour strayed across Alex's face about asking the morose Sergeant Johnson, who wanted her out of the group. 'I'll ask, but don't be optimistic as we have an increased security level after yesterday's attack. Firearm trained officers are always in demand.'

21

Jane smoothed down her black police skirt and checked her hair in the mirror. Pleased with her immaculate appearance, she straightened her shoulders as she mentally encouraged herself to find ways of overcoming obstacles in her career path. The imminent meeting about the failures in Brighton with her Superintendent had the potential to set back her career unless she focused the blame on the Sergeant. Perhaps her request to move him from her command would be listened to sympathetically. A disaster for her might be twisted to her advantage with careful planning. Several deep breaths, as she strode along the corridor, didn't quell the internal tension but exuding calm and with her senses on high alert, she knocked on the door.

'Perfect timing.' The Superintendent's face brightened and he opened his hand to indicate they should sit in the low-level comfortable chairs at the coffee table in his office. Jane knew little about her newly arrived senior officer. Despite the casual chairs and the warm greeting, she would remain wary of his approach.

'You are an excellent officer, Jane, but…' His expression stalled and grew serious as he dropped into the chair opposite. 'But you are under pressure.' Jane's eyelashes fluttered against her cheek as she meekly lowered her eyes.

Not wanting to rush her reply. Should she ask for his help? The Superintendent waited. Her hands moved nervously in her lap. His eyes focused intently on her. She re-crossed her legs. Her skirt slid up her thigh, but she did not adjust the hem. Finally, she raised her eyes and her lips curved into a smile, 'It's a stressful time.'

His eyes moved from her legs and roamed slowly over her body to her face. 'Work or private life?'

'Both, I have to admit I'm not on top of either.'

'Perhaps it will help you relax, if I tell you I will not act over the Brighton incident and will not discipline Drummond, is that what you wanted?'

'I'm not sure.'

The Superintendent rubbed his hands together, 'There seems to be animosity in your section. Why does Sergeant Johnson want Drummond out?' Jane avoided his eyes as embarrassment surfaced and flicked at a non-existent thread but didn't answer. 'Perhaps an office romance that has gone wrong?'

'I'm not sure, but I am trying to reconcile them.'

Leaning forward, he rested his elbows on his knees, 'What do you want me to do with Johnson and Drummond. Off the record, what do you think? I can transfer either or both to other divisions.'

Grimacing, she weighed up the possibilities. 'Johnson isn't that bright but is going through a bad patch so leave him where he is.' If she removed him quickly from her command, it could cause more problems for her. Her faced distorted with the pain of saying she wanted him to stay. 'Alex Drummond is a mystery to me, what do you think of her, sir.'

'I would agree a mystery, but a brave officer. Why such a beautiful, talented woman wishes to be in the front line is beyond me.' Jane's eyes sparkled as his line of sight moved across her body, lingering on her breasts. He remained resting on his elbows, leaning forward.

'Unofficially, I can guess the problem?' He rolled his shoulders.

'Yes, it might help to hear your understanding.'

Taking a deep breath, 'Any department which is mainly men, but has two beautiful women, is always likely to have difficulties.'

Jane tilted her head on one side and a questioning gaze passed between them, 'What solution do you propose?'

'Neither you nor Alex can remove your beauty, so we need to talk it through when problems arise, don't deal with it in isolation, Jane. I'm always here to listen to your concerns.'

'That's such a comfort,' she re-crossed her legs and kept her eyes on his face, but his eyes were elsewhere.

22

Alex desperately wanted to re-establish her old relationship with Tanya, which had been broken when she joined the police. Tanya, she loved to bits, but she had an attribute that Alex had always found intriguing. She pointed out the obvious in no uncertain manner when everyone else had missed the point. Alex's life outside of the police force had been the thrust of her comment. Alex sighed. Her sister had been right again. If she returned to her former life of Modern Pentathlon with her sister, her job might be forgotten or passed into the background of day-to-day talk. If Alex attempted to engage again, then her parents and Tanya would be pleased, but the commitment to find the killers would remain.

Although still very fit she had let her skills in the Pentathlon diminish. While rarely beating her sister she could come close, whereas now she was not in the same league. Time for a different approach.

She entered the shabby vestibule that smelled of waste and burned coffee. Sergeant Johnson lounged on a chair near the coffee machine, focusing on his notebook. Excited voices, intermixed with laughter, resonated from a distant office and echoed in the near empty space. The coffee machine and a well-used kitchen cabinet didn't soften the noise. An intense man, pleasure rarely softened his granite like face, so Alex expected little response.

In the shelter on Brighton seafront, he'd been livid with her. His nagging would continue. Her actions would reflect on him as he would be expected to control his team of constables. Pushing these negative ideas aside, she bounced across the space, dumping herself on a chair next to him with a grin, 'Any chance of a change of rota next weekend?'

He blinked through half-closed eyes, but his expression didn't reveal his thoughts. No doubt he would prefer to avoid her until the disciplinary procedures had been completed. 'Why do you need it at short notice, it's not like you?' His voice didn't hold the edge she'd expected. Had he softened his attitude towards her?

'Someone has dropped out of my sister's team and she wants me to be a substitute.'

'What type of team? Martial arts?'

'Modern Pentathlon. She hopes to be in the England team for the next Olympics.'

'Athletics?'

Alex shook her head and chuckled. 'No, the modern version involves swimming, running, riding, shooting and fencing.'

A quizzical frown appeared on his forehead, 'Can you do all those?'

'Yes, I've been doing them since a young girl. I'm not as good as my sister, but I can still give most a good run for their money.' The surprise registered on his face, which then relaxed into a slight grin, an unusual occurrence. Alex had decided when she first joined the police force to reveal little about her background as it would cause jibes about rich lifestyles.

'Okay, I'll check the rota and see what I can do. I can't come next weekend, but I assume it's open to the public.'

'Yes, although crowds are small, but are you interested?'

'I would like to see an event, it sounds good.'

Alex found her Sergeant a mystery. If he attended an event, would he use it as an opportunity to ask her out? Her colleagues maintained he hadn't married as he was too dedicated to the police, but the hungry expression that flashed across his face when he believed no one was watching made her wonder. Today, his handsome features were shadowed with fatigue. Too much work and no play were Alex's conclusion. She didn't want him to ask her for a date although he was a good looking man, who exuded confident masculinity. At the present time she did not want a man in her life. It would be too complicated but he would be hard to resist.

23

Mustafa locked the door of his restaurant from the outside as he left after a successful evening's business. Normally happy to relax with a cup of tea after a busy time, tonight would be different. His world had changed. Close to midnight, he scurried through the back streets towards Paddington. The damp drizzle and wet ground sparkled in the constant stream of headlights. Shouts and laughter from late night revellers pierced through the continual drone of cars and taxis.

Pulling his jacket tight and his woollen hat down to his eyebrows, his mind focused on his daughter. He shivered about adopting an authoritarian approach to Doha. Sadness clouded her eyes when he refused to be questioned. But he needed to make her safe. His only distant relative had been reluctant to take Doha without a satisfactory explanation. Mustafa had only visited their house in Manchester once. Poor and overcrowded, but he had nowhere else to send her. Tomorrow he would make another attempt to persuade them.

Sweating and puffing, he turned off a well-lit main road into a side street leading to a trading estate. The chilly wind penetrated his chef's trousers. The poor lights in this little-frequented area made him wary, but he reasoned that only he and one other knew of his journey. His friend would not betray him. The metal gates, with rusting wire mesh, led to single storey warehouses. Some were empty, others had the smell of garages, but with no light, most remained anonymous. Mustafa slowed as he crossed the uneven concrete.

The lights beamed from a warehouse where an articulated lorry unloaded. He recognised the name of the courier company, the night's activities preparing for deliveries the following day. The courier firm wasn't the reason he had come. Staying in the shadows, he passed the laughing and joking voices. A weak light illuminated the sign across the front of the next building, Kay Foods. Pushing open the door, he strode into the dark and shadowy reception lit by a single desk lamp. The smell of raw meat and disinfectant filled the atmosphere.

An old man, practically bald, in a thick green well-worn sweater wrenched his eyes away from his crossword. A German Shepherd dog, lying on the floor next to him, growled. 'Business is closed,' sneered the man with a dismissive wave of his hand.

'I'm meeting Abdul.'

The old man scoffed. The dog roused himself to standing and growled again. Mustafa's eyes focused on the menacing teeth of dog which were revealed as it curled its lips back. The man at the desk caught his collar, 'Name?'

'Mustafa Mohamed.'

Grunting, he nodded towards the door and still holding the dog's collar, returned to his crossword.

Mustafa pushed open the door into the dimly lit warehouse. The smell of fresh meat became overpowering. Large butchery benches now cleaned and scrubbed smelled of disinfectant. The sound and vibrations of huge fridges lining the far walls of the warehouse echoed in the empty space. Two men stepped from the shadows inside the door, one roughly grabbed his arm. Mustafa sneered at him and rapped his hand hard on the man's arm, forcing him to release.

'Gun?' grunted the man, scowling at Mustafa.

He opened his jacket and spread it wide, 'No, now get out of my way. Where is he?' They hesitated. 'Where?'

One man pointed to a flicker of light under a solid door. Pushing past the men, he strode across the warehouse, around the wooden butchery benches and without knocking threw open the door. Two men reacted and their hands dived inside their jackets. He scanned the office; three desks and several filing cabinets filled the room, lit by a single lamp. 'I'm Mustafa Mohamed.' One pointed to the door at the far end, but the other kept his hand inside his jacket.

He approached the door and knocked.

'Come in.'

Abdul in his shirt sleeves, with his company tie loosened, sat behind the large desk in a high-backed chair. Two guns lay on the surface. As he entered Abdul's hand had moved to one of them.

'Peace be with you,' mumbled Abdul as he opened the flat of his hand to indicate the chair.

Mustafa perched on the edge, 'What news, Abdul?'

He shook his head, 'Even my contacts cannot tell me whether our old enemies are in the country.'

'What about the Brighton attack as the news mentioned the occupant was Egyptian?'

'I have little information to offer you my friend as the incident was a kidnap attempt to snatch the daughter of a Government minister.'

Mustafa took a deep breath, 'Any connection with our past?'

'Not that I know, she has grown up in a privileged environment away from Cairo.'

Mustafa rubbed a hand across his face to ease the tension pulling at his temples, 'Someone must know!'

Abdul's expression darkened and a shadow of alarm touched his distinguished face, 'I am seriously worried, which is why I've moved to this office as protection is easier.'

'That doesn't help me.'

'I can give you two men.'

'Don't be so ridiculous.' A glazed look of despair spread across his features, 'What would I say to my customers? Please ignore the two thugs with guns standing in the corner.'

'I know, my friend, calm yourself, I will do my best for us, but it will not be easy.' Mustafa stared at his face where the anguish was visible by the lines of worry etched across his forehead, 'Keeping themselves secret from my contacts show they are determined and well organised.'

'But the police captured three, only one escaped.'

'I spoke with their lawyer, a friend of my wife's, they have refused to reveal their names.'

'What do we do now?' he flung out his arms in a gesture of despair.

'Have you sent your daughter away?'

'She goes soon.'

Abdul nodded and picked up a gun from the desk and

a box of cartridges and offered them to Mustafa.

'It's a sad day.' Mustafa reached across and with shaking hands stuffed the gun and box into his jacket.

'I will do my best.' Abdul came from behind his desk and hugged Mustafa, 'But prepare for retribution! Someone out there wants to resurrect the past.'

24

Alex's stomach tightened as the early morning meeting could decide her future. The escalation to the head of the Special Escort Group had taken place quickly and she had been summoned to appear before Chief Inspector Jane Craddock. Alex had never gelled with her chief. As two women in a man dominated department, they should be kindred spirits, but no bond had formed. Alex stood in front of the desk in the sumptuous Scotland Yard office with a highly polished desk and black leather high-backed chair. The lavender air spray had remained in the unventilated office since the early morning cleaning. The bland magnolia walls had regimented pictures of London scenes but gave no character to the room. This meeting might establish the first steps towards trouble for her. Disciplinary charges could be laid.

The door opened but Alex didn't move and stood square, close to attention although it wouldn't be demanded.

'Good morning, Alex, you had better be seated.'

'Good morning, ma'am.'

Alex studied the Chief Inspector when she came into view behind the desk. Always immaculately presented in her uniform, the white blouse gleamed. As usual her brown hair, without a strand out of place, had been tied in a tight bun which accentuated her delicately carved features while her large blue eyes were vivid and questioning. An attractive woman.

'Once again you have not obeyed the rules, but you are a mystery.' Alex expected the usual files of notes, but the Inspector made no attempt to place paperwork in front of her. Her voice lacked its usual stringency. 'Compared to your colleagues, many of whom have over a decade of service, you have only two years' experience, but you have progressed at a remarkable rate. You have immense talents which can only benefit the police, but you must abide by the rules.' Alex stared at the edge of the highly polished desk as anxiety spurted through her. So far, the Inspector had been complimentary. Was she building up to the unwelcome news? 'The gung-ho manner which you have adopted must be stopped.'

'Sorry, ma'am.' What else could she say as she wasn't prepared to reveal the truth and hadn't formulated a plausible explanation?

'Your case for disciplinary action has been passed up the chain of command in Scotland Yard. Sergeant Johnson believes that you're a liability to his group and will endanger both yourself and your colleagues.' Alex stared at her commanding officer as tension rippled down her spine, causing an involuntary shiver. 'Don't misunderstand me, no one doubts your bravery and yesterday you were exceptional again in protecting the target of the kidnap snatch. When people join my team, they are exemplary police officers who follow the rules under difficult circumstances, but you make little sense to me.'

Her normal conversational voice surprised Alex. Why had she opposed her Sergeant? 'Anything I can explain, I'll be most willing,' offered Alex, hoping to mitigate a potential reprimand.

'I see from your record you hold a first class honours degree in languages. The background report shows that you had the prospect of a glittering career at the United Nations. Your decision to join the police is commendable.'

'The police saved my life,' Alex's voice sounded quiet and slow.

'Yes, you had to endure the tragedy when your husband and a friend were killed. But I cannot tolerate even a hint of revenge in your actions.'

She must be guessing. Panic jabbed hard at the pit of her stomach as no one knew Alex's inner thoughts. 'There is no revenge, ma'am,' keeping her voice slow and steady with an effort of iron will. 'I want to support the people who saved my life. I don't know who the perpetrators were that terrible day and I have not tried to pursue them.' She gulped; the lie had slipped effortlessly from her mouth.

'Has the other major incident in your life in which you were heavily involved with the police affected your outlook?'

'I don't think so, ma'am. While terrifying at the time the result exonerated me.'

The Inspector leaned back in her chair and fixed her penetrating blue eyes on Alex's face, 'But you killed a man.'

Alex wanted the meeting with Jane Craddock to be over. Why did she want to pry into her past? It was not relevant to what happened in Brighton and had resurrected old memories that were best forgotten? But if she showed any extreme reaction, her Inspector would pounce and use her police questioning and training to examine every detail. She had to remain calm and unflustered, but it would be difficult as the images of what had happened with the rapist returned to her. A dark night. Panic had filled her. The rapist had died.

Alex rested her hands in her lap as she waited for the next question. 'What was your reaction when you were charged with murder?' The Inspector studied Alex's face.

Her mind drifted to the terrible event, but she brought it back to focus and her current situation. 'Dumbstruck, that no one believed me it was self-defence.'

'How long did you have to endure the charge hanging over you?'

'Two days, but then they found DNA evidence and identified him as a serial rapist in the north of London and the police had been after him for months. He had tried to rape me, but I fought back. In the struggle, he landed on his own knife.' The Inspector stared at her. 'The attack was six years ago, ma'am, and while I will never forget the incident, it no longer causes me concern.'

The Inspector stood, crossed the room to look out of the window towards Whitehall.

The silence weighed heavy, but Alex wouldn't break it.

Without turning, 'Why haven't you applied to be a detective, you have the intelligence and capability?'

'Detective work does not appeal to me and as I enjoy my current role, I have no wish to transfer to another area or to seek promotion.' Did her words sound convincing? She waited to be picked for transfer to the intelligence services, but would that selection ever come?

The Inspector twisted around and lent against the

windowsill, 'You could rise through the ranks of the police service and overtake me and many of your colleagues. You could earn serious money and contribute majorly to the police.'

'I'm happy as I am.'

'Sergeant Johnson has outlined the reasons for disciplinary action, but the investigation will not be quick. He has requested a suspension which I'm not prepared to authorise at this stage.' Alex's shoulders relaxed; she would have another chance. The Inspector returned to her desk and in a livelier voice, 'The Egyptian Ambassador wishes to thank you.'

'Jack is prepared to represent the Metropolitan Police. I wish to avoid such an occasion.'

'In your role at the United Nations you would have been meeting senior diplomats. Your manner shows you would be at ease, but I will not command you to attend.'

'I would prefer not to go, ma'am.'

'Very well, Jack can represent us at the embassy. Despite this conversation, I do not understand what motivates you. You are a mystery, but I intend discovering what drives you forward. You must have dreams and aspirations for the future, but why are you keeping them hidden?'

25

A shudder ran through Fatema's body as she prepared food in the restaurant kitchen wearing a chef's apron to protect the delicate fabric of her pale blue yalek. Her world had been transformed. The blissful years of peace with two wonderful daughters had evaporated. The death of Mariam, when she had been killed in Leicester Square almost three years ago, had sent her into such despair she had been lucky to survive. Only the desire to protect Doha had dragged her from the dark days, but she feared for her remaining daughter. Would their enemies resurface to claim revenge?

A knock at the back door. Fatema froze. Mustafa had left her alone in the house with Doha. She had no gun. Sweeping the long carving knife into her hand, she crossed to the door and flung it open. A smart man in a business suit stood in the yard. His bushy eyebrows held a deep frown. A shadow of alarm crossed his face as he reached out and took the knife from her. Without a word she entered the kitchen, knowing he would follow.

The door from the restaurant opened and Doha bounced in. She stopped and examined the man in the smart suit who carried the large knife.

'Is this your daughter, Fatema?'

Fatema grabbed the worktop for support. Unable to form any words, she nodded.

Doha's frown didn't lift, but she crossed the kitchen with her eyes fixed on the knife and offered her hand, 'I am Doha.'

He smiled for the first time and placing the knife on the work surface he shook hands, 'I'm an old friend of your mother and father, my name is Abdul Kadir.'

Doha's lips creased into a small tentative smile, 'Pleased to meet you, Mr. Kadir.' Fatema watched the exchange but could not utter a single word.

'You are truly a beauty, Doha, much like your mother when a young woman.'

'Thank you, sir.'

Fatema gulped, her voice strained as she forced the words out from her tightened throat, 'Are you packed and ready to leave?'

'Yes, mother, I'd rather not go as I shall miss my schooling, but father insists.'

'Your father is right, it's for the best, my dear.'

Fatema patted Doha on the shoulder, 'We haven't seen Abdul for many years and therefore meeting him again has come as a surprise.'

'Where do you know my mother and father from, Mr. Kadir? I haven't met you before, so it must've been a long time ago.'

'Yes, but our lives have changed since then. Isn't that true, Fatema?'

'Yes, for the better. We were blessed with two wonderful daughters that brought joy into our lives.'

'Is your second daughter at home?'

Doha gulped and grabbed her mother's hand.

Again, he glanced between them, 'I can see from the expression on your faces I have spoken the wrong words.'

'My sister was killed in an attack in London.'

Abdul's eyes opened wide and he stared at her.

Fatema whimpered, 'We only have Doha now, which is why we hope she can visit distant relatives.'

Fatema's body quivered. She struggled to form words. 'Explain to Abdul about Mariam.'

Doha led Abdul into the empty restaurant, they made themselves comfortable at a table, Fatema leaned against the door frame but didn't speak.

'Is it too painful for you to talk about your sister?'

'No sir, it is tragic and obviously I wish I still had an elder sister, but I'm happy to share fond memories of her.'

'Please go on,' he rested his hands on the table and his expression softened.

'She was six years older than me.'

'Do you have a picture of her?'

Doha slipped a mobile phone from the back pocket of her jeans, flicked through the photos, then turned the screen towards him.

'A beautiful young woman, I'm sure your father has great pride in his family.'

'Yes, sir.'

'If it's not too stressful for you, can you tell me how she lost her life?'

While it might cause a lump in her throat, Doha would explain without becoming overwhelmed by emotion which would happen to her mother.

'Mariam attended university and met another student on the course and they became great friends. She and Alex were always together.'

'Did you know, Alex?'

Doha gave half a grin, 'Yes, she visits us regularly and has become a great friend to me. Alex married a famous film star, Matthew Drummond, but her and Mariam still met regularly.'

'Did Mariam have a man herself?'

'No, several men courted her, but she hadn't chosen one.'

A puzzled frown crossed his face, 'Didn't your parents arrange a suitable marriage for her?' He glanced at Fatema.

'No, mother and father maintained that as we have grown up in an English culture, they would allow us to make the choice for ourselves.' Doha swallow deeply, 'Alex, her husband and Mariam were attending Leicester Square Odeon when they were caught in a terrorist attack.'

His eyes widened, his mouth dropped open and he sat as rigid as a statue.

Doha licked her dry lips, 'Mariam and Matthew were killed, but Alex survived.' He seemed not to be concentrating. His eyes had glazed over and his mouth remained opened, but he didn't speak and stared at Doha.

Finally, his eyes refocused, 'You said Alex visits you?'

'Yes, although she is busy with her job.'

'What does she do?'

'She is a brave police officer.'

Abdul Kadir's shoulders slumped and he stared at the table.

Fatema crossed the room and sat down with a loud agonising groan. 'Mariam was so beautiful.' Then she lowered her head onto her arms and sobbed.

26

Alex manoeuvred her Yamaha Supersport motorbike onto the drive of her parents' house in Ongar and parked next to her father's E-Class Mercedes. The gravel crunched under her feet as she crossed the wide expanse in front of the house and smelled the fresh grass. The country air gave a contrast to the fume laden atmosphere of central London. Removing her helmet, she ignored the drizzle that settled on her face and tensed at what her parents would say. They continued to be unhappy about her role in the police force. In previous years she would have rushed into the house for hugs, but times had changed. Life had moved on.

The sight of Tanya's car sent a wave of pleasure coursing through her. To see her sister again would be good, although they had recently met for lunch on the South Bank. Sergeant Johnson, to Alex's surprise, had changed the rota so she could take part in Tanya's Modern Pentathlon Team. Nipping through the side gate and into the utility room, she hung up her riding leathers, 'I'm home.'

Her mother greeted her with a warm smile and wrapped her arms around her, 'Your dad cancelled his trip abroad.'

'That's great, where is he?'

'Come through.'

She led the way to the extensive conservatory overlooking the rolling hills in the distance with a freshly cut lawn in the foreground. 'Dad, great to see you,' she hugged and kissed him. The wall hung television was set to a news channel. Alex closed her eyes as she recognised the rerun of the Brighton attack. The story kept hitting the headlines as witnesses were being interviewed. She picked up the remote from the coffee table, 'Shall I switch it off?'

'It's about you and your colleagues.' He shook his head so she couldn't switch off the news. Alex's mother sniffed and tears ran down her face. Her father, without taking his stare from the television, nodded towards the screen, 'Did you make that chase?'

Alex could brush off references to the police raids, but this had been specific.

'Yes, being the nearest, I began the pursuit.' She wrapped her arm around her mother, who sobbed. Her father stood and took his wife from Alex. 'Please, please Alex. I beg you to resign from the police. It is not a suitable career for you. You can see how the job upsets your mother and the dangers you face will not leave my mind. Neither of us can live with the tension and stress of you pursuing armed and dangerous people. It's too frightening and traumatic for us as a family. Tanya tried to explain our viewpoint, but you won't listen. Why are you so stubborn, Alex?'

Staring down the garden a silent groan reverberated through her body. It was so difficult to keep her secret from those she loved but there was no other way. Her mind was made up. 'Please don't distress yourself, mum, we've been through these arguments many times. My life changed when I lost Matthew and Mariam and I'm only here because of the bravery of the police officers who rescued me. My way of repaying them is to join the fight against evil people who wantonly take lives.' Alex had a pang of misgiving about not surrendering to her parents' requests, but her drive would never cease until the killers faced justice.

Her father led her mother from the conservatory. Alex didn't follow as it would exacerbate the tension. Tanya bounced in, gave Alex a huge hug, but her animated expression vanished in an instant. 'I've upset mum and dad, they keep following the attempted kidnap case, why do they heap the agony on themselves?'

'It's terrifying for us. As a little girl, you had a stubborn streak. Nothing has changed. Will you give up your job?'

'No, I won't.' She scowled and twisted away from Tanya as another argument hovered in the air between them. The television pictures flicked through the scenes from the Brighton attack. Alex wanted a change of topic but glanced up to see a news article about Egypt. The presenter talked over the pictures and about the current trade delegation. Newsreel footage showed various scenes past and present from Egypt. Alex watched abstractedly until she saw the interlocking crescents symbol displayed on a fluttering flag. Her legs turned to jelly and she sank down onto the sofa. That symbol had changed her life.

27

Mustafa wrung his hands together as he waited with Abdul in the back seat of his smart Mercedes. Two men, Ali and Malik, climbed from the front seats and peered along the Mayfair Street. The bright sunshine made the scrutiny of the street easy. Ali, the driver, with a broad frame and deep forehead, squinted his narrow eyes as he focused on a man at the end of the street who turned and marched away. With intense concentration, Ali opened the door of the car for Mustafa and Abdul to emerge. Glancing around, they climbed the steps. The door to the Egyptian Embassy opened for them. The bodyguards returned to their seats in the car.

'Welcome to the Egyptian Embassy.' A young woman gave a slight bow. Abdul presented his business card. Mustafa tugged at his ill-fitting suit jacket as he surveyed the opulent hallway with its rich gold embellishments on the elaborate plasterwork. These were lavish circles compared to the squalor of the distant Cairo days. He gulped; those days had returned to haunt him. 'This way, please.'

Abdul with an eye for a pretty face followed her. She knocked and entered. The only occupant of the room, filled with exotic Egyptian pictures and finery, sat in a wing-back chair near a window. The round, nearly bald man wore a bright yellow and black kaftan. He had been reading documents. He signed the top one, then stood to greet his visitors.

'Peace be with you, Abdul and Mustafa.'

'Thank you, Ambassador. I appreciate you agreeing to meet.'

'Come and sit,' he handed the signed documents to the young woman, 'please ensure we are not disturbed.'

A servant served coffee, which he placed on the table between the men before discreetly leaving. 'No formality, you have always referred to me as Hamada and I am happy for that to continue.'

Abdul acknowledged with a nod, 'Congratulations on rising through the Government ranks to the prestigious job of Ambassador to the United Kingdom.'

Hamada gave a dismissive wave of his hand, 'My rapid promotion has resulted with help from my friends,' he winked, 'such as you. Why the meeting? You were mysterious on the phone, so I assume it is not about company business.' The Ambassador rolled his shoulders, ignored his coffee and stared out of the window.

Mustafa waited. Would this meeting be as valuable as Abdul had suggested? Would the outcome allay the fears about his family? After a few minutes, Hamada faced Abdul, 'You have been helpful to me in the past. Is it time for me to return those favours?'

Abdul gave a knowing nod, 'It is difficult to explain, but there have been unpleasant incidents concerning myself and Mustafa. We wish to know if it extends to others in the Egyptian expatriate community in London.'

A serious frown crossed the Ambassador's face, 'Tell

me more.'

Abdul sipped his coffee, 'It would waste your valuable time to explain the details, but the news reported an attack on the Egyptian trade delegation in Brighton.'

'Yes, a serious and unnerving occurrence.'

'Is there a link between the attack and the unpleasantness shown towards myself and Mustafa?'

'I cannot give you diplomatic information,' he took a deep breath and his face became watchful, 'but as we are friends, I can share some facts with you.'

'Have the British police tracked down the culprits?'

'Three were captured after the outrage but they have refused to give their names. If they had come from Egypt, I would have expected them to ask for the Embassy's support, but I have received no such request.'

Mustafa moved in his seat. Abdul had wanted a low-key approach, but would it bring the results they wanted?

'I believe from the television news a gunman escaped.'

'Yes, but how the attack could have happened and then the specially trained British Police allow one to escape is beyond me.'

Mustafa peered over his coffee cup as he took another sip. The Ambassador appeared relaxed and confident in his role. Mustafa stared at Abdul to urge him to come to the point of the meeting.

'I'm not sure how to phrase my next question so as not to offend.'

Hamada grinned, 'Abdul, we are friends from past days, please speak your mind.'

'Why was the young woman attacked?'

The Ambassador rubbed his chin, but his eyes never left Abdul, 'She is the daughter of the Ministry of Trade and helps her father in his work. She is lively and person-able, so I can find no reason for her to be attacked.'

Mustafa finished his coffee.

The Ambassador's distinguished face became som-bre, 'Cairo in the past unites those in this Embassy today.'

Mustafa frowned; the man had not taken their plight seriously.

Abdul's mouth was tight, 'I don't understand.'

'Shani, the young lady attacked in Brighton has a boyfriend called Ibrahem who like you is a successful busi-nessman but principally in Egypt.'

'Tell me more.'

'Your father and Ibrahem's grandfather ran two rival businesses in downtown Cairo thirty years ago.'

Mustafa scowled behind the Ambassador's back as he led them from his office. Cairo thirty years ago had been filled with deadly violence. There was no romantic view perceived through rose-tinted glasses. His attitude annoyed Mustafa, who wanted the dangerous and violent times to stay in the past. Someone wouldn't let sleeping dogs lie and had resurrected the old animosity. Who would they meet? Please let it be a stranger. Someone with no connection to his past life.

Abdul interrupted, 'Could you apply pressure to the British police to investigate Egyptian militants in this country?'

The Ambassador jolted himself back to the present, 'The police have been lacklustre in their approach and have not visited me with an update. I shall speak with the British Foreign Office and demand answers. It is time for you to meet Ibrahem Khan and Shani.' The Ambassador led them through the opulent hall. Mustafa rubbed his face and then squeezed the bridge of his nose. Perhaps Ibrahem Khan knew little about the rivalry from the old days. Abdul's family and the Khans fronted Cairo businesses but used them to hide their gangland activities. Violence and terror were everyday occurrences. Mustafa had become Abdul's best friend and so joined with the Kadirs.

The Ambassador led the way through the reception hall and down the stairs to the basement, 'Ibrahem and Shani are keen on martial arts. Just before your arrival they intended visiting the gym for a judo session.' The surroundings in the basement were less opulent, but the bright white walls smelled of paint. Hamada opened the door and entered the gym. Mustafa recognised the facial resemblance of Ibrahem to his grandfather. He shivered at meeting a Khan again. They stopped their match and crossed to meet them.

Ibrahem offered his hand with a relaxed smile, 'I don't think we've ever met before, Abdul or you, Mustafa.' Mustafa's stomach clenched. A whisper of chilly air crossed his skin as a wave of apprehension jangled through him. Abdul's father would have been appalled that he was prepared to shake hands with a member of the Khan family and Mustafa's hand trembled as he grasped the outstretched hand.

'No, we have never met.' Mustafa's heart hammered, as images of the massacre in the Souk thirty years ago plagued his mind.

'My grandfather would expect us to be at war with each other.' Ibrahem spoke with an expression of pained tolerance, though his gaze was alarmingly direct.

'Yes, you are correct, Ibrahem.' Abdul studied him for a long moment, 'Our grandfathers had a different view of life, but they were distant times in the slums of Cairo, it's a changed world now.'

'But we can never detach ourselves from our roots, can we?' The broad grin stayed on his face, but his words sounded harsh and unforgiving. Mustafa had no wish to continue the conversation as every fibre in his body warned him about this young man. His grandfather had been a killer.

Abdul gave Shani an ingratiating smile, 'I don't believe I've ever had the pleasure of meeting you.'

'No, we have never met,' Shani grinned with flashing eyes, no doubt captivating Abdul who always had a wandering eye for beautiful ladies in his youth and he had not changed.

'I'm sorry to hear about the attack.' Abdul adjusted the lapels of his jacket and straightened his tie.

'Terrifying, but the police were wonderful.' A faint smile lined her lips and she lifted her chin defiantly. 'Although we've been disappointed, they've not been able to pinpoint the group responsible and their motives.' Mustafa's jaw twitched, but he remained silent. With no new names from the police, Mustafa's suspicion fell on Ibrahem. He suddenly appears in this country and then the memories are re-kindled, coupled with a violent attack. Too much of a coincidence.

Abdul smooth business voice never faltered, although Mustafa gagged for words from his constricted throat. 'Yes, it is galling as in the broader Egyptian community there are concerns about the perpetrators.'

Ibrahem grinned, 'I'm sure it is an exaggeration about subversive plots. It is an isolated group seeking money and nothing to do with the old groups from Egypt. The police should have found them easily.' A shadow passed across his face like a flickering memory.

Shani touched the Ambassador's arm, 'A policewoman saved me. Can we invite her to the Embassy to update us on progress?'

'I doubt a police constable would know, but I will invite her.'

'It is so unusual to find an Arabic speaking police officer. Her bravery stopped the kidnappers from abducting me.'

Mustafa didn't want to progress the conversation in the presence of Ibrahem, so hoping to deflect them from the current train of thought, 'Is she of Egyptian descent?'

'No, she has an English name, Alex Drummond.' Mustafa drew in a stuttered gasp as an explosive current of shock twisted his stomach into a hard knot.

28

Alex stared at the silent phone after she had rung to confirm she would change her mind and attend the Egyptian reception. The interlocking crescents on the old Egyptian film story gave a little hope that she could find clues to their origin. Ignoring the drizzle, she dumped herself on the ornate metal bench away from the house. She needed to plan, but the pressure from her family and at work made her quest more difficult. Dampness seeped into her trousers from the bench, but her mind sought the best approach.

At the Egyptian Embassy, she might ask discreet questions about interlocking crescents. Someone would know their origins and connections to Egypt. Her mind ticked at another problem. Officers were only expected to use the police computers about their current case. While involved in the kidnap attempt, others had taken over the investigation and follow up. Using the computer system for her own investigation could land her in more trouble.

The Sergeant had free access to search as he had become the unit's link with other enforcement bodies and civil organisations. Should she become more friendly? Perhaps becoming closer to Sandy Johnson could be a good ploy? The way he watched her, he would be interested, but it would be a complex route to go down. She'd leave making an approach until after her meeting at the Embassy.

Intending to comfort her mother and father later, she would deal with the recent argument with Tanya. She'd been abrupt and sullen with her once again. Their discord always centred around whether Alex would leave the police force. She couldn't, as it was the only route that might bring success but she couldn't allow the gap between them to become wider. The hassle of her family wouldn't disappear. Harmony with Tanya would be her top priority. Despite their argument, Tanya would go to the basement gym on her own and practice her skills.

Alex flexed her shoulders, jumped from the bench and trotted towards the house. She passed through the plain white door from the hall and down the spiral staircase to the basement. Ignoring the whirring and gurgling emanating from the boiler room, she pushed open the door to the gym. Tanya in her fencing outfit had limbered up with a series of exercises she had perfected for flexibility and speed of movement. Alex nipped into the small changing room, slipped on her breeches and jacket, then picked up her gloves and a mask. Without a word, she joined Tanya on the fencing mat and plugged herself into the electronic scoring equipment.

Flexing her shoulders, she would need to be at her best to give her sister a suitable match. They squared and saluted to start. Alex immediately received the first touch, which registered on the system with a ping. Tanya shouted, 'Concentrate!'

Backing down the mat would be the only way to stop Tanya achieving more hits. Alex had become rusty with lack of practice, but her sister had not only superior skill but it was coupled with determination, generated by the earlier argument and she intended taking it out on Alex.

After being wholly beaten several hits against two, Alex removed her mask and flicked at her hair. Hot and sweating, she towelled her face. Tanya placed her arm around Alex's shoulder as they entered the small changing room. They returned their gear to the lockers and stripped off to shower. Alex guessed that Tanya would speak about the raid.

'We need to have a serious talk, but you're not in the mood,' her voice was crisp and clear. Closing her eyes against the shampoo, Alex tried to blot out the anxiety about her family.

'Are we still having the event next weekend?' Alex wanted to change the subject.

'Yes, and I'm expecting a superb performance from you. Forget your damned police work and get a life back!'

29

Mustafa swore and cursed as he pushed through the crowds of shoppers in Oxford Street. With no time for delays, he had taken the shortest route from his restaurant to meet Abdul in Soho. It was imperative that he found more about the events in Brighton and the people he had met at the Egyptian Embassy.

His sole aim would be to protect Doha. Would sending her to Manchester to stay with distant relatives make her safer or remove the little protection that he and Fatema could provide. He swore as a shopper's umbrella caught him on the head. Reaching a side turning, a car blasted its horn as he stepped from the kerb. Giving an irritated wave of his arm, he scurried across in front of the car. Dark clouds covered the sky, but he didn't hesitate and took an alleyway filled with rubbish bins.

Although his knees ached, he quickened his pace at the sight of Abdul in the distance. The night clubs of Greek Street were closed, so only a few tourists hampered his progress. His friend moved from foot to foot. The agitated stance worried Mustafa. What had caused his anxiousness as he had Ali and another bodyguard on either side of him?

'Peace be with you, Mustafa.' Ali gave him a nod.

'And with you, my friend.' They half hugged as they touched shoulders. 'What news to you have for me?'

Abdul looked down at the pavement. 'I have tried my contacts again and had a follow up call with Hamada at the Egyptian Embassy but I have obtained no further information.' They moved to a close huddle as two police officers strolled along Greek Street towards them. The conversation halted until they passed by, taking no notice of them.

Mustafa closed his eyes and rubbed his hand over his face many times. 'I need information, Abdul. Protecting Doha is imperative, but I must know who wishes to pursue us. The anonymous letter has sent a shock wave through me and Fatema.'

Abdul squeezed his shoulder, 'Calm yourself, my friend. We need to assess the implications of what happened at the Embassy earlier. All those years ago I valued your opinion and I need to know your thoughts.'

Mustafa hunched his shoulders and stared at the wall in front of him, 'We have three events. The Brighton attack, the anonymous letter and the appearance of Ibrahem Khan in London. It would be typical of the Khan family to send the letter and carry out the attack to instill the fear. It resembles their actions from the old days.'

Abdul shook as head as he meandered along the backstreet in the shadow of the buildings, 'Ibrahem cannot be responsible for the attack as the target was his girlfriend. Their reactions to each other show they are lovers.'

Mustafa lurched forward after Abdul so he didn't need to shout. Snarling at the first drops of rain, he pulled his jacket tighter. 'A Khan arrives in the city and we receive a letter resurrecting the devastating event thirty years ago in Egypt. It is too much of a coincidence.'

'I can understand your reasoning for the letter, but the attack makes no sense.' Abdul stopped walking, 'It could be a coincidence.'

Mustafa shook his head, 'I do not believe in coincidences. There will be a reason for the perpetrators to attempt the kidnap, but it will not become clear until the attackers have revealed those who have paid them. I hope that the police solve the case soon, as it could have serious implications for us.'

A group of Japanese tourists approached laughing, pointing and taking photo as they gabbled away. Mustafa grimaced and indicated an alley leading to the back of the shops and clubs. Ali stepped in first and nodded to indicate the area would be safe.

Abdul eyes narrowed. 'Why?'

'Ibrahem Khan knows about us. We were at war with the Khans in Cairo. Who will he suspect is behind the attack as soon as his fiancé arrives in London?' He caught Abdul's arm until his friend stared into his face. 'It is us. You, me and Fatema. The Khans were notorious for their cruelty, do you believe they have changed?'

'No, I do not. Ibrahem's eyes still held the evil from the old days. I will do my best to secure further information. Hamada is my best chance of inside information.'

'No, Abdul. You have too much faith in him.'

Abdul glanced around to the empty alleyway and moved closer, 'Hamada owes me a great deal as I helped him up his career ladder, so he will yield information.'

'I'm sorry to speak ill about your friend, but his skittish eyes looked those of a coward. Hamada takes bribes,

Ibrahem has money the same as you. Whether it is money or threats, I believe the Egyptian Embassy is under the control of the Khans.' Abdul closed his eyes.

30

Alex, in dress uniform, stood next to her police partner Jack, for the presentation to the Egyptian Ambassador. Jack had admitted he couldn't relax in such plush and luxurious surroundings. The building from the outside appeared modest for Mayfair, but inside the resplendent rugs and ornaments showed quality and value. The Egyptian Ambassador opened his hand to Alex to indicate other people to meet, 'You have already met this young lady, Shani Zaher.'

Shani looked so different to when she had transferred her from the ambushed car to the Police Range Rover. Today, her elaborately patterned white blouse with gold thread contrasted with slim, elegant black trousers. A multitude of rings and bracelets were complemented by delicate make-up on her olive skin. Jet black hair flowed over her shoulders.

Her face lit up with excitement as she grasped Alex's hand in hers, 'We will have a private conversation shortly.'

A tall dark Egyptian man stepped forward and shook hands with Jack and then with Alex. 'I am Youssef Zaher, the Minister of Trade for Egypt. I remain in your debt for saving the life of my daughter. While it is impossible to repay such bravery, I shall use my utmost power to offer you compensation.'

'We were doing our jobs and are well trained to deal with such circumstances. It is kind of you to offer this reception on our behalf.'

'You're most welcome and perhaps you will allow me to introduce you to other guests who are keen to meet you.'

Jack raised his eyebrows as they reached the end of the queue and the introductions. Alex had guessed it would be a showcase affair, but when it finished, she might pursue her ulterior motive of coming here. Could she find any information about interlocking crescents?

Shani's father, Youssef Zaher, approached Alex and took her by the elbow to one side, 'My daughter has taken a particular liking to you and I can see that you are approximately the same age. The Ambassador will arrange a formal presentation of an award to you and your colleague but, from my family's point of view, my house is open to you. Could you join us for a weekend when your duties permit?' His honey coated words hung in the air.

'Thank you for the offer but we do not expect rewards for doing our job. I appreciate your generosity so please do not take offence if I decline as I'm busy at work with extra duties.'

He chuckled not bothering to hide his amusement, 'I've already spoken with your Inspector Craddock who told me you are a modest lady. I will speak with her again and we will discuss your invitation.' With no reason to alienate Shani's father or the Egyptian Ambassador, Alex stayed quiet.

Shani appeared, and rested her hand on Alex's shoulder, 'Father, I appreciate you want to thank Alex for her efforts, but will you leave us to chat in private.'

'That's a wonderful idea. I shall take my leave now. Once again thank you Constable Drummond and I hope we meet again.' With a slight inclination of his head, he moved away.

Alex was guided down a long corridor by Shani and through a door which opened into a large walled garden and then towards a luxurious summerhouse set among the early spring colours. An unseen blackbird serenaded them from the blossom of a cherry tree. The garden was a hidden gem in the hustle and bustle of London.

'Come and sit with me as I wish to know you better. Perhaps you will visit me and advise me about London as life in the Embassy is stilted.' She laughed. Alex nodded in agreement. 'In return I can tell you about Egypt and show you our country house. I appreciate you have your duties, but we could spend time together. Also, it would give me pleasure to introduce my fiancée who will also wish to thank you.' Alex's mind raced. It would offer her a wider range of connections for her pursuit of the symbol. 'While I find the memory distressing, have you managed to capture the escaped attacker?' Shani's voice quivered.

'No.'

'Do you know the attackers' background and why they made the kidnap attempt?'

'It's not information that comes down to constables. Although from those arrested, I would guess they come from Egypt or a neighbouring country. Enough about the attack.' Shani nodded. 'Let's talk about Egypt. I've been intrigued with an Egyptian symbol.'

'How wonderful, what is the symbol?'

'Interlocking crescents. Does it hold meaning for you?'

'The moon is part of Muslim symbolism, but interlocking crescents are not significant to me.' Shani's deep brown eyes focused on Alex, 'It means nothing to me but when you visit our house, there will be several people there who know the history of Egypt and you'll be free to ask them.'

Without a moment's hesitation, Alex changed her mind about the invitation.

31

Fatema chopped and meticulously placed each piece of salad in a line of bowls ready for lunch. Mustafa would be with Abdul all day as they attempted to find information about the anonymous letter. The operation of the restaurant didn't concern her as she had been doing the tasks for years and had substituted for her husband on the rare occasions when he could not cook. Abdul, she knew and trusted from the old days, but he had money, influence and could pay for elaborate protection and even if he offered, it would not be workable for a restaurant. There had to be another way.

Satisfied the salad bowls were to her liking she moved into the restaurant, checked again that every item matched her expectations, raised the blinds and changed the sign to open. Doha must be protected. If the sender of the anonymous letter knew their address, a simple search or observation would reveal her daughter. While she had agreed with her husband's plan, she considered it time to work out her preferred solution. Threats in London would be difficult to carry out. But time wasn't on her side. Mustafa and Abdul would build a joint solution, but she wanted one of her own that could be implemented at a moment's notice.

Returning to the kitchen, she awaited lunchtime customers and meanwhile she would devise her own plan. She jumped as the door swung open but relaxed with a smile as her daughter entered.

She grinned at her mum, 'Dad is out so I will help in the kitchen and serve.'

The radiant face brought a gulp, as tears ran into her eyes. She hugged her daughter so she could blink them away. They parted and Doha gave a quizzical look. The tremble of the bell alerted them to the restaurant door being opened. Doha bounced, 'I'll settle them and find out their choice.'

The brief period gave Fatema time to recover her composure. Her fledgling plan would have to wait until later for further consideration. Doha skipped into the kitchen, 'Two usual guests who want Koshari.'

A standard Egyptian lunchtime meal and variations on it made it their most popular dish. Fatema set to work as Doha waited to serve.

'Mum, may I ask about dad's decision to send me away?'

'It's for the best, so I hope you do not wish to challenge your father's intention.' Fatema's brow creased with worry and she continued to mix the ingredients with increasing vigour.

'You have made your decision but have not offered me an explanation, however I will accept your wish that I leave these premises for a period.'

'That is what you have been told and I don't expect you to question the decision.'

Doha stood up straight, 'I do not intend challenging, but by sending me to Manchester my schooling will be disrupted, so may I make another suggestion.'

'Very well.'

'I've met Alex's parents before. They live in a large house on the edge of London, which is near to a tube station. If I stayed there, then I could travel on the tube to reach school.' Fatema frowned. 'Mrs. Drummond has mentioned frequently that I would be welcome to visit and stay with them.'

'It might be a possibility.' Coldness crept up her spine and fear gripped her chest. It was vital to keep Doha safe. Events seemed to shift out of her control. 'We can ask relatives, but they are only friends and I would not like to impose on them.'

Doha sloshed the water around the large sink preparing for the dishes when the diners had finished, 'If I spoke with Alex, perhaps I might be able to stay for a short period until my exams are complete and then go to Manchester.'

'But you must apologise for asking.' Too many mixed emotions swirled within her chest. Alex would protect Doha and would defend her against trouble. Sending her away was the only solution. It would be so difficult. But she would tell Mustafa that she had agreed.

'I appreciate that mother.' Doha readied to serve the meals, 'When did you know Mr. Kadir?'

'In Cairo before we moved to London, we were good friends.'

'Both of you?'

Fatema place the Koshari under the serving lights, 'Too many questions. Serve the food.' She didn't want Doha to probe about her previous friendship with Abdul. Why had life become so complicated?

32

Jane worked late to cope with the busy work load but gave a sigh of satisfaction as she pressed the send button on her keyboard. An up-to-date report for her Superintendent. Becoming close to him would aid her career so she would make sure she was viewed in a good light and the blame for the Brighton incident would be placed on others.

With a flourish, the door of her office open and Sergeant Johnson strolled in. Jane's lips tightened and the deep lines of a frown formed.

'You've bloody let her off,' sneered Sandy Johnson as he slumped on the chair in front of her desk.

Banging down her pen, she crossed the room, glanced outside to the empty open plan office and slammed the door. Sandy's eyes followed her. In a slow deliberate movement, turning, she leaned against the door and rested her head back. He shuffled in his chair at her uncharacteristic relaxation, but a cocky smirk formed as he crossed his legs and leaned back. With the office quiet, she would deal with Sergeant Johnson. The formal route could wait as that might become complicated and lengthy if she asked the Superintendent to transfer Sandy to another department. An informal approach was her first strategy. The arrogant look that radiated from his eyes irritated her.

Sauntering towards him, she flashed a sudden wide smile. Leaning across, she placed her hand on the back of the chair. A grin of amusement flicked at the corners of his mouth. With faces only a few inches apart, she stared down into the mocking brown eyes. Her expression one of pained tolerance, 'Ever since you've been in my bed you've become insulting and patronising.' How he spotted her in Swindon was a mystery, but he had used the sighting to his advantage.

The grin continued and for one long moment they stared at each other, 'But you enjoyed it.'

'I told you it was a one off,' she snapped back, 'and I allowed you the benefit of the doubt over your blackmail attempt.'

The angry retort hardened his features and his smile slid away to be replaced by a lustful expression, 'You were willing.'

'Only because you threatened to spread gossip that you'd seen me entering a swingers club on a night out,' she hissed between almost sealed lips.

The grin returned, 'As long as we understand each other? You like sex, so why not with me?'

'Yes, I understand you, Sandy. A lazy, incompetent Sergeant who is trying to tell me how to do my job and hide your own inadequacies. Then you have the audacity to blackmail me because you can't pick up a woman.'

Scoffing in her face his eyes narrowed, 'Just get rid of Alex, she's a liability with her own agenda.'

'She's not interested in you, that's why you want her out. We have been told to recruit females and you want her removed so you can prey on the next one.' Her hand slid along the back of his chair. 'I promised you one night in my bed so you didn't blab about my visit to the club. But you don't want to stick by our agreement.'

He laughed in her face.

'So, I will not stick by it and I'll use an unorthodox way of dealing with you.'

She leaned forward, their faces remaining a few inches apart. He kissed her on the cheek. In a rapid movement, her hand slipped from the back of the chair to around his neck. Tensing, she tightened her arm muscles as the heel of her wrist pressed against his windpipe. Then she yanked his head back, knowing the constriction on his throat would prevent the noise. Before he could grab her arm, her other hand smacked into his groin. She grabbed and twisted, then hissed, 'Don't tell me how to do my job. Is that clear?' Giving the windpipe another wrench back, she drove her hand down once again on his trousers and twisted. She gritted her teeth with grim satisfaction as his face paled from the pain.

Although a large man she used her position and grip along with the shock of the pain to unbalance his chair and dumped him on the floor.

'Now get out!'

33

Alex drove into the underground car park at Scotland Yard after another routine assignment. As she cleaned her bike, her mind drifted to the Egyptian Embassy. Chatting to Shani had produced no results. Her one hope rested on visiting their country house, where enquiries among the many Egyptians, in a casual setting, might produce answers to the sign of the interlocking crescents.

Striding around the corner of the car park, she bumped into Sergeant Johnson. With no form of greeting, 'We need to have a chat, Alex.' His voice sounded strained with anxiety.

'Are you okay, your face is pale, and you are limping.'

Waving a dismissive hand, he leaned back against the wall, 'We need to talk,' he spluttered in a croaky voice.

These chats resolved nothing and drove a wedge between her and the Sergeant. A nagging doubt crept into her mind. Perhaps he's waiting for the opportunity to ask her out, but because they argue the atmosphere is never right. What would be the best approach? Friendly and open or awkward, then rely on the visit to Shani to further her cause.

'What about? I'm back from a long patrol and I am

late clocking off,' she sneered and folded her arms across her chest, as she decided.

'We are busy because of the enhanced terrorist intelligence, it goes with the job,' he gave another dismissive wave of his hand.

'I could manage a few minutes now if you want to talk.'

She didn't move, hoping to keep the meeting brief. Moving from one leg to the other, he appeared in discomfort. His eyes slowly moved up and down her body. The leathers covered her figure and gave a shapeless appearance, but she suspected his desire, 'You need to ingratiate yourself with senior management.' Is he expecting a more friendly approach to him? 'I want you out of my team, you're a liability.' Here we go again. She swallowed the sigh that rose in her throat. 'But senior management thinks differently, although they're not happy at your cavalier approach, so it's time to mend your ways.'

Alex wouldn't justify her actions and had no interest in currying favour unless for her benefit. His eyes studied her face. She didn't look away but concentrated on keeping her expression neutral. 'We don't want you to get hurt and neither do your colleagues who value you highly. So please think about your actions, take incidents calmly and wait for backup.'

Dismissing the platitude, 'Thank you, Sarge, I'll be more careful.' Alex then reverted to silence, signalling the end of the conversation.

'Why are you so reluctant to attend the Egyptian events?'

'Praise is embarrassing.'

'The Met Police has a public image to maintain. We

often receive bad press, so any opportunity to bolster the image should be welcomed. You expressed to the Minister of Trade from Egypt that you are reluctant to go to a weekend party.' Although she'd agreed with Shani to go, the message had not percolated through, so she remained silent on the subject. 'In order to encourage your participation, Inspector Craddock has allowed you to treat it as duty, not rest days.'

'I'll try to be more cooperative, so yes I will go.' The Sergeant grimaced as he moved his briefcase to his other hand. 'Has there been any progress on the Brighton kidnap attempt?'

'No, the fourth person hasn't been traced. The three in jail are refusing to speak. They have the usual solicitors who speak Arabic, but still refuse to put in a plea or recognise the court.'

'Radical militants?'

'It would appear so, but the motivation in trying to kidnap a fellow Arab is unclear. As usual there are several groups which have come out of the woodwork claiming rights to the attack, but they do not fit the profile of the ones in custody.'

It was frustrating that she had no authority to use the computer, as she wanted to compare the Brighton and Leicester Square attacks. The concept provided her with a small fragment of hope.

'They will be charged and found guilty even if they don't attend the court, but my guess is they will continue to refuse to speak.' A bland and monotonous response from the Sergeant.

'What nationality were the ones who attacked Shani?'

'Not recognising the court is their only statement

about militancy, the Egyptians think a group of criminal warlords in the Middle East are trying to extract money. Kidnappings are popular in places like Lebanon and Syria.'

Superficial news and no hint of any information useful to her. 'Thanks, Sarge.' Perhaps the time had come to change her approach to the Sergeant. A handsome man. She could do worse. 'Have you considered coming to the next Modern Pentathlon event?'

The eyes focused on her face then drifted over her body showing he wanted it to become a date. 'I would like to come, please drop me the time of the next one?'

Looking at him full in the eye for a long moment, 'We might be able to kill two birds with one stone.'

'I don't understand.'

Alex gave a forced laugh, 'You can then learn more about the event.' She stopped talking and looked down.

'What is it?'

'We've not hit it off between us so it might be an idea to have a quiet chat away from work.'

'Brilliant idea.' His words were delivered with unusual enthusiasm. He studied her, allowing his eyes to rake slowly over her while a slight smile lifted the corners of his mouth. She had no doubt what he wanted.

34

Fatema placed her head in her hands. Her elbows rested on a restaurant table. Next to her was a pile of napkins freshly laundered waiting to be folded. All was quiet for the moment but how long would that last? Someone wanted to resurrect the conflicts and hatred from the past. Ever since the first letter had arrived with the press cutting, she had been watchful of the post. After years of glancing at the envelopes, she recognised most of them. If they were from the usual suppliers or advertising, she would pop them on top of a cabinet in the storeroom for her husband. Mustafa would try to protect her from the worse aspects of life, the same as he had done when they arrived as forlorn refugees decades ago. The burden couldn't be his alone and she would stand next to her husband and face the past. Her mind raced. Doha, her only remaining daughter, never left her thoughts. She might need to return to the old days to protect her.

Opening her eyes, she scrutinised the single photocopied sheet placed in front of her, but face down. The badly printed envelope had only the restaurant name and address. Her mobile phone, placed in position next to the single sheet, beeped. The message read ten minutes.

Doha had gone to school. Mustafa would be out for another hour. Controlling the emotions that racked her would be difficult, but she had to formulate a way forward. In ten minutes, he would be here.

Moving across the room she pulled the restaurant window blinds closed, then stepped into the storeroom and fetched the steps. Despite her large size, she made little fuss of climbing them to open a high cupboard. Mustafa reached it easily without the steps, but she and Doha couldn't, which is why he had hidden it there. Pushing a few small boxes aside her hand slid to the back of the shelf. Her fingers touched the cold metal. Picking up the gun, she climbed back down the steps and returned to the restaurant. She had guessed Mustafa would protect them, so earlier she had searched until she'd found it.

The neat arrangement on the pristine white tablecloth of the photocopy, the envelope and her phone were now completed by the careful positioning of the gun. At the end of the organised table, a pile of ironed but unfolded napkins. Methodically, she began the folding operation she had done for years. In some ways the rhythmic sequence helped to calm her mind.

The back door rattled as it opened. She waited. Abdul stepped into the restaurant. He took in the contents of her table. His eyes opened wide. Instinctively, his men placed their hands inside their jackets. Fatema snarled and barked in Arabic, 'You two elephants get out into the yard, I shall protect Abdul.'

His eyes twinkled with amusement, 'Do as she says, I will be safe here.' The two bodyguards nodded their acceptance and closed the door quietly behind them.

Fatema waited for Abdul to sit next to her. His gold

cufflinks in his brilliant white shirt flashed in the restaurant spotlights. Even after all these years he remained a handsome man. Unlike herself and Mustafa who were both now round and overweight, Abdul had kept his tall slim physique. The A4 sheet remained face down. She remained silent as she waited for him to settle. She didn't need to see his face. His expressions wouldn't have changed over the years.

Without a word, but with methodical precision, she flipped over the sheet of paper. The gasp from next to her and the ragged breathing showed the same shock as she had suffered. Abdul didn't touch the paper or envelope and his olive skin had paled as his eyes scanned the old grainy photograph.

'Did it arrive this morning?' Fatema nodded as she lowered her gaze and tried to hide her inner misery from his probing stare. She huffed at the image of herself thirty years ago. She had been a good-looking woman. Slim and not ravaged by age and fat.

Abdul had rested his elbows on the table. He was shaking as he let out a long audible breath. 'We were lovers then,' his voice dropped almost to a whisper.

Fatema swallowed deeply, as she focused on the picture taken in a desert area outside of Cairo where she was flanked by the only two men that had significantly affected her life. Abdul on one side and Mustafa on the other. Abdul in the early years had been her lover, but Mustafa with his unwavering loyalty had won her heart. They left Egypt together to escape the violence and arrived in England to build a new life together.

Abdul tapped his finger on the paper, 'It's where we used to visit for shooting practice.'

Fatema focused on the automatic weapons that each of them held, then stole a slanted look at him as a small sigh escaped from her lips, 'I was the best shot.'

'Yes, Mustafa and I never equalled you.'

She let the silence develop, so Abdul could organise his mind. Automatically, she picked a serviette and folded it with the usual precision and placed it on the completed pile. The rags of tension pulled at her temples and her mind was a turmoil of fear and bewilderment. Swallowing hard to keep the tremble from her voice she lifted her chin and boldly met his gaze, 'Mustafa tries to protect me.'

'Of course, he does.'

'I must make the best provision for Doha,' a knot rose in her throat and her voice cracked into a sob. 'I need to know what the threats mean. I must keep her safe.'

With a crack in his voice, 'Please God, let her remain unharmed. I have made provision for her; she will never want in her life.'

'Thank you, Abdul. That is such a comfort. I will do my utmost to protect her.' The shiver from his hands resting on the table rippled the smooth surface of the white tablecloth. 'Now the truth, Abdul. Don't spare my feelings, I need to know.'

'Ibrahem Khan arrived in this country at the same time as we received the letters. Mustafa and I met him at the Egyptian Embassy.'

Fatema had a sharp intake of breath. The past flooded back with alarming clarity. 'The battle for the control of the slums still makes me shiver today. Did he recognise you, as he was only a boy then?'

'Yes,' his voice took on a new note which frightened her. 'The evil in his face and the icy contempt in his eyes were unmistakable.'

'Then send your men to visit him.' Fatema snapped back without a moment's hesitation. He must be stopped.

35

Alex followed Shani into the ultra-modern country house in Hertfordshire. This was too good an opportunity to miss as it would be her best hope of finding the significance of the interlocking crescents. Shani beamed with excitement, 'I'm so glad you came, the house is secure with guards and cameras around the periphery of the estate, so I can relax.'

'How large is the estate?'

'About thirty acres so plenty of space for riding.'

The white textured stone cladding complemented the extensive glass of the rectangular blocks linked with ingenious stairs and corridors, all visible from the outside. Occupants would be vulnerable without stringent security. The taxi that had brought Alex from the station had undergone several security checks before approaching the house.

Shani led the way down a glass tube linking the main building to a distant part of the complex. 'We have the afternoon to ourselves, my father and boyfriend, with other guests, will arrive for the evening meal.' They entered an open airy space at the end of the corridor which had been cleverly air conditioned, so it had been a pleasant walk in the glass tube even though the sun had been shining for hours. Shani caught Alex's hand, 'Every time I think back to Brighton, I go cold and shivery.'

'The shock of the traumatic attack will take time to leave you.'

'You were athletic in saving me. Are you a sports woman?' Shani opened her hand to a long couch. After-noon tea comprising scones, cream, jams and a steaming pot of Earl Grey had been set on the low level table. 'Your room will have a maid allocated, so please ask her for any-thing you want.'

'Thank you.'

'Which sports do you prefer?'

'Running, riding, swimming and fencing.' Alex left out any reference to shooting.

Shani made a mock face of disappointment, 'That's a pity?'

'Why?' Alex took in the extensive luxury with the wall coverings made of intricate weaves which exuded class and money.

'Judo and karate are my sports.' Alex couldn't prevent her eyebrows from rising. Shani was immaculately styled and sat with elegant lightly patterned black trousers and a cream blouse. Her long black hair had been perfectly set and with impeccable makeup she didn't appear a sports person.

Alex made herself comfortable, Shani had relaxed so a conversation should be easy. 'I'm a purple belt in judo.'

Shani clapped her hands together, 'That's excellent, I'm one better a brown, would you like a match?' It hadn't been what Alex had expected. 'I'm confined in large hous-es and under high security and so have little chance to attend outside gyms. Often I only see my instructors and a few of his students when they visit me.'

'I didn't bring my gear.'

Shani bounced with excitement on the couch, 'We have plenty to spare.'

'If you are sure?'

'Yes, yes. Please Alex. We are free this afternoon so it will be such fun to have a judo session.'

Having finished their afternoon tea, Shani opened a nearby door.

'Very impressive.' Alex surveyed the large gymnasium full of modern equipment and recognised the latest brand of treadmill that had recently been introduced into the gym she attended. Alex guessed the judo area, with mats already in place, measured the full fourteen metres square as used in competitions.

Shani led her to a stock cupboard where she soon found the correct size jacket, trousers and a tee shirt. The individual changing rooms were luxuriously equipped with private sauna and steam room as well as a full range of hair and body products. Shani lived a life of luxury.

When Alex emerged from the changing room Shani bubbled with excitement. 'This is so thrilling.' After the bow of the ritual rei, Alex acted cautiously as her belt level was lower in the hierarchy. Shani moved with speed and agility and caught Alex off balance with a spring hip throw. Alex suspected Shani to be a black belt. The throw had been delivered with speed and intensity. Alex crashed to the floor with the full force of the throw. The thick mats ensured no injury, but the venom hadn't been expected. Snarling, with intense piercing eyes, Shani waited for Alex to take up her position again.

Alex recovered herself. This would be a demanding match. Shani intended winning.

36

Fatema would allow Abdul time, so she folded another napkin. She chose not to speak to allow him time to assess the different options, but she hoped he would devise a method for dealing with the threat either legally or illegally although she would distance herself from the latter. Spending time in jail could not protect Doha.

'I can't go back to the old days,' his voice fractured with emotion.

Fatema crashed her fist on the table. Abdul jumped, 'You have the men, we do not!'

Shaking his head and with a groan, he buried his face in his hands. 'They are to protect me, not to attack.'

'You have the money and can pay them well.'

Leaping from his chair, he moved to a mirror on the wall of the restaurant and opened his eyes wide. Without blinking, he stared at his own face, 'All these years haven't changed you, Fatema. You were ruthless then, the determination in your voice is the same. If I don't look around, I can hear that beautiful woman's voice urging us to enter the Souk with our guns and deal with the Khans.'

'Nothing has changed. In Cairo, the Khans threatened us, now they do the same.' Her voice remained slow and calm.

Spinning round, 'You incited carnage then.'

With her eyes fixed on his face, 'Nothing has changed.'

With slumped shoulders, he refocused on the mirror. Fatema waited, he had never liked to be rushed. He opened his eyes wide and gaped at his reflection, 'I see before me a successful businessman, not a gangland killer.'

'Needs must.' Fatema folded another serviette.

'I cannot do it,' he moved back to his chair, 'do not make me.'

She waited until he twisted around wanting to see his face, 'If we do nothing we will be killed. The Khans were ruthless. They will not have changed.'

'It might not be them.'

Her eyes narrowed as she scowled, 'Don't squirm, it doesn't become you.' Picking up the gun, she checked it was loaded.

He gently took it from her and replaced it on the table. The agony in his face had disappeared. 'Ibrahem's girlfriend, who has no links with Cairo, was attacked.'

'If he believes you to be responsible, he will come after you.'

Shaking his head. 'Think, Fatema. This photo.'

He dragged it across the table in front of her, 'Have you seen it before?'

She glared at the picture, 'No, but I assume you have.'

'No, never.'

Fatema's quiet voice had an intensity and iciness as her hand rested on the gun, 'Only a select few took part in target practice, so who took the picture?'

'The recruit to our gang.'

Fatema folded the napkins in silence, Abdul sat next

to her in a daze. The layout of the table hadn't changed. Arabic shouting echoed from the rear yard. She recognised Mustafa's voice berating the bodyguards. Flexing her shoulders, she transferred the last of the napkins to the finished pile. Mustafa strode into the restaurant; he paused as his eyes slowly traversed the table. A sharp intake of breath came as he concentrated on the gun, then his eyes moved to the envelope and the single sheet. With shortened breath he spluttered, 'Another one.'

Fatema nodded, but Abdul remained motionless. Mustafa crossed to pick up the sheet, glanced at the grainy photo, and closed his eyes.

'Have you ever seen the photograph before, Mustafa,' Abdul struggled to form his words.

'No.'

Mustafa pointed to the gun and turned his weary face towards Fatema. She narrowed her eyes, 'I want no secrets from either of you. The old days were terrible. To God, I have prayed they would never return, but they are here. In Cairo we never sat around with indecision, we took action.' Both men shook their heads. 'If we do not, the Khans will kill us and then our lovely daughter.' She focused on her husband, 'Do you remember the recruit who would have taken this picture?'

Mustafa nodded, 'Was he the man with the interlocking crescents tattooed on his forearm?'

Abdul nodded, 'He had joined us, but we were unsure of his background until he proved himself. Then, as we trusted him, he came to the shooting practice with us.

Mustafa rubbed his face, 'Why don't we explain to Alex, she will help us.'

Fatema smashed her hand down on the table, toppling the neat pile of folded napkins, 'You are no husband of mine coming up with such a ridiculous suggestion that we should involve the English police.'

Mustafa cowered away from his wife, 'Alex represents the law, we could speak with her and explain.' Abdul shook his head.

The shrillness of Fatema's voice penetrated the restaurant, 'How do you propose we explain to the police about our Cairo days? Admitting we were killers is not an option.' Mustafa hesitated but chose not to speak, Abdul sat with wide eyes staring at Fatema. 'Ibrahem Khan has been received into the Egyptian Embassy as a successful businessman. How can you convince Alex he is a killer; you have no evidence and cannot cite the past?'

Abdul rubbed his face, 'We'll get nowhere if you don't stop arguing. My bodyguards are a temporary option. It wouldn't be difficult to evade them. Ibrahem has a business that specialises in explosives. I've only withdrawn from my business for a temporary period, it cannot run without me, then I become an exposed target again.'

Mustafa mumbled, 'You have your men.'

Abdul gave a dismissive wave of his hand, 'How will they protect me from a bomb.' Silence descended, Abdul picked up the photo and stared at it again. Mustafa's hands covered his face and his body shook.

Fatema picked up the gun, turning it over in her hands. Mustafa lowered his hands and with an expression of horror stared at his wife. Abdul took the gun from her and returned it to the table. Fatema's steely voice made them wince, 'What do we know about the man who took this picture?'

Mustafa glared at Abdul who rubbed his face, 'Very

little and it's a long time ago.'

'Think!' urged Fatema.

'He visited the Souk wanting to join us.'

'How did he prove himself?'

'By breaking into the Khan's family house where he stole money and jewellery which he willingly gave us to buy guns. I remember his interlocking crescent tattoo and the shooting practice.'

'What happened after that?' A confused expression spread across Mustafa's face and his brow creased with concern.

Abdul squared his shoulders, 'Events took a disastrous turn a few days after that photo.'

Mustafa dropped onto a chair and put his head in his hands, 'The day after my birthday.'

'The Souk?' Fatema's voice was low and flat.

Abdul nodded, his expression grim, 'The Khans raided us but we had the weapons.'

'A terrible day,' shivered Mustafa.

Abdul's voice shook, 'After the carnage that day we fled and never returned to the Souk.'

37

Alex applied her make-up for dinner. The evening would be tense and difficult, but she wouldn't be deterred from pursuing her reason for attending. She needed to have some easy and relaxed conversations. Choosing a low-cut satin turquoise dress with a leg slit, she nodded in anticipation as she expected to be lavished by men throughout the evening.

Her mind drifted to Shani. The aggression during the judo hadn't been expected. Perhaps it resulted from the exhilaration of an activity for which she had considerable skills. Being cosseted in a high security environment must frustrate her.

It could be another wasted attempt to search for information, but she would be embroiled in Egypt's culture and that gave her hope. A light knock sounded on the door which gently opened. Shani popped her head in.

'Come in.'

Perched on a chair near the dressing table she twisted around as Shani approached, 'I enjoyed the judo earlier. We could become good friends as we have many shared interests in sport. My father and the Egyptian Ambassador will give you gifts, but I wanted to give you a personal thank you before this evening, so I have a little present for you.' Shani passed Alex a small black velveteen box.

'Thank you.'

'It's a brooch so you can wear it this evening if you wish.'

Alex opened the box and gulped. She tried to hide her emotions but found it difficult. Shani studied her carefully. Alex took a deep breath, 'Thank you, it is delightful, but what made you choose interlocking crescents?'

'We talked about the symbol when we met at the Embassy, so I asked a jeweller to make a small brooch as a gift.'

With shaking fingers, Alex picked the brooch from the velveteen pad. It would be traumatic to wear it tonight, but her mind cleared as she studied the sparkling gemstones set on the edge of the silver shapes. The different arrangement of the crescents gave her tension some respite. It wouldn't raise suspicions if she asked for an explanation of the symbolism in Egypt. With a delicate kiss on the cheek, Shani slipped away, allowing Alex to complete her make up for the evening.

Alex smoothed down her satin dress, touched her hair and checked her reflection in the mirror. With trembling fingers, she attached the small brooch as her mouth became dry with tension. She picked up her shawl to accompany her low-cut dress. Leaving her room, she glided down the stairs, apprehensive of what the evening might bring.

Shani's father waited at the door as she approached the lounge, where the chatter of several people caught her attention. 'Welcome, Alex, please make yourself at home.'

'Thank you, Mr. Zaher.' Declining wine, she took an

orange juice from a passing waiter. A tall young attractive man entered the room and gave Shani's father a hearty handshake. Others in the room nodded in his direction.

Shani beckoned Alex. 'Please meet my fiancé, Ibrahem Khan. This is the wonderful police officer who saved my life.'

Taking Alex's hand, he bowed and kissed her fingers without taking his eyes from her face, 'I shall always be eternally grateful to you.' He kept holding her hand. His piercing brown eyes never left hers.

Ibrahem liked the ladies, but the lingering eye contact made Alex uncomfortable. Shani didn't notice. Finally releasing her hand, his eyes travelled the full length of Alex's figure, 'You are the most beautiful English woman I have ever met.'

A servant announcing dinner gave Alex the chance to move away from the uncomfortable situation. Choosing where she sat at the dinner table was impossible as the places had been allocated. Ibrahem took Shani's hand and led her into the dining room and to a middle chair down one side of the table. Youssef offered his arm and accompanied Alex to her seat opposite Shani.

The table, set with large floral displays along its length, had antique silverware and cutlery which had been systematically set out on luxurious cream linen. Alex had a tinge of uneasiness as Ibrahem sat next to her. It would be an uncomfortable meal. Hoping to talk to Youssef on her other side, she turned towards him but after muttering a few words, he began a conversation with people further down, leaving her no option but to speak with Ibrahem.

He gently touched her hand, 'Allow me to pour you water.'

'An interesting pair of cufflinks.' Alex had caught sight of another variant on the interlocking crescents.

'They are a family heirloom.'

'Shani gave me this delightful brooch.' He pretended to examine it closely, although his eyes moved to her cleavage, which gave Alex a shiver. 'Does the symbolism represent a tradition in your family?'

'I believe their relevance to my family goes back to our ancestors and the days of oppression, but that was a long time ago. Since then my family has risen in society and run leading businesses in Egypt.'

As much as she didn't want to, she forced her lips into a smile, 'Tell me more about your ancestors and their struggles, it sounds an interesting story.'

He laughed. 'Unlike modern day Egypt, my country has been under external forces many times in its history with the division of land, invasions and suppression of my people.' Alex wasn't sure why he'd laughed, 'In the history of my family, one group seem to have been the greatest oppressors.' He paused for effect and with a wave of his hand, 'The British people.'

'Not recently, I hope.' His intensity frightened her.

'No, in the days of the Empire, but old wounds lie deep.'

Throughout dinner, Alex had been aware of the full force of Ibrahem's intensity as he had monopolised her to the extent she had no chance of talking to other guests at the table, which she didn't enjoy. Even the multiple courses, including her favourite, Kushari, had been spoilt by his forceful character. While a handsome man and at ease with opulent surroundings and high-powered business, he did not relax. His face was watchful and his sharp calculating eyes bored into her while his conversation was stilted and uninteresting as he seemed intent on talking about himself. Alex wanted to avoid him for the rest of the evening.

Youssef tapped on a glass as he rose to his feet and addressed the dinner guests, 'You are good friends and colleagues to me, Shani and Ibrahem, but tonight this special dinner has been arranged for one reason.' Alex gulped, please don't let it be me. 'Alex Drummond, who is sat next to me, showed unprecedented bravery as an English police officer in saving the life of my daughter. She is our honoured guest tonight.' Alex's face flushed as she received a round of applause, and she forced a tremulous smile to acknowledge the praise.

As they left the table, Ibrahem caught Alex's arm to guide her to the lounge where coffee waited. Shani joined them as he handed Alex an Egyptian coffee from the waiter's tray.

'Shani has told me you are an expert at judo, I am not as good as her, but perhaps we could have a match.'

'Our busy schedules would be hard to dovetail.'

Grinning, he gave a dismissive wave of his arm.

Shani placed her empty coffee cup on the side table, 'It is hot in here and I feel flushed. Ibrahem will you take me onto the verandah so I may enjoy the fresh evening air?'

'My darling.' He offered his arm.

Shani declined and caught Alex's arm, 'Please join us.' Alex had not made progress on her evening's quest. She allowed herself to be guided to the verandah doors by Shani. 'Have you been talking about the interlocking crescents with Alex?'

'Yes, I have been explaining about my family and their difficulties with the English.'

'Oh dear, my phone has buzzed in my bag. Alex chat with Ibrahem while I go to answer it.'

Being left alone with Ibrahem on a dark verandah sent a shudder through her.

He grinned, his teeth flashing white against his brown skin, 'A most enjoyable evening when I have the pleasurable company of two beautiful woman.' She inclined her head in response to the compliment.

'Now we are alone, a question has been bothering me, would you mind?'

'Depends on the question.' Alex kept her expression under stern restraint as she moved into the light from the lounge window.

'I'm intrigued to know why such a beautiful woman, who is used to good living, has become a police constable. Even I could understand if you were a senior officer or climbing through the ranks, but a constable?'

'It's an enjoyable job, I've good friends and colleagues in the police force.'

He laughed, 'I suspected you would be evasive and not answer my question.'

'I'm not avoiding your question; my answer is the truth. You are right in your supposition, I come from a wealthy family, but my parents encouraged me to choose the career that suited me the best. I started work as a translator, but it became a boring job and I much prefer the police.'

'The light is catching your hair; you are a beautiful woman.'

The conversation had become embarrassing. He

needs reminding that he has a fiancée, 'How long have Shani and you been engaged?'

Again, he laughed, 'You are an evasive lady. We became engaged a year ago. My business covers a variety of activities, including ones which involve me with the government. I first met Youssef at a government meeting about export licences and subsequently met Shani.'

Curiosity surfaced so trying to sound casual she delved for further information, 'What do you need export licences for?'

'Part of my company is involved in building demolition and therefore we have a wide variety of explosives.'

'Do you export them?'

'Yes, but only to local countries.'

'When do you return to Cairo?' Shani rejoined them.

'As soon as I have finished my business in London.'

Shani caught Ibrahem's arm, 'I wish you didn't do your business in the poorer areas of the city. Why do it personally? You visit dangerous areas in downtown Cairo.'

He touched her hand, 'Don't worry about me, Shani, I can look after myself and I have several friends in that part of the city despite it being poor.'

With a serious expression, Youssef joined them and fixed his stare on Ibrahem, 'Did you know Abdul Kadir is in the country?'

'Yes, I met him at the embassy.' Ibrahem's eyes focused on Alex, 'I'm surprised the British authorities allowed him in with his past reputation.'

Taking her leave after midnight, Alex plodded up the stairs to her room. The pursuit of the interlocking crescents appeared a forlorn hope. Ibrahem originated from a large family empire that had once used interlocking crescents as its logo. From what she gathered, the business had a national reputation and made the family rich, so pursuing the emblem would be a futile attempt. Throwing herself onto the bed, she gave a long, low sigh as tears rolled across her cheeks. How could she find the people who killed her husband and friend?

Alex sprawled on the bed, her mind racing with the frustration about her lack of progress over the past two years. She hadn't switched on the light in the room when she'd entered, as the darkness matched her mood.

Brushing the tears away, she scrambled to her feet. Kicking off her shoes, she stepped through the French doors onto the dark balcony. Voices reached her from below. Normally, she wouldn't listen to a conversation, but her mind twisted and turned trying to find a clue to follow through. Tucking herself into the corner of the balcony, she concentrated on the words spoken as she recognised the voices of Shani and Ibrahem.

They spoke in Arabic. Alex adjusted to a position to eavesdrop on the conversation. Ibrahem's voice became a whisper, 'Well done, you have become close to Alex and that might be to our benefit to have the inside knowledge from the British police.'

'I refuse to see Alex as part of your plans as she is becoming a good friend whose company I enjoy and I will not permit you to involve her in anything that could compromise her. Also, she is only a constable, so she won't have access to the information you need.'

Alex crept back to her bedroom with more thoughts clouding an already complex situation. She would have to find out more. Ibrahem had secrets. What were they? Why did he want police information? Was he involved in illegal activities? Her mind spiralled through a range of possibilities, but no conclusions presented themselves as she didn't have enough information.

38

Fatema wrapped the scarf tight around her head, 'Before he left, Abdul stated he required two hours. It's gone midnight.'

'Please calm down,' whispered Mustafa as they scurried side by side through the dismal, deserted back streets of Paddington.

Fatema tugged at his hand, urging him forward, 'It pained me to let Doha have a sleepover at a friend's house this evening, but we must defend her, and one gun will not be sufficient.'

'Abdul doesn't want violence.'

'No one wants it!' she dragged him forward and along the road to the warehouse, 'except the Khans. Can you convince me they have become peaceful?'

'No,' mumbled Mustafa.

'They were barbaric killers then and nothing has changed. We need to stop them before they come for us.' Tears trickled down her cheeks and her voice fell to a whisper on the last few words.

Sweeping past the courier company where the laughing and joking broke the distant drone of traffic, Mustafa pointed to the single light in the corner building. Fatema took the lead and thrust open the door of the reception with such force that it crashed into the wall with a loud echoing thud. The German Shepherd dog stood and growled. The night watchman snarled, 'Couriers next door,' and returned to his crossword.

Fatema crossed to his desk. The dog moved forward and growled, but the man made no attempt to control it. Ignoring the aggression of his dog, he became aware that Fatema stood in front of his desk without speaking. Finally, he lifted his head. The barrel of the pistol which she held glinted in the desk's light while her eyes stared at him with deadly concentration.

The gun loomed too close to his nose to focus. He gulped and the colour drained from his face. Fatema spat out the words, 'Show me into Abdul's office.' He hesitated and his hands gripped the edge of the desk. 'Now!' The dog growled again, Fatema pointed the gun at the dog and her eyes darkened. 'Be quick otherwise…' She flexed her hand around the gun.

The old man staggered from his chair and sneered at Mustafa. His broken voice stammered, 'You've been here before.' The old man narrowed his eyes and glowered at Fatema.

'Meet my wife.' The man drew in a stuttered gasp. 'She doesn't like delays.'

The man hissed, 'Sit,' to the dog, which did as instructed, as he lurched towards the door.

Fatema grasping the gun in front of her followed the man and snarled, 'No tricks.'

In a theatrical fashion, the man hoisted his hands above his head as he stumbled into the warehouse. The two heavies stepped forward. Fatema slipped the gun into the folds of her jacket and forced her way past them, 'Out of the way, you elephants!'

Abdul and two bodyguards strode from the end office into the warehouse. He stopped when he noticed them and placed the large holdall he carried on to a butchering bench. With no lights in the warehouse, the doorway from reception and the office provided the only relief from total darkness. The weak light failed further as the old man returned to reception and closed the door with an echoing thud. The shadows of the bodyguards danced across the wall as they moved in the eerie silence.

Fatema moved close to Abdul as she wanted to see his expression. He glanced down at her hand still gripping the gun. One of his heavies stepped forward. 'Stay, she would never harm me.'

For the first time that evening, Fatema's voice lost its sharpness. In a flat but normal voice, 'You are right, Abdul.' Her eyes studied the long holdall on the bench, which had the word Cricket etched onto the outer surface. Over a metre long it had been designed to take cricket bats. Fatema unzipped the bag and peered inside. The semi-darkness prevented her from obtaining a clear view. She placed her hand in and found the cold metal. Rummaging, she located the short barrel of a pistol, then she moved her hand towards the end. Another barrel of cold steel, then at the far end a third. 'Pistol, automatic and rifle,' mumbled Abdul. Fatema's fingers explored the space under the barrels. The small cardboard boxes produced a satisfied nod and her finger prised the lid open. The bullets clinked as she ran her fingers through them. Her eyes left the bag and slowly rose to Abdul's face. She nodded, 'You have done well.' He shook his head. Fatema stared at him in cold triumph and hissed, 'You will do what we agreed tomorrow.'

'If I can, Fatema, it will not be easy.'

Without moving her glare from his face, 'I want to know Ibrahem's plans.' Mustafa and Abdul grimaced, but nodded.

Fatema returned her attention to the holdall, 'Are they ready for action?'

'Yes, modern ones, not like the old.'

'I'll work out how to fire them.' She attempted to lift the bag but dumped it back on the bench, 'Too heavy,' she stared fixedly at a van parked in the corner and her expression hardened.

Abdul responded with a wave of his hand and with a weary voice, 'Take the van, we'll pick it up from the restaurant tomorrow.'

'Don't forget, Abdul,' She paused and snorted with derision while her voice had a bitter edge, 'I need to know whether Shani Zaher is a threat to us as well as Ibrahem Khan.'

39

Alex marvelled at the young woman who had blossomed into adulthood over the past year. While slender, she no longer appeared small, but a beautiful woman. Even from a distance, she noted the stiff neck and strained pinched muscles on Doha's face as she hesitated on the other side of the road. What had prompted the flurry of text messages with the pleas to meet? Judging by Doha's expression, it must be urgent.

Alex continued to perform her job as she was on duty. Whitehall had been quiet at six o'clock when she had started her shift. She glanced behind as the Prime Minister in Downing Street held an impromptu press conference, but her focus would be on anyone approaching the gates. She patrolled backwards and forwards across the end of Downing Street. Another assignment away from her home group. Why did Sandy Johnson want her out of the team, perhaps because he had other intentions towards her?

Doha spotted her and crossed the road, but then hesitated, Alex grinned, 'You can come close unless the gun frightens you.'

She shook her head, her voice low and soft, 'Where shall I wait for you?'

'I've been told I'm on extended duty so do not know what time I will finish but stand next to me and we can talk.' Doha's body stiffened as she stood next to Alex, and a nervous smile played along the edges of her full lips. She didn't want to alarm her young friend but had to say, 'If I say go, don't question. Leave as quickly as possible.' Doha nodded as she carefully examined the gun and the various items on Alex's belt.

Having satisfied herself, she shuffled her feet and gave a visible shiver, 'Mum and dad have a gun.' Her words sounded shaky and clipped. Doha's sorrowful face gazed at her. Alex attempted to keep her expression neutral, although the surprising news had alarmed her. What was happening at the restaurant? Neither Mustafa nor Fatima were aggressive. Why would they have a gun? Alarm bells sounded and unease rolled through her.

Forcing her expression to remain bland so as not to worry Doha, 'Do you know how long they've had it?'

'No, it has been hidden. Early this morning, I noticed a high cupboard slightly open in the storeroom. I climbed the steps but it would not fasten so I checked to find the problem. The pistol lay on the shelf under plastic bags.'

'Do you know why they have it?'

'No, but Dad is behaving strangely and although I've asked, he won't reveal the problem. He wants me to live elsewhere, but my only relative who lives in Manchester already has a full house. I don't want to go, but dad is insistent and won't discuss it.'

Alex's mind whirled with this information. Doha needed her help, which is why she had requested a meeting. 'The situation sounds serious; do you want me to speak with them.'

'Yes, please. Something happened the day of the kidnap attempt in Brighton and they have been nervous ever since.'

'Okay, I'll visit them.' Alex studied a group of enthusiastic tourists who created a great deal of noise, but they appeared harmless. 'Do you want to come and stay at my parents' house; my mum would love to see you again?'

'Yes, please.' Her desperate gasp clipped the silence.

'I'll ring mum and arrange it.' Doha's expression was tight with strain. 'What is it? What's the matter?'

'Just after my parents became nervous, a man who I'd never met before visited the restaurant and spoke at length with mum.'

'Did he appear threatening?'

'No, he wore a business suit and had an expensive gold ring. He knew my parents from a long time ago, but they wouldn't discuss his visit.'

'Do you know his name?'

'Yes, Abdul Kadir.'

40

Jane followed Vincent into his flat after a boozy lunch. She wanted information from him. Although she referred to him as her boyfriend, their relationship remained on a casual basis. His laid back attitude to life often irritated her but he made her laugh and his love making was sensuous and breathtaking. Throwing his jacket onto a chair, he grinned and straightened his shoulders, 'Is your Sergeant still being a pain?'

'Yes, I want to get rid of him but no one else in Scotland Yard wants him because he's devious and useless.'

Although not her flat, she flicked on a table light in the small lounge as the curtains hadn't been opened. She crossed to the corner table and poured herself a large gin.

'I'll fetch the tonic from the fridge, pour me one.'

'How do you live in this dump?' She sneered at the old décor and poor furniture.

'I can't be bothered to decorate.'

Vincent took his drink and dumped himself in the middle of the two-seater sofa. The reflected light glimmered over his handsome face and the dark shadow of stubble roughened his jaw line while his intense watchful eyes gave her a lingering look, 'You asked me to find out about one of your constables, Alex Drummond.'

'Yes, that reminds me, I wanted to talk to you about her,' She expelled her breath in a slow steady hiss as she perched on the edge of a chair and swung her legs over the arm. Her short red silky skirt slid up her thighs, but she did not pull it down.

'Investigating her is difficult.'

Jane laughed and shook her head in mock disbelief. 'The great MI6 can't find the background to an English police officer.'

Vincent scowled at her laughter, 'I'm only doing it un-officially, but how the hell did she get into the police force.'

The alcohol induced good humour disappeared from Jane's face. She wriggled in her seat and her skirt slipped further up her thighs while her mouth thinned with a hint of displeasure, 'Tell me more.'

'Her mother's Algerian.'

'For Christ's sake, not every Arab is a bloody terrorist, you've got enough in your own department.'

'They do undercover work.'

Jane took a slug from her glass and placed it on a near-by table, 'Other relatives.'

'Yes, I have traced her mother's side of the family, but their links appear dubious.'

'Tell me!'

'Terrorists against France.'

'That's bloody years ago,' Jane sneered, 'I wasn't even born then. Anything else?'

Vincent sipped and then smirked. A long pause fol-lowed before he spoke, 'She's a killer.'

A quizzical expression crossed Jane's face, 'Alex has recorded no deaths since she joined the unit. At Brighton, she'd been armed, but didn't shoot as she couldn't get a clear shot.'

The smirk remained on his face, 'The self-defence case.'

'A known rapist attacking women, he'd already killed two.' He didn't respond but his expression radiated superiority as he settled back on the sofa with exaggerated casualness. 'What do you know, Vincent, tell me?'

'Have you read the court case and the background?'

'No, should I?'

'It makes interesting reading.' He picked up the bottle, leaned across and topped up her drink. 'I don't know for certain.'

'Get on with it. She convinced me it was self-defence.'

Vincent lounged in his chair and for a long moment they stared at each other before he spoke, 'The rapist liked overweight, older women. He was large, sported a big beer belly and was fifty-five years old. None of his victims before Alex possessed the capability, youth or agility to fight back.'

'Why did the prosecution miss those clues?'

'A young, beautiful woman pleads self defence when a known rapist attacks her in the park. Whose side will the public be on?'

'So, you don't think they tried hard.'

Vincent raised his eyebrows and his mouth straightened into a hard line, 'The prosecutor would have attempted to uncover any background information, but he was inexperienced as he had only been in the job for three months since leaving law college.'

Jane nodded, 'Place a junior on the case against a talented defence lawyer.'

'Exactly, so it never reached court.' Vincent stood, downed the rest of his drink and crossed the room. 'Fit, quick and ruthless sums up Alex. It would be a pleasure to welcome her to MI6 apart from her Algerian connections.'

'She's staying with me; I've plans for her.'

He bent over Jane, kissed her briefly on the lips and slipped her stretchy figure hugging top over her head allowing her breasts to swing free. She groaned in anticipation as his hand slid up the inside of her thigh, 'Alex has terrorist links in the family and is a killer.' Jane didn't care as she had more pressing thoughts on her mind.

41

Alex passed under the portico into London Zoo, having completed her early shift in Whitehall. Had it been wise to come? Early for her appointment, she wandered past the Butterfly House through a small crowd enjoying an exciting visit. As she stepped into the Land of the Lions, she scanned the crowds but didn't recognise Shani until she approached her.

Looking petite, she wore flat shoes and a plain black dress that reached her ankles. Her usual flamboyant style of dressing had disappeared. Tugging at the tightly wrapped hijab, she lowered her head keeping her eyes downcast as she drifted towards Alex. 'Thank you for coming,' Shani whispered. Keeping her eyes fixed on the ground, she added, 'Shall we watch the lions? Meeting you in private is important to me, so I had to come without bodyguards or official police support.' Alex's suspicions increased, but the tense expression on Shani's face showed the meeting was significant.

Alex waited as a lion climbed on to an old railway truck in the enclosure. To appear a tourist, she consulted the guide leaflet that she'd been given at the entrance.

'I have a problem and I need your help.' Alex had

wanted to avoid the Egyptian Embassy as she had exhausted the interlocking crescents connections when she'd visited, so she would be wary of committing herself. Shani didn't need encouragement to continue, 'Ibrahem, my fiancée, has cancelled his return to Egypt.'

'Any reason?'

'We have received death threats and he doesn't want to leave me.'

'Has he told the police?' Alex didn't want to become involved. She wasn't a private investigator and after the eavesdropped conversation she had become wary of Ibrahem. He seemed to have the strange idea that she might provide him with information. He was best avoided. A pity, as she liked Shani and had enjoyed her company.

'My father insisted he spoke to the Ambassador who has consulted the police.'

Alex nodded her approval, 'What did they advise?'

'As he is not a diplomat, he would not be protected and they advised caution but suggested his bodyguards did not carry weapons. They recommended leaving the country earlier than planned, but he wishes to stay. They advised I remained in the Embassy until my return to Egypt, but if I have pressing Government business, then they will provide an escort.'

'How was he threatened?'

'A phone call. A woman's voice. It originated from a public telephone so the caller couldn't be traced.'

Alex's curiosity rose to the surface, 'What type of accent?'

Despite the change in her fashionable appearance, Shani's eyes remained sharp and alert as they focused on Alex's face. 'Ibrahem told me, a London accent but not a native, although he couldn't determine the origin.'

'There's nothing I can do, Shani, I'm allocated to protection roles but do not choose who I accompany. I'm a mere constable and must follow orders from my Sergeant. I can't pick my assignments.'

Shani nodded, 'There are other ways which may benefit you, me and Ibrahem.'

Alex had mistaken her opinion of Shani. Initially she appeared to be a spoilt young woman, raised in a household with limitless money, but she detected a shrewd, intelligent female who would plot and plan to achieve her aims. Pausing as other people stopped nearby, they waited for them to take their pictures and move on. Her mind whirled. What had Shani meant? She remained silent and waited to hear what else Shani had to say.

'There are groups in Egypt who wish to overthrow the Government and large businesses.'

Alex raised her eyebrows in a questioning manner, 'Islamic militants?' Shani's studied the lions with her face turned away. What was she thinking?

'Yes, perhaps,' Shani wandered along the path and stopped to admire the antics of the monkeys, 'but also organised crime thrives with unstable governments and weakened businesses.'

'Why did you want to talk to me.' Alex needed some answers. Strolling side by side, they meandered along the edge of the monkey enclosure as though they were two friends enjoying a pleasant day out. Appearances were so deceptive. A flicker of apprehension swept through her as she waited to hear what Shani had to say.

'I have information about Egyptian militant groups in the UK.' A bitter smile curved on Shani's lips. 'The Ambassador suspects it would have been one of these groups who attempted my kidnap. They are based here, but their main target is in my home country. It is easier for them to meet here and join with other groups wishing to destabilise governments in the Middle East.'

'How do you know about them?'

They passed down a footpath to watch the flamingoes. 'My government tracks them in the same way as your MI6 department would track people in Egypt who are a potential threat to the UK. I will give you their names.'

'Why?' A whisper of cold air crossed her skin and she shivered.

'The English police may not be aware of them. If they are not active in the UK, then no harm is done, but if they are behind crimes because they try to raise money for their illegal activities in Egypt, you will receive the credit.'

Something about this entire conversation nagged at Alex. Worry mingled with irritation. Why was Shani doing this? What was she hoping to achieve? With growing concern, she glanced across at Shani hoping to find an answer in her expression, but Shani had turned her head away. 'Aren't you passing on information that might get you into trouble, Shani?'

'Yes, but we are friends and you will not implicate me. If the people are plotting acts against the Egyptian Government and they are arrested for crimes in this country, then it is to our benefit.' Shani caught Alex's hand, 'I am convinced it will be the same group of dissidents and militants that wish to murder my boyfriend and I wish to protect him.'

Shani carefully eyed a group of tourists that approached. She stood to one side but never took her eyes from them. Satisfied that none were taking any interest in her, she again caught Alex's hand. This time a piece of paper was pressed into her palm. She caught it between her fingers and transferred it to her pocket.

Shani headed towards the exit. Alex hadn't had time to think through her best approach going forward. Could she trust Shani? Possibly, but not the others she had met at the Embassy and country house. They would involve her solely for their own purposes and would have no interest in what happened to her. A dilemma struck her. She wanted a low profile to pursue her own aim but couldn't hold on to the information in case a senior officer found out that she had been given names and had not passed them on. If her police colleagues ignored them, that was up to them.

'Please come to the Embassy or the house again, Alex. I enjoy your company and we could have another judo match. It is safer behind the security cordon as I can relax.'

'I understand.'

'Please can you do your utmost to protect my Ibrahem?' Shani stopped at the exit to the zoo and caught Alex's hand, 'We will become close friends.' Alex fixed her eyes on Shani's face but remained non-committal. 'Before you leave here, will you meet Ibrahem?'

Alex didn't wish to meet the lecherous man, but Shani wanted to draw them together. *Has she noticed the way he ogles women?* 'Why?'

'To give you information that I do not understand.'

Against her better judgement, 'I'll meet him.'

'Thank you, Alex, you will not regret your decision.'

Had Shani considered the implications?

'Where and when?'

'He's in Regent's Park. He is concerned for my safety and so we have separated as we have death threats, but he will watch as we leave, if I nod, he will approach you.' Shani nodded as she strode through the exit.

42

Alex, wary of Ibrahem, intended the meeting would be conducted in a public area close to other people. She allowed Shani time to clear the exit. Ibrahem crossed the road further down. Alex twisted away but walked at a slow pace. Within a minute, a deep voice at her side broke through her thoughts. 'Alex, it's good of you to meet.' They proceeded along the pavement beneath the avenue of large trees, following the outer circle in Regent's Park.

Hoping to keep the conversation brief, Alex opened the questioning, 'You have information for me.'

'Yes, it's complicated.'

Alex wouldn't give him encouragement, so without turning and keeping her voice steady and monotone, 'I'm listening.' For the first time she glanced at him. The flashing eyes and the smug self-satisfied expression had vanished. Perhaps outside of the security cordon he became nervous.

'Abdul Kadir is in the country.' Alex pricked up her ears at the mention of the name. The stranger who had appeared at the restaurant which had concerned Doha. Alex didn't like coincidences and wanted further details. He needed investigating.

'When did he arrive?'

A moment's hesitation forced her to surmise that the question had surprised him. 'He runs an international business so comes to England frequently.'

'I don't understand why you are telling me about him.' Ibrahem had slowed, but Alex kept walking. She wouldn't stop to make the conversation appear intimate as she didn't trust this man but was curious to discover what he had to divulge.

'He led an infamous Cairo gang many years ago when he was young, but has now become a businessman.'

'If the immigration office sees him in that light, then he may visit and leave as he pleases.' The road took a circular route through Regent's Park, so she intended walking until he had imparted the information and she could leave.

'Why are you telling me about Abdul Kadir?'

'Can we stand, I'm becoming out of breath.' She didn't believe him, but she stopped and waited. He appeared flushed and nervous, unlike the confident man at the dinner on the estate. 'It is rumoured he resorts to his old methods when pressed.'

'Who's pressing him?'

'In the past my family opposed him frequently. I met him at the Egyptian Embassy by accident and soon after I received death threats.'

Alex didn't believe Ibrahem had useful information. Why didn't he leave the country and the problem would be solved? Her only concern was the significant change in him. He appeared drawn and nervous. 'Why would a businessman issue threats?'

'Abdul will allow no one to stand in the way of his success. Outwardly he is smooth and charming but underneath intimidating and manipulative. He uses his money to fund those on the wrong side of the law, so no one rivals him.'

The deep-throated roar of a souped-up car caught their attention as it started about fifty metres in front of them. Both stared in that direction. The car had parked in a space facing them. The deep red Subaru with darkened windows and gleaming chrome had broken the quiet bird-song of the afternoon park.

Alex strode away.

'Alex, wait, please.' The car roared but held no interest for her.

Ibrahem let out a yelp as the car shot forward from the parking space. The back wheels spun and screeched on the quiet road. 'Killers!' shouted Ibrahem pointing at the car which rapidly closed the fifty metre gap between them.

Alex tensed and focused on the approaching car. Her attention travelled to the registration plate, but Ibrahem enveloped her with his arms and forced her through a gap in the hedge. Swept off her feet from the sudden movement, she lost balance and with the momentum of his weight fell through the bushes, landing heavily. She glanced back long enough to see the darkened driver's door window open.

Alex lost her brief view of the driver in black, with no noticeable face, before Ibrahem landed on top of her and knocked the wind from her body. The car roared past and disappeared into the distance. 'They were killers. I had to save us.' Alex stood and stepped away from Ibrahem. She remained unconvinced. The incident appeared contrived. 'I will give you more information. Please help me stop them, Alex.'

43

Jane opened her eyes and studied the dark red ceiling. A shiver of revulsion shuddered through her as she smoothed her hand over her naked body.

'Are you still going out with Vincent?' Sandy Johnson propped himself onto one elbow next to her. The bedroom with dark blue walls and black bed linen flooded with light as he switched on a bedside lamp.

'What's it to you?'

Sandy moved closer on the bed; the smell of his aftershave strengthened.

'I want to know where I stand.'

'I can tell you exactly where you stand,' she rolled her head on the pillow to snarl at him, 'You're a disgusting, blackmailing pervert.'

He gave a snigger of a laugh, 'I chatted to people you met at the swingers' club. Interesting information!'

'You must have followed me, so you're a bloody stalker.'

'Fanciful information, you've no proof.'

Jane sneered, her tone sarcastic, 'Fifty miles from London and you are there. You followed me, you scumbag.'

He laughed and his eyes deliberately slid up and down

her body. Wriggling with unease under his harsh scrutiny, she jerked the sheet to cover her nakedness. Not looking at him would ease her conscience, so she closed her eyes. As he ran his finger along the outside of her thigh, she shuddered.

'You've had your fun; this is the second and last time.'

'There's nothing you can do about it, so we'll be together when I decide,' the sneering grin greeted her as she opened her eyes.

'That's where you're wrong.' The quizzical expression pleased her, 'You're still chasing Alex.' His brief intake of breath revealed the truth. 'Every time you see her your tongue is hanging out like a rabid dog.'

'What's it to do with you?'

'I've known you too long, Sandy. You're desperate to get her into bed. If you leave me alone, I could help.'

He grunted, 'Go on.'

Opening her eyes, 'I might give you a good reference as a past lover and suggest she makes a play for you.'

He sneered, 'You overrate yourself. Why would she take any notice?'

Jane's voice changed to a serious tone, 'She has her own agenda.'

'What's that mean?'

'She's always asking questions and wants information.'

'So?'

'I could suggest that you might be indiscreet, pillow talk, with confidential information.' He remained silent, but his eyes twinkled. 'I'll decide on the next step, but never attack me again, I was bruised for days.'

Jane giggled.

He yanked away the sheet covering her body.

'So have your fun for the last time, next time you can have Alex.' His hand roughly kneaded her breasts molding and reshaping them while his open mouth came down on hers with a harshness that took her breath away.

Releasing his grip on her swollen breasts he ran his fingers up the inside of her thigh making her gasp with a mixture of anticipation and pleasure. Desire warmed her body. Then in a sudden movement he stopped. 'Turn over, face down,' he snarled.

She opened her eyes and stared at his lecherous face, 'Do we have a deal?'

'Yes.'

Rolling over, she rested her head on the pillow, 'I only hope Alex wants a pervert.'

Then his large strong fingers yanked at her hair and pushed her head into the pillow. All words and thoughts deserted her as with a loud growl the full weight of his body pressed into her.

44

Alex approached the appointment with her Inspector with a mixture of emotions swirling through her. Doubt, frustration and determination all played their part in the tension that was building up making her stomach roll. The list of names that Shani had passed on were impossible for her to investigate on the police computer, although she would have preferred an opportunity to satisfy herself their identities were unimportant to her quest. The meeting would be difficult but to pacify Inspector Craddock she had emailed the names to her. The smallest snippet of information could help her mission.

The door of the Inspector's office was open wide as she approached. The smile worried Alex, although she had no reason to suspect her boss of false misrepresentation. The Inspector opened her hand to the seat opposite her desk.

'You've done well, Alex,' Jane studied her computer screen and rubbed her chin. Alex had passed on the list from Shani and a detailed account of Ibrahem's view of Abdul Kadir. 'There is nothing significant on the police computer about the names, but we need to check with a variety of Government agencies.' Her eyebrows furrowed in confusion, 'Did you believe Shani volunteered the information to protect her boyfriend?'

Alex didn't respond to the question immediately as something hadn't been right about the meeting at the zoo, but she couldn't pinpoint her unease. It lurked beyond reach in the recesses of her mind. She allowed a silent sigh and focused on the Inspector's now unsmiling face. 'Yes, when in the company of her boyfriend she appears attached to him, although I'm not convinced the relationship is reciprocated.'

'Leave the names with me. I'll keep you informed of the feedback from other agencies, especially immigration as they will lead us to an investigation, particularly if all have a concerning background but have done nothing illegal. It happens in this country as compatriots from the host country will offer help, support and can easily become embroiled for recruitment to terrorist activities either here or abroad,'

Alex assumed the end of the meeting and stood ready to leave, 'What about the mention of Abdul Kadir's friends?'

'That's tricky,' Jane made a steeple of her manicured fingers, 'we have no names.'

'Do we follow it up within our group?'

'Yes, while we pass on acquired material, we are on the ground with the diplomats so need information.' Hope bubbled up in Alex. If she became involved in the investigations, she could search the police systems for knowledge about the interlocking crescents. A thin smile edged Jane's lips, 'I'll ask Sergeant Johnson to give you time in the office and to help you. He's good with computers and has built up links with other agencies, so he should be able to find out more about Abdul Kadir and his friends.' Alex now had a legitimate reason to work with the Sergeant as her boss had given her permission. Perhaps this would lead to a breakthrough in her pursuit. A flicker of uncertainty made her shiver. But would she have to become involved with him to get the depth of information she needed?

'Before you go, Alex,' she nodded to indicate that she should sit again.

'Yes, ma'am.'

'Off the record, what do you think of Sandy Johnson?'

Was this some trial? Alex had to think fast. What type of response did she expect? Her mouth went dry and the words seemed to catch in her throat, 'We seem to rub each other up the wrong way, I don't know why?'

'That's my observation. Will you try to improve your relationship with him? He controls the information that flows in and out of this group and I wanted to assign someone to help him as he's overworked.' Alex didn't hold the same impression, but it sounded a good opportunity. 'He's old school, brought up through the police service working with men, so finds us females difficult.' She gave a short laugh. 'Will you smooth out your relationship with him by taking the initiative?'

With the chance to get unlimited access to information, Alex bubbled with excitement, 'Yes, ma'am.'

45

Mustafa stood on the pavement, nodded at his greengrocer neighbour and waved at the departing Mercedes driven by Marwa Drummond with Doha on board. The mid-morning sunshine shone on the restaurant window. In his methodical, but absent-minded way, he re-entered the restaurant, closed the blinds and locked the door. Weak in the legs and with a racing brain, he leaned against the door frame with his hand covering his face. Keeping Doha safe was of prime importance and she would be well cared for by Alex's family. When would this nightmare be over?

Fatema shuffled into the restaurant wearing a full-length black dress with a hijab. Mustafa glanced at her from between his fingers. He rubbed his forehead and a shiver ran through him at the sight of her expressionless face. 'Lock the back door, Mustafa, we want no surprise visitors.' Her words were flat and business-like as though dealing with awkward customers.

After securing the back door, he returned. In his absence, she had laid the guns, cloths and the container of cleaning fluid on the table. Next to her lay a tablet computer on which she had brought up the instructions of how to clean the semi-automatic weapons. Mustafa ran his fingers through his thinning hair in despair. Leaning against the door the sight before him sent a cold shaft of fear snaking through him, so powerful that he sank down onto a nearby chair. The woman seated at the table frightened him. Every day she sat at the same table folding napkins. Today with the same expression she cleaned guns.

'Marwa Drummond is an agreeable lady,' Fatema struggled with a catch on the gun, 'and Doha will be happy to stay with her.'

'Yes, she assured me that Doha will be well cared for at their home and she would be pleased with the company.'

Fatema gave a small nod of satisfaction as she placed the reassembled gun on the table, 'Being with Alex will be the best protection we can give her. Marwa and her husband live in a large remote house which has heavy security.'

Mustafa stared at his wife and shuddered as she picked up the pistol to clean it, 'Abdul is concerned that we are too close to a British police officer.'

Fatema stopped cleaning and hesitated, 'He is not the man I remember. In the old days he was cunning and never frightened.'

'Life changed for us when we arrived in this country,' Mustafa shuffled on his chair, 'I am now trying to cope with the recent changes in you.'

Her face softened as she lay down the gun and reached across to touch his hand, 'In Cairo, we had a fearless youth, death surrounded us but we became fighters,' she paused and a shadow touched her face, 'we had luck but our fighting and planning skills allowed us to survive and win our freedom.'

'Those days were long ago; we live in a different age.'

'You brought me to this country and I became a contented wife and mother. I've never minded the hard work and revelled in the safe environment in which we lived.' She pushed the gun away, 'then Mariam was murdered.' She gasped and drew in a long hissing breath. Her eyes watered, but she rubbed the unshed tears away with the back of her hand.

'It nearly killed you.'

'Yes, I couldn't cope with the injustice for such a beautiful girl.' Tears streamed down her face. 'When the police made no progress in finding the killers, I agonised whether we should try ourselves.'

Mustafa's eyes opened wide, 'You never shared those ideas with me.'

'No, but that caused my internal anguish. We still had Doha, so I could not risk her upbringing if you and I were taken with the revenge.' His mouth dropped open, but no words formed. She cleaned another gun, 'The threats we have received are not empty. Whoever it is will know we have a daughter. Think of the Khans. How would they attack us now?'

He nodded, but his expression remained grim, 'I understand.'

'Sending Doha away will only give us a short time to prevent the attack. We need to find those who threaten our daughter and deal with them.' Mustafa shivered. Her voice low and flat, 'I will give my life providing I take out those who wish to kill my precious daughter.'

46

'It's a dangerous game, Alex. You're not experienced at undercover work.' She sat with Sandy in the corner of the office, which prevented anyone else in the room from seeing his screen. The surprise had registered on his face when Inspector Craddock had asked him to take Alex through the method for tracing undesirables who were not British residents. Alex, keen to get on with the search, had to wait for him to make himself comfortable. In the tight corner, he brushed against her several times. Perhaps this would be the opportunity to search the computer, she needed to keep him sweet, she'd do anything to help her quest, so she moved closer.

'It's not undercover work, I'm only seeing Shani.'

Sandy's eyes opened wide as he switched on his computer, 'I never expected you to get involved with the passing of names. If the wrong person at the Embassy finds out, they might come after you.'

'Yes, I understand, but I want to help Shani. While she has the privileges of money, she is a lonely soul and I like her.' Did her words sound convincing?

'Who are we checking first?' Sandy drew the keyboard towards him.

'Ibrahem Khan, he's Shani's boyfriend, but I don't think he can be trusted.' Alex hadn't mentioned the souped up Subaru that had shot past them in Regent's Park. As a police officer, she should have made a better effort to read the number plate, but had missed it and despite Ibrahem's pleads afterwards that if he hadn't pushed her into the bushes, it would have been a drive-by shooting, she hadn't been convinced. Her mind wandered, late afternoon, not a time for fast cars. In the evening it would have been a suitable explanation. Why couldn't she see the driver's face?

'I need you to come with me, Alex.' Jane Craddock approached the crammed corner and unusually a smile crossed her lips. Alex wanted to delve into the people's background. It might lead to the results she wanted. When Sandy became bored, she would volunteer to carry on. It would be her best chance in the two years she'd been in the police force. She didn't want to miss the opportunity. She frowned, 'Now?'

'Yes, it's important.'

Her mouth tightened as a shot of nervousness ran through her, 'Where?'

'No questions.'

Sandy opened his hand to show Alex should go, 'We'll catch up later.'

'We need to change out of uniform.'

This statement aroused her curiosity. Where were they going? 'Any clothes in particular?'

'Doesn't matter, whatever is in your locker will do, but I've arranged to meet in half an hour.' Her mind raced as she changed into an old tee shirt, jacket and jeans. The sudden decision from the Inspector both intrigued and alarmed her. Alex met her at the exit door from New Scotland Yard. To Alex's surprise, the normal immaculately dressed Inspector had changed into a pair of baggy trousers with splodges of paint, a thick dark blue fleece and dark green trainers. The Inspector led the way from the building and headed along the embankment towards the Houses of Parliament. Alex had no clues as to the destination but she wanted to return to Sandy and pursue the tracing of the names.

The Inspector's harsh voice cut through the noise of the traffic and brought Alex back from daydreaming. 'You are an inexperienced officer, caught up in complex matters and you are about to become immersed. Does that give you concerns?'

'No, ma'am. I'll follow orders.'

'You must promise to leave your gung-ho approach behind as it won't be suitable going forward.' Alex nodded, but didn't speak. 'No one doubts your bravery, but we want you alive.' The message made Alex shiver, but she couldn't ask questions so would have to wait. She guessed a political meeting at the Foreign Office, although she struggled to understand the reason for changing from her uniform.

The Inspector didn't turn towards Whitehall and the Foreign Office but crossed the road towards the Houses of Parliament. Ignoring the entrance, she carried on walking and answered her mobile. Would this be the next part of Alex's training in the police force? From being on the outside a few weeks ago, she had been accepted far more. Her personal chances of success would increase if she managed to search the computer systems without the worry she might be caught. Sandy would be the key to unfettered access. How far to lead him on?

Finishing her call, the Inspector crossed Vauxhall

Bridge. Alex had a good idea of where they were heading, Vauxhall Cross, the headquarters of the Secret Intelligence Services. The Inspector made a brief call, 'Yes, I know. We'll meet you there.'

Passing by the block-built building which faced the Thames, she led the way to Vauxhall gardens passing to the far side and then stepped through the gate into the allotments. Alex's eyes searched the area. But the early season onions and late sprouts showed it to be a real allotment. The Inspector perched on the edge of a pile of pallets. 'We'll wait, he won't be long.'

Alex scrutinised every movement in the street, but no view caused her suspicion. What a strange place to meet? A few people drifted through the park. A thick set man, a few years older than her, wearing a dark jumper and jeans with cropped hair hurried across the grass, came into the allotment and approached them. Jane stood and gave the man a wonderful smile, the most significant one that Alex had seen. He hugged and kissed her on the lips. Breaking away, he caught both her hands, 'You're looking superb, Jane.'

A slow secret expression crossed her face, 'Behave yourself, we're here on business.'

Alex received a radiant smile from the scruffy man and held out her hand, which he ignored. He enveloped her in a hug and kissed her on the cheek, 'Great to meet you, Alex. I'm Vincent. Two beautiful women. What more can I ask?'

Despite the circumstances, a shiver of excitement passed through her as Vincent studied her face. She concentrated on him. Unlike her past men, who were tall, dark and handsome, Vincent didn't have those features, but her legs went weak as their eyes locked. What was it about him? Not looks. Manner? Not sure. Charisma? Yes, he had loads.

'Business,' the Inspector snapped her fingers and they exchanged a look of subtle amusement while her voice had lost its usual harshness.

'Sorry about the ridiculous place to meet,' he glanced at the Inspector.

She shook her head, 'I've not explained.'

He focused his attention on Alex, 'As you might have guessed, I come from the Legoland building back there on the Thames, MI6. It's too complicated to negotiate your entry into the building, as your positive vetting hasn't been completed, so you do not have the security clearance.'

If they investigated her, please don't let them discover a reason to reject her. She'd never shared with anyone her real intentions in joining the police. Her record at the United Nations had been impeccable.

'I'll leave you with Vincent.' Glancing at him a slow secret expression covered her face, 'Give me a time and day?'

A lopsided grin adorned his face and his eyes twinkled with mischief. 'Perhaps.' She gave a gurgle of laughter as she strode away towards the exit. Alex observed the exchange with intense curiosity. Were they lovers? She waited, allowing the silence to lengthen as apprehension about this strange meeting made her stomach muscles clench. Why had she been set up to meet MI6?

Alex scanned the allotments while she waited for Vincent, who busied himself in a ramshackle lean-to shed. He flashed a wide grin and straightened his shoulders, 'While we are here, we can make ourselves useful. I'll fill you in as we go.' He unlocked a small wooden trunk made of old pallets and handed Alex a trowel. Picking up a second trowel, he then selected two small paper packets.

'You plant the carrots in that row,' indicating a smooth line in the tilled soil, 'and I'll do the cauliflower.' Alex read the instructions on the packet and began her task, although her mind continued to spin with questions about this strange meeting.

'How are the people at the Egyptian Embassy?' Vincent planted the cauliflower seeds without looking at her.

The question showed that he had been briefed about her recent background encounters, 'Shani wants to be friends, I'm not sure about Ibrahem's motives for wanting to talk with me.'

He chuckled, 'I can guess and I don't blame him.'

'Yes,' her mouth twitched with a mixture of embarrassment and amusement, 'but the other day his confidence had gone.'

'Have you met Abdul Kadir?'

'No, but he's been mentioned by several people who didn't expect him to be allowed into the country.'

'He runs a multi-national company and is the height of respectability these days.'

'But not in the past.' Alex stopped seeding to observe the reaction in Vincent, but he didn't lift his head and continued his meticulous planting. 'Has he left the past behind?' Alex would not mention that her friends had met him.

'Do your best to ingratiate yourself with the Embassy, it's a good opportunity for us to obtain inside knowledge.' After delicately stroking the soil onto the top of the seeds, he straightened up with a groan and rubbed a hand across his lower back. 'Once your security clearance is through, I'll fully brief you, although we only want you to watch and listen.'

'Why has your department become involved?'

'We are interested in one name on the paper Shani gave to you. Also, we need intelligence about Abdul Kadir. We're not sure how the Egyptian pieces fit together, which is where you can be useful.'

As he'd been talking Alex tried to keep her opinions hidden. This was another great opportunity to further her cause. A surge of optimism filled her as she carefully raked the soil across the drill of carrot seeds. It gave her another chance to study Vincent. What was it about him that appealed to her? His warm gold green eyes were without doubt his best feature. They were lazily seductive but at the same time sharp and assessing.

47

Despite a good evening out that had finished in a VIP night club, Jane's two current issues, Alex and Sandy Johnson, would not leave her mind. She had to deal with both, but she needed more information about Alex.

Hammering on the door she tapped her toes with impatience as she waited. Where was he? Why wasn't he answering? When the door finally opened, she glowered at Vincent and pushed him out of the way as she strode down the short gloomy hallway. 'I want words with you!' she snapped. Wearing a flowing blue dress, black jacket and strappy high heels she stood in the middle of the lounge with a thunderous expression on her face. Rubbing his bleary eyes, he ran his fingers through his short dishevelled hair and yanked at his boxer shorts which were in danger of slipping, 'For Christ's sake, Jane, it's six o'clock on a Sunday morning.' Dragging on his dressing gown, he tied the cord and dumped himself on the couch with an exaggerated groan. 'I was having such a wonderful dream before you interrupted. Now I'll never know how it ended.'

Peeling off her jacket, she threw it onto a chair and with hands on her hips she remained standing in the centre of the lounge, 'I want an explanation from you.'

'Oh God, you are in a mood.' He raised a hand to his forehead in mock horror while his eyes squinted with a twinkle of mischief.

Jane ignored his humour and her bright blue eyes impaled him with an unblinking glower. 'I had a drink with Sandy Johnson last night.' She didn't elaborate any further. Vincent didn't need to know that she'd had another steamy love making session with her Sergeant. His domineering and demanding style was becoming addictive. A grin crossed Vincent's face. Had he guessed? He raised his eyebrows, but she chose to ignore him and carried on with her tirade, 'he saw you being lovey-dovey with Alex.'

'You and your slimy Sergeant together,' he put his arms behind his head and rested back against his hands while a wide grin creased his lips. 'I would have loved to be a fly on the wall for that conversation.' His comment hit home. What did Vincent know? Had he found out about her sex with Sandy Johnson?

'Are you spying on me?' Jane's top lip curled, and she gave an impatient huff as uncertainty swept through her. Trying to gain the upper hand she opted for a verbal attack. 'Just because you work for MI6 you think you're a super spy, don't you? But we both know that you use your work connections to pick up the dross on everyone you meet.' Pausing for breath she waggled her finger at him, 'You are a dirty-minded stalker.'

Vincent waved his hand in dismissal, but the grin did not leave his face, 'I learned it all from you and your dodgy sergeant.' With a loud chuckle he rearranged his gaping dressing gown.

Her mouth thinned with displeasure and twisting away from him, she gave an impatient shrug. This conversation was not going according to plan. Why was he laughing at her? 'Are you going to dump me so you can try it on with Alex?'

'Face reality, our relationship fluctuates as you chase other men at every opportunity.'

'At the beginning when we were casually dating that was true, but our relationship has developed, so I assumed we'd settled down as we hit it off and have fun together.'

Allowing a long silence to develop, he stared idly around the room, 'Are you in it for the long term, Jane?'

Tilting her head on one side, she gave him a broad smile, 'I am, are you?' Having Vincent all to herself was what she wanted. She didn't want to share him with anyone, especially Constable Alex Drummond. The little indiscretions that she indulged in were not important. Besides Vincent wouldn't find out. He had no realisation how important men were in her life. She had a large appetite for them. With difficulty she suppressed the small smile that threatened to surface on her pouting lips and turned away.

The silence between them stretched. He hadn't answered her question. Jane wandered over to the drinks table and moved the bottles into a neat line, 'Have you seduced her?'

'Who?'

'You know who I mean. She is beautiful; her elegance and poise are complimented by her perfect skin colour.'

'Fancy her yourself, do you?'

She glanced over her shoulder at him, 'Don't be silly, I only like men. You didn't answer my question.'

'No, I haven't been to bed with her.'

A small grin crossed her face and she narrowed her eyes, 'Is that because you haven't tried or because she won't have you?' She laughed, 'You need two reminders.'

Vincent gave a nervous laugh, 'What reminders?'

Jane crossed the room to stand in front of him as he sprawled on the couch. His face remained impassive. Jane's arms crossed her front and she peeled the blue dress upwards in one smooth movement and threw it to join her jacket on the nearby chair. She stood naked except for the high-heeled stilettos.

Vincent grinned, held out his arms and opened his dressing gown. She accepted and with a deft movement straddled him. Pushing her breasts into his face, she whispered in his ear, 'First reminder, I'm much better in bed than her, I can guarantee that.'

His hands moved up to cup her breasts and he grinned again, 'What's the second.'

She placed her hands on either side of his head and nestled her fingers in his hair. As she wriggled on his lap his grin widened. Faces inches apart, her mouth curved with amusement, then she twisted her fingers through his hair and yanked hard. He yelped. She shifted again but didn't let go of his hair and using her flexibility she shifted her position and drove her stiletto heels into his thigh on either side of his groin. The loud yelp filled her with a sense of superiority. Leaning forward she tickled his ear with her tongue and whispered, 'Second reminder, I can get nasty.'

48

Alex concentrated on the computer screen as she struggled to discover the best way to search for links to the interlocking crescents. Changing tack, she examined the information that had been found about the people on the list passed on by Shani, but nothing of interest emerged. What next? The details she required would be there somewhere. It was a question of finding the right words for the search. She tapped the keyboard in frustration.

Jane appeared next to her desk. Her expression was stony and with no preamble, 'The Superintendent wishes you to represent the Metropolitan Police to brief the Egyptian Ambassador on the updates to the kidnap attempt.'

This came as a surprise to Alex, and she struggled to maintain a neutral expression. 'For updates to diplomats, normally one of the liaison units or you would go, ma'am.'

'Yes, I understand our usual protocol, but the Ambassador rung the Foreign Secretary and mentioned your name, so it's come down the chain of command. They know and trust you.'

Keeping a straight face to disguise her enthusiasm, it would give her a legitimate reason to delve further as she would be expected to deliver information. 'I don't know how the investigation has progressed.'

'You can read the case updates, but those captured are not talking and we have no further information about the one who escaped.'

'Do we have progress, otherwise we will be in for criticism?'

'Unfortunately, no.' The Inspector's face darkened and her whole demeanor seemed to grow in severity.

'It will not please the Egyptians.' Why had they placed her in such a difficult position?

'Never mind,' Jane snapped back, 'stick by the usual statements. It's a complex situation and we do not know whether the incidents require a great deal of manpower to investigate or are only internal issues in Egypt. That is why we have involved MI6.' Alex wanted snippets of information but sensed that the Inspector kept anything usefull to herself. 'Did you have a good meeting with Vincent?'

'Yes, we chatted for a while and will discuss the Egyptians next week.'

'He's good at his job.'

'I'm sure he is.' But as he had asked her out, mixing her private life with her job added another complication she did not need. Becoming involved with him would be too soon after Matthew. Another complication was his involvement with Jane, who was her boss. It had the possibility of being complicated and messy. Gauging it to be the end of the meeting, she closed down the computer and pushed her chair back, 'Are you sure you want me to visit the Embassy?'

'There is no doubt, the Met Police seniors want you to go. They have requested you attend as soon as possible.'

Alex shoulder's slumped, 'I'll go today if they will see

me. Do I assume as it is an official visit, I go in uniform in a police car?'

'Good question, Alex. No, in your casual gear in a taxi.'

49

Mustafa scanned the dark dungeon-like club in the basement of a tired concrete building that housed decaying industries and businesses. Ali sat on a half-broken chair at the next wooden table. 'How do you know of this place, Abdul, it is far from your normal luxury?' He placed his hand to his face to stop the insipid smell of sweat mixed with cannabis from entering his nose.

Raised voices near the dingy bar escalated to shouting and swearing until bouncers appeared. The quieter, seedy atmosphere in the semi-dark returned. The card players only allowed a momentary distraction to check on the noise then returned their attention to the money piled in the middle of their game.

Abdul, in old clothes with a scruffy anorak that he hadn't removed, sat hunched in the corner. His shapeless body gave the appearance of a down and out, but his steely eyes sparkled. 'Sometimes it is necessary to do business with those you would prefer to avoid.' Abdul's eyes attached to a man in a dark jacket, jeans and a woollen hat who had entered. Mustafa remained quiet.

The man hesitated until he received a nod from Abdul, and then he approached. He slipped into a chair at the table and gave a perfunctory nod. The man slipped a packet to Abdul. Without a word, he left the club.

Abdul whispered, 'The go-between for the guns.' Mustafa gulped and stared at the two pints of lager in front of them, which had been bought to look normal. Neither would drink from them.

Abdul moved closer to him, 'What's the latest with Fatema?'

He let out an audible sigh and rubbed his face, 'My wife has transformed from a home loving, hard working mother into a possessed evil spirit.'

Abdul nodded, 'She has returned to the old days.'

'I fear for her.' Mustafa hung his head.

'Yes, so do I.'

Mustafa opened the palms of his hands and raised his shoulders, 'But how do we get through to her?'

'We must think of a way.' Silence fell and they allowed the noise and smells of the club to wash over them as they stared at their untouched lagers.

'What do you think will happen, Abdul?'

'I hope that the threats are to unnerve us as our enemies have moved to a psychological war. This is twenty-first century London, crimes especially murders are usually solved.'

'They never caught the killers of my Mariam.'

Abdul's hand rubbed his face, then he patted Mustafa on his shoulder, 'I'd wish I'd known her.'

'I should have attempted to contact you when you first arrived in this country with your business. I regret it now,' mumbled Mustafa.

'Feeling sorry for ourselves will not help.' Abdul sat up straight, 'I am concerned you have a police officer as a friend, I want you to break away from her, we are better on our own.' Mustafa's wide eyes stared at his friend, but he didn't reply. Abdul carried on regardless, 'I hope Fatema wanted the guns for defence although she speaks aggressively, just like the old days.'

Mustafa shook his head, his eyes focused on Abdul's face, 'She is convinced Ibrahem Khan is responsible for the threats and he is the one who endangers us.'

'So, what is her plan?'

He shook his head, 'Some bullets for the rifle are missing.' Abdul tilted his head on one side in a questioning manner, 'Despite her attempts to clean away the evidence, the rifle has been fired.'

'Has she been to target practice, like the old days?'

'That is my guess, although she goes out for long periods and will not tell me where she is going.' Mustafa dropped his head in his hands, 'I believe she intends killing Ibrahem Khan.'

50

Alex took a deep breath, paid the taxi outside the Egyptian Embassy and approached the main door which opened before she rang the bell. The servant bowed, 'Welcome, Constable Drummond, please follow me.' She had become recognised within the Embassy which worried her. The servant knocked gently on the largest door in the corridor and entered.

He stood to one side and bowed again as she stepped into the room, 'Constable Drummond.' Alex expected a formal meeting with the Ambassador and perhaps his security adviser, so it came as a surprise to see Shani and her father seated alongside the desk. Shani jumped from her seat and hugged Alex. Both men nodded indulgently. Not the meeting she had expected where heavy criticism of the Metropolitan Police would be forthcoming.

The Ambassador waited for Shani to finish her enthusiastic greeting and offered Alex a seat. Again, not what she had expected. The Ambassador, a man with a large face and wearing a bright red patterned kaftan, had an open and friendly expression. 'Thank you for coming to meet with us.' Despite the Ambassador going up the chain of command at the Foreign Office, he appeared relaxed. 'I believe you will give us an update.'

Flustered by the less than ideal situation, Alex took a deep breath, 'The captured men refuse to talk and the escaped man has not been identified.' The constant stare of Shani didn't waver, but she would not return the look. 'We have received the identity of suspects and are following them through.'

'Where did the list come from?'

'An anonymous source, sir.' Alex focused her eyes firmly on the Ambassador and didn't glance at Shani.

'Alex, thank you for the update, but the lack of progress gives me concern.'

'Yes, I can appreciate your unease.'

Confusion flashed through her as the Ambassador had addressed her by her first name. 'I shall point out to your Foreign Office that you gave us an excellent briefing, but I would wish to keep the pressure on them and hence the Metropolitan Police to come up with an answer.'

'Yes, sir.' Assuming the meeting to have ended, Alex pushed back her chair and rose to her feet.

The two men stood. A flash of eagerness crossed Youssef Zaher's face, 'I hope you don't have to rush off as Shani is looking forward to your company this evening.'

'I've no plans.' She tried to keep the reluctance from her voice.

Shani leaped up, 'Excellent, we have a gym downstairs.'

A look of amusement flickered on Alex's face, 'A judo match?'

Shani nodded and giggled, 'Yes, please.'

The Ambassador laughed, 'You ladies are experts at martial arts. It frightens me that such beautiful people can have that aggression.'

As they descended to the gym, Shani gripped Alex's arm and gave her a small squeeze, 'You haven't visited, which is a pity because we have become friends.'

Her thoughts drifted to her Inspector and Vincent, who both wanted her to visit more often. 'I'm sorry, Shani,' Alex lied, 'I had to be with my family but I've no pressures now so may visit you as many times as you like.'

'That's excellent. As well as judo we can visit the estate in Hertfordshire and ride.'

Alex would begin her search for information with innocuous questions. 'Aren't you spending time with Ibrahem?'

She shook her head, 'Although he is my boyfriend, he neglects me.' She giggled. 'He has to visit other businesses, despite the threats, so your company would be most welcome. Everyone in this building admires you for your bravery in tackling those evil people.'

Shani caught Alex's hand as they reached the changing room door, 'Thank you for meeting Ibrahem and I'm sorry the meeting didn't go well.' In the subsequent confusion, Alex had nearly forgotten about the meeting in Regent's Park. She harbored doubts about the Subaru car but why she doubted it after the other incidents she wasn't sure. She remained apprehensive. 'Ibrahem was glad he spoke with you. He believes the information he passed on will help protect him.'

Shani had become a mystery. Demure and innocent looking until she began a judo match, then an aggressive and uncompromising young woman took over. There appeared no reason for her continued presence in the country.

The facilities in the basement gym were more primitive than in the country house. Shani led Alex into the compact changing room. Judo kit, the right size, had already been laid out for her on the bench. Shani had expected a match.

Despite trying to think of different approaches, she was at a loss of what questions to ask. She would have to report back to Vincent and Inspector Craddock but didn't have one piece of information.

'I'm afraid sharing facilities here is necessary.'

'It doesn't concern me, providing you are content.'

'Yes, no problem for me.'

They stripped to their underwear. Shani faced her. Alex's eyes were drawn to a tattoo of interlocking crescents at the top of her leg. Although difficult to stare, she was convinced they were the arrangement of the interlocking crescents for which she searched. A skimpy bikini would cover the tattoo. Had Shani deliberately set this up so she would see it? They had discussed interlocking crescents more than once and Shani had given her a brooch.

It would have been easy to make excuses about not sharing a changing room so she could have easily obscured it if she didn't want to reveal it to Alex. Her mind reeled with possibilities. Shani popped on her judo jacket, 'Did you notice my new tattoo?'

'No,' Alex lied, allowing her a deliberately longer scrutiny which confirmed her earlier glances.

'I liked the brooch I gave you and as I've been thinking of a discrete tattoo for some time it seemed the perfect symbol.'

51

Alex had arrived at Mariam's restaurant perplexed by the call from Mustafa asking for an urgent meeting. With his wife and daughter out visiting friends and the restaurant closed as usual on a Monday, he led her into the back yard. With no preamble as to the purpose of the meeting, 'Alex, can I beg of you to protect my wife and Doha should anything happen to me.'

'I will, but nothing will happen to you,' Alex moved uncomfortably at the direct plea for help. Alex hadn't met Mustafa for several weeks and she saw a changed man before her. The Egyptian cigarette gave a pungent smell in the late evening as it drifted across the yard behind the restaurant. Alex wrinkled her nose up at the sweet sickly smell but needed information. They stood in the backyard gazing up at the overcast, moonless sky.

Mustafa flexed his shoulders, drew a deep breath of the spicy cigarette and exhaled puffing the smoke into the night sky, 'When I first met you as a bright friend for my Mariam, I was pleased that she had chosen such a wonderful person.'

'Doha is with my parents who dote on her, but did you know she found the gun you are hiding?' A shadow of discomfort crossed his face.

Shaking his head mournfully, his shoulders slumped, 'I need it close by and feared she would find it, which is why we wanted her out of the house.' Pausing, he eyed Alex in a questioning manner, 'Will you arrest me?'

She'd agonised on her journey to the restaurant as to her approach. 'Tell me why you need a gun.' Avoiding the discussion of an arrest might be the best approach for this evening. Alex lowered her voice. 'You are not an aggressive man, so you must fear an attack?'

'It is a long story which had passed into fable, but history is resurrected.'

'I'm not leaving.' Alex folded her arms across her chest and leaned against the wall to emphasise her words. 'I want to know the details.'

He sighed and lit another cigarette, 'The gangs around here remind me of my youth in Cairo. We started young and in harmless groups. Older years brought more daring and the first stealing. Moving into manhood, we had no jobs or prospects, so we blamed the government and the large successful businesses. The extreme circumstances we suffered bred violent discontent. I'm ashamed of my history, but at the time I willingly joined the militants.'

'Is it people from your past who are causing trouble?'

'I wish it were that simple, my dear Alex. If it were so, I would visit them and pay them off as they would respect me as I became one of their leaders.'

'Were you never arrested?'

'Do not compare the policing in London with my days in Cairo. No-go areas were common. We ruled the roost; the police couldn't come and arrest us without causing riots, so they stayed away.'

Moving to the end of the yard and despite the cold night, he sat on a rusty crooked metal bench. Alex shivered as the chill crept through her insubstantial jacket and she flicked up her collar and stuffed her hands into her pockets. Sitting nearby, she waited as she didn't want to break the flow as it might reveal a clue which could lead her forward in her own investigation.

Leaning forward, he positioned his elbows on his knees and stared at the slabs through the darkness. 'Violent groups divide because they cannot agree and ours split into two factions. Rivalry developed with the associate violence over territorial and control issues. The modern press would call it gangland violence with beatings, killings and riots.'

'Your Cairo days must have been over thirty years ago, surely the gangs do not still exist.'

'You are right, many left Egypt to avoid the repercussions, but it is their descendants who have revived the cult and intend taking an international stage. The young are forcing the old to join their campaigns, so violence abounds here and in Egypt.'

'Do you know the leaders' names?'

'Such knowledge would place you in danger.'

'You know that will not frighten me.' Alex tensed, 'My colleagues would only need one crucial piece of information to help eradicate the behaviour.'

'The leader of my gang is now an important figure but is resisting violence. But the pressure may be too strong for him to ignore it for long as the new factions must be stopped.'

'Will you tell me his name?' She suspected it would be Abdul Kadir.

Rubbing his chin, 'Despite the years that have passed, I will not encourage the police to take him.'

'How will we stop the violence, Mustafa?'

'He is a highly articulate man who I sincerely believe has renounced violence.' This could be the crucial information that Alex needed. 'I cannot inform on him, even to you.'

Alex had to break the impasse they had reached. 'Does the symbol of interlocking crescents mean anything to you?'

His shoulders lurched and he buried his face in his hands, 'Please no more, you know too much.'

'The name. I must have the name,' she hissed.

'I cannot. I cannot,' he cried. 'He once saved my life so I could not live with letting him down.'

Alex racked her brains for a different approach. The silence hung between them. The cold night enveloped her, but she ignored her shivers. In a low but firm voice, 'I want you to take me to meet him.'

He shook his head, 'The men around him are violent.'

'I want to meet him.' Again, he shook his head. 'I will be an unarmed defenceless woman, let's prove your friend has given up violence.'

52

Alex weighed up her options. Should she ring Inspector Craddock or Vincent to report that Mustafa Mohamed would meet a key person of the investigation? No, she couldn't betray him, and she yearned to discover information for her personal pursuit so she had to trust him.

The dark night had intensified as Mustafa, without speaking, led her through the back streets of Paddington. He hadn't told her where they were headed. He puffed away on one cigarette after another. From the main road, he took a side road and stopped. The anguished face stared at her, the creases on his forehead intensified by the subdued street lighting. 'Are you sure? There is time to turn back.'

Alex didn't hesitate. 'I'm in no doubt. I want to meet him.'

Taking a deep breath, he lit another cigarette and lengthening his stride turned into a rundown business trading estate a little way down the road. Alex had memorised the route and location, but there were no secrets about the name of the dilapidated 1960s trading estate. Some buildings had been refurbished and appeared more prosperous, while others had old signs and showed decay. Many hadn't been painted for years. Randomly working weak floodlights gave a shadowy appearance to the area.

From one building, a mass of lights shone out and a hubbub of loud voices filled the night air. A courier firm readied itself for the nightly transfer. 'This way.' Mustafa strode past the bright lights and passed into the darkness at the far end of the estate. They headed to the last building. A faint glow from reception showed an old man at a desk. The night watchman.

The sign along the front of the windowless concrete building announced Kay Foods. Her eyes searched the length of the sign which remained in the shadows. A single crescent gave the logo of the business. Her stomach muscles tensed.

Mustafa entered reception where an old man sat reading a newspaper in the weak light. The man grunted and didn't lift his head. With a nod Mustafa passed him, led Alex through a door and into a low lit warehouse where the space had been filled with butchering benches. From one side a dull drone indicated walk-in fridges and freezers.

Voices echoed in the warehouse. Lugubrious chatting in Arabic, but nothing significant only idle conversation. The men tensed as Mustafa and Alex marched towards them, one muttered, 'Mustafa' and they returned to their conversation. Several heavy men came as a surprise as they entered an office. She counted five. They didn't chat. They tensed, the nearest to the door dropped his hand inside his jacket. The others freed their hands and stood watching her every move, but Mustafa ignored their presence.

'Is he in?' A brief nod, but no words. Mustafa scowled. Their intimidating sight seemed to hold no fears for him. Alex admired his singlemindedness and determination, a different man to the one she had known over the years.

The poor soul must be struggling with the trauma in his life which had been ignited by past times. Giving a hard rap on the door, he didn't wait for a reply and shoved open the battered wooden door and strode into the office.

The man behind the desk tensed and his arm shot to the open drawer to his right. Another gun, although it remained hidden from view. The thickset man in his fifties, wearing a smart business suit, despite the time of night, adjusted his position behind the desk. Alex recognised the features of Egyptian descent. His chubby fingers were covered with rings and his open shirt front revealed a gold medallion. The scowl and tension etched across his face made Alex gulp. She had descended into the depths of the lion's den to obtain information.

Despite his large size, he skipped from behind the desk, the scowl disappeared to be replaced by a welcoming grin, 'Mustafa, my good and loyal friend, peace be with you.' They hugged and touched cheeks.

Old friend sprung to Alex's mind, but the scowl returned as he regarded her with a calculating and unfriendly scowl. Then twisting his face away, he muttered a few words to Mustafa.

'She is fluent in Arabic,' Mustafa dumped himself on a seat. The man shouted in Arabic, 'Ali. Come. Stand guard.' A large man entered and stood with his hand inside his jacket.

'We will speak in English. Ali cannot understand.'

'I won't make you suffer the indignity of a personal search, Constable Drummond.'

'I am not armed. Mustafa maintained I could trust you.'

Mustafa nodded, 'You are right, Alex, I trust my

friend to do right by you.'

'Do you have a name?' He ignored the question and eyed Alex up and down, 'Everything Mustafa has said about you I can see to be true. Dealing with that attack on Shani makes you a resourceful and deadly lady.'

Ignoring his comment, she fired another question, 'Do you know the attackers?'

'They are not my men. My name is Abdul Kadir.'

Despite the tension, a small smile crossed her lips. 'You know Ibrahem Khan, I believe.'

'You are well informed. I have known Ibrahem for many years and met him recently at the Egyptian Embassy. Why did you want to meet me?'

'I wish to protect the people dear to my heart. Mustafa and his family have long held a place in my affections. Unfortunately, I could not protect my husband and Mustafa's other daughter from being killed during a terrorist attack.'

'I heard. Do you wish to arrest the assailants?'

'My greatest wish is to stop the violence being perpetrated toward Mustafa and his family. I wanted to meet with you. I believe you hold the key to prevention and a peaceful resolution.'

'You assume I hold more power than I do.'

Alex gave a gentle shake of her head and nodded towards the guys in the outer office, 'You understand the undercurrents which come from your home country. The only arrest I would wish to make is the man who killed my husband and best friend.'

'Would you arrest them or kill them?'

Alex didn't answer, but her eyes narrowed and a surge of tension scoured through her body.

Mustafa's voice cracked with emotion, 'Please Abdul,

use your skills and influence to end this renewed blood-shed. We are old men now who have renounced violence for peaceful means. Despite the men here, I know you well, my friend. You would prefer the dark days of our youth to stay there. I would give up my life to stop this mindless violence which will descend on to my wife and daughter.'

Abdul focused his attention on Alex. 'Coming here on your own without the backup of your police force is either brave or foolish.'

Alex wouldn't be daunted and ignored his words. 'I presume this is your business?'

'My family owns it.'

'The authorities have allowed you into this country despite a record in the past. It's time we moved on.'

Resting back in his chair, 'You are a stunningly beautiful woman but so single minded it frightens me. I have never met an English police officer with your intensity. I suspect that if you thought me responsible, then you would not hesitate to take me out.'

'I am not an assassin; this is England where the police arrest people they do not kill them.'

Silence filled the air; his piercing eyes never left her face. 'I wish I could believe you.'

53

With the shock of meeting Abdul Kadir on the previous evening filling her mind, Alex had another summons to Inspector Craddock's office as she returned to her base after a standard escort duty.

Alex's tension had grown. Mustafa's connections with Abdul Kadir and the hidden gun at the restaurant caused her concern. The conversation had moved on from the reason he'd obtained it, but she had been caught between support for a friend and her duty as a police officer. Why had she allowed herself to move into such a dangerous position?

Why hadn't she persuaded Mustafa to go with her to the police? The reason was obvious. It might solve the immediate problem, but she had a sniff of finding the killers she wanted as interlocking crescents produced a reaction in both Mustafa and Abdul. When the symbols had been mentioned they'd become wary. After a quick glance at each other, they had focused their attention on the ground and had refused to continue the conversation. They'd gritted their teeth and remained silent.

Forcing herself to be calm and composed, she knocked on the Inspector's door and held her breath as she waited for the reply. 'Come in, Alex.' Jane waved a hand towards the single chair and waited for Alex to settle herself. 'During the two days you have been off duty we have had a call from the Egyptian Embassy.' Would it be another social occasion? She'd had enough of those. Possibly another judo match would lead to closeness between her and Shani which might allow her to discover whether the tattoo was a recent addition as she suggested or something older and more significant.

'Yes, ma'am.'

'You know Youssef Zaher and his daughter Shani.'

'Yes, ma'am.'

'He has been dismissed from his post in the Egyptian cabinet for taking bribes. He will have no appeal.'

Alex opened her eyes wide at the unexpected news. Did it change her approach? Would it affect her quest? To conceal her innermost thoughts, she focused on keeping her voice calm and controlled, 'May I presume they will no longer be at the Embassy and my involvement with them will cease?'

'Yes, do not meet with Shani.'

That's a pity, but perhaps Abdul Kadir would prove to be a better link to her husband's killers. From their brief meeting, it was obvious he understood the underworld of Egypt. Could she deal with him and extract the information? A difficult task, but he had the key and she needed it.

With a curt dismissal, she left the Inspector's office and trudged her way along the corridor towards the changing rooms, where she dumped herself on the bench and gave a silent groan. Life had become more complicated. In her early days in the police force, she had imagined pursuing her quest to a successful conclusion. It hadn't worked out. The tension and stress of meeting Abdul had made her uneasy all day. Moistening her lips, she sat up as her phone vibrated with an incoming call. Shani's name flashed on the screen of her mobile. They had exchanged private numbers at the Embassy. Needing to dismiss her, the best ploy would be to answer.

'Alex, it's Shani.'

'What do you want?' Alex couldn't hide the aggression in her voice.

'My father has been stitched up by lies and rumours, none of which are true. He has lost his position in the cabinet and we are desperate for help.'

A sense of rising irritation made Alex's whole body tense, 'There's nothing I can do about your predicament.'

'Can we meet? I need to see you.'

'No, I've been told by my boss to avoid you, so I can't meet.' The deliberate harshness in Alex's voice would signal an end to the conversation.

'Please, Alex, it would mean so much to me as you are my best hope.'

'No, Shani.' Alex expected the call to be dropped.

'Do you remember the last judo match we had?'

'Yes.'

'You noticed my tattoo of the interlocking crescents.' Alex stayed silent. 'You are interested in them, I'm not sure why, but I have been investigating and can give you more information.'

Would meeting her be a con? While she wanted to be rid of Shani, one clue might help. The mention of interlocking crescents meant a great deal to Mustafa and Abdul. Perhaps with a little more information the whole picture would become clear. 'Where?'

'Can you come to a club near the Elephant and Castle this evening?'

'Which one?'

'The Walworth Harlequin, near the flyover.'

It didn't have a good reputation but would be a large and busy club, which would suit Alex. 'I'll be there within the hour.'

54

Fatema curled her lip as she contemplated the indecision and inaction of Abdul and her husband. Why did they have no urgency? The Khans were killers and would inflict the greatest amount of pain by taking Doha first. A pang of regret flooded through her as she gazed with unseeing eyes from the London taxi. The driver found it amusing that she wanted him to follow another cab but after a scowl from her and the rustle of notes, he complied without another word.

Her wait, down the road from the Egyptian Embassy, had been profitable. She had seen Ibrahem and his girl-friend, Shani, emerge from the building. Although not having met either before a quick internet search had given her pictures although she would have recognised the Khan visage anywhere. Uncertain of her plan, she would first become familiar with his movements. Planning in modern London was so unlike the olden days in the Cairo Souk. She hadn't planned decisive action for thirty years. Strangely, the taxi from the Embassy had taken him and Shani to a poor run-down neighborhood that she had not visited before but that held no concern for her. She would deal with any trouble that came her way.

Ibrahem's cab pulled into the side of the busy road, 'Drive past them. I want to give them no suspicion they are being followed.' The taxi driver flicked her a glance, but the laughing and joking he had at the beginning of the journey had evaporated. 'Pull in!' He complied. Glancing at the meter, she thrust two twenty pound notes to him for a twenty-five pound fare.

He breathed a sigh of relief, took the money and relaxed his shoulders as she left the cab. 'Thanks, luv.' The taxi accelerated away as soon as the door clicked close. Fatema took her time to flick her hijab across the bottom half of her face. Not that Ibrahem or Shani would recognise her. Fatema's eyes never left the pair. She moved cautiously, so she did not trip on the voluminous ankle length black dress. Clutching a large black handbag close to her side, she walked towards them as they stood in the middle of a wide pavement outside a nightclub.

Without losing sight of the pair, Fatema drifted towards the huge concrete pillars of a flyover. She didn't wish to bring attention to herself. Positioning herself near a bus stop, she could wait without arousing suspicion. With fierce concentration, the pair finished their discussion and to her surprise wandered towards the run-down club, nodded to the two bouncers, and entered.

Another taxi arrived and a young woman in black emerged, her black scarf covered her face, She marched into the club, but she held no interest apart from giving Fatema an idea. A busy club, loud music in dark surroundings and a disguise. It could be the perfect spot to kill Ibrahem. The possibility swirled around taking on different options, but whilst the plan might work, Doha kept coming to her mind. If she were imprisoned for killing Ibrahem, she would hardly see her daughter. Could she devise a way of effecting the kill, but escape? Her mind whirled. In Cairo she had made many attacks during the gangland wars. She found that creating confusion and panic made it easier to pick out a target. During the aftermath, she could affect her escape.

Watching the entrance foyer of the club from the bus stop, her mind oscillated. Should she involve Abdul and Mustafa or deal with the situation on her own? The Abdul of the old days had been corrupted by his wealth, so why would he take part in a murder plan. Screwing up her eyes, she sighed at Mustafa's indecision. If he had evidence of a plot to murder Doha he would act, but with the current knowledge of the Khans, he would side with Abdul. She would make the plans to kill Ibrahem. Shani presented a problem. What to do about her? Could she find out more? No, it would not help her cause. If she became a witness as she would be close to Ibrahem, Fatema would kill her as well, but if she were not there during the ambush, she would not pursue her.

As she leaned against the concrete pillar, her hand slipped into her bag and her fingers followed the contour of the cold metal of the pistol barrel. Determination gripped her. Eventually she would kill him.

55

Alex had tied up her hair, darkened her make-up and had dressed in black trousers and a matching jumper, completing her outfit with flat shoes. Despite close examination by the door staff at the Walworth Harlequin Club, she entered the dark and claustrophobic atmosphere, laden with the smell of alcohol and perfume. The deep throbbing sounds of seventies dance music enveloped her.

Ignoring several men who spoke to her, she bought a bottle of Bud and leaning against the bar waited for Shani to arrive. Alex recognised the weak voice behind her and twisted around to face her. Shani barefaced, without make-up, appeared pale, even though her skin had the tone of an Egyptian. Ibrahem stood behind her, his face drawn and tense. So, he hadn't left England yet, despite the death threats. 'In the corner,' he grunted and jerked his head.

He had chosen a small round table tucked in the corner near to a fire door. The busy club had a boisterous atmosphere as the members succumbed to the spirit of the evening. It boomed with noise. Impatience wrapped itself around Alex. She didn't want to be in this raucous environment and Ibrahem's presence didn't help. She distrusted him. The quicker she found out whether Shani had anything interesting to reveal, the happier she would be. As soon as they were settled, and with no preamble, Shani leaned her head close, 'I'm in desperate need of your help.'

A groan of annoyance almost escaped Alex's lips. 'What help do you need from me?'

Shani glanced at Ibrahem and a frown flitted across her features. 'I passed you a list of names of people we know to be dangerous. The leaders of those men have conspired to remove my father from office and have found out that I handed the list of names to you and the police.'

'How do they know? You were discreet.'

Ibrahem leaned forward, 'They have spies everywhere and take drastic action. You will remember the attempted drive by shooting in Regent's Park.'

Alex remained unconvinced. Something about the whole scenario didn't add up. Keeping her opinions to herself, she grimaced, 'I passed on the names to the other departments in the police.' Her voice was low pitched and cold, hoping that it would stop this conversation in its tracks.

'We know that the police haven't visited them or arrested them.' Shani slipped her hand across the table. Alex reached out and took the paper from inside her fingers. 'These are the addresses of those people.'

Why were Shani and Ibrahem so keen to have them arrested? Something niggled her. She'd agreed to meet Shani hoping to gain some information about the interlocking crescents. Had Shani lied to persuade her to meet at this shabby club. Why couldn't she have been honest? With a sigh, Alex concealed the paper in her pocket. 'I will pass on these addresses to my colleagues.'

Shani caught Alex's hand, 'Please be careful, these are

dangerous people and I wouldn't want you to be hurt.'

'What will you do now? Are you returning to Egypt?'

'Father wishes to work out the politics of how we can return. The way it has been set up against us means he is in disgrace. Before we depart, we need to establish the truth and convince others. It is unlikely we will stay in the UK for long as we will carry no diplomatic privilege which will be withdrawn shortly by the Ambassador.' Tears filled her eyes, 'We are not sure where we will go, but Ibrahem is still in danger from the threats.'

'The interlocking crescents?' She didn't want to miss her opportunity. It was the only reason she had agreed to meet.

'They go back before Ibrahem's generation and come from Egypt.'

Ibrahem's face hardened and he scowled, 'The key to their meaning lies between my father, who is now dead and Abdul Kadir, who knew him well. He runs a reputable business and so might be prepared to meet you and discuss the origins of the interlocking crescents from my country.'

The mention of the crescents had produced a strange reaction from both Abdul and Mustafa, so their origins must lie in the militancy of their youth that someone was trying to resurrect. Why was Shani associated with the symbol?

Shani touched Alex's arm, 'You have to work out whether the symbol has substance, but I believe it is too common to be important.' Ibrahem's mouth tightened and he rose to his feet, signalling the end of the meeting.

'Goodbye Shani, I don't expect we'll meet again, especially if you're leaving the country.'

'I shall miss you, Alex.'

Ibrahem glanced around and nervously raked his hand through his jet black hair, 'If you are leaving, we will walk with you to the door.' Why did he appear so agitated? Why did he want to accompany her? Was it to ensure she would leave the premises? She didn't like him and distrusted his offer.

After crossing the noisy floor of the club, Ibrahem pushed through the double doors into the entrance foyer where receptionists and several bouncers lingered. Alex contemplated the small snippet of information she had received. How to tackle Abdul, to force him to reveal what he knew? Did Mustafa also hold the key? Did he know more than he was prepared to reveal? One bouncer opened the outside doors.

Two large men who scrutinised new arrivals moved back from the doors as they exited to the pavement. One of them gave Alex a wink, but she didn't respond. She concentrated on the area outside the club. Being with Shani and Ibrahem might be dangerous.

56

Buses pulled into the stop, but Fatema ignored them. Trailing Ibrahem would be time consuming and difficult. Mustafa, already suspicious, might close the restaurant and follow her. Until she could think through a foolproof plan, aimless tailing of him would be high risk.

An idea came to mind that could give her more time to produce a plan. Ibrahem lived at the Egyptian Embassy. She would increase the number of anonymous calls to threaten his life until he become too frightened to leave the building. Then she would extend the threats to his girlfriend who would tell the Ambassador or the police. It would restrict their movements and delay his plan for Doha.

Fatema's mind had been drifting, but sharp focus returned as she spotted Ibrahem and Shani inside the open door of the club. The halogen down lighting extenuated with blue lit surrounds showed clear definition in the foyer through the full glass doors. She dropped her hand into her bag and caressed the barrel of the gun. He and Shani chatted as though they had not a care in the world, but Fatema wouldn't be deceived. The young woman in black that had entered the club after them came into the foyer.

Alex! Why was she here? Was she with Ibrahem and Shani? They'd entered the club at nearly the same time and were leaving together. Why? Alex wasn't wearing her uniform and her eyes showed apprehension as she peered into the street. Could Fatema trust her? Her world had been turned upside down. She gulped; Doha was staying at her house, but Alex was associating with Ibrahem Khan. She had assumed that Alex would be on her side. She wasn't a stranger to her family and had been Mariam's best friend.

Should she tell Mustafa and Abdul? Her husband had a right to know that their daughter was in danger and it might be the evidence he needed to act rather than dithering. Abdul, no doubt because of his current dubious background activities, wanted them to drop all connections with her but he would baulk at dealing with a London police officer.

No other explanation sprang to her mind as to the collaboration in a social scene between Alex and Ibrahem. The three hovered in the foyer. Ibrahem and Shani looked calm, but Alex's eyes flicked around and she moved with agitation from foot to foot.

If Alex had betrayed her family and befriended a Khan, would she succumb to their bidding? Would she harm Doha? She would be prepared to eliminate Ibrahem, but should she kill Alex as well?

57

Alex left the club as Ibrahem and Shani held the door for her. After the bright lights of the foyer, the gloomy overcast sky gave the urban area a grey appearance. Little information about the crescents had been revealed but she had the addresses from Shani which could be useful. Alex would not keep them to herself but lie about their source as she had been instructed not to meet with Shani.

The sudden movement and the squeal of brakes fully focused Alex's attention. The outside bouncers fixed their gaze towards the car. A figure dressed in black, wearing a balaclava, jumped from the car and raised a gun. Three young women nearby screamed.

Alex, with the sole intention of survival, sprinted two steps and dived behind a concrete pillar which supported a nearby flyover. The gun fired several shots and as no bullets whistled near her; she was unsure if they were aimed at her. She didn't look back to check on whether Shani and Ibrahem had been shot. Keeping the concrete between her and the gunman, she scurried across a road and disappeared down a pedestrian walkway in front of the shops. Then sprinting at full speed, she focused her energy on distancing herself from the situation.

Turning the corner, she jumped on a bus about to pull away. Greeting the driver, she paid her fare and resisted the urge to look over her shoulder. Passing to the back of the bus, she tucked into a corner and settled down. Gasping for breath, she shivered violently while her heart hammered in overdrive. Who had been the target of the gunman? Was it Ibrahem? Had the death threats against him been real? The traffic halted, so she waited patiently on the bus which finally crept forward. It seemed the safest place. It wouldn't pass the club as it was headed in the opposite direction. It proceeded at a snail's pace as it negotiated the busy slow moving traffic. She would remain huddled in her seat until it arrived in an area that she recognised and then disembark to return to her flat. Another incident. They were becoming too frequent.

No reason surfaced to suggest that she had been the target. Either Shani or Ibrahem or possibly both had been the focus of the gunman. Perhaps Ibrahem's fear in Regent's Park had been genuine. The target would become clear when the incident was reported on the news. The bus trundled from the locality as wailing sirens filled the air.

58

Fatema pulled her hijab up to her eyes, Ibrahem and Shani did not know her, but Alex would recognise her although in the traditional clothes with only her eyes visible she expected to escape being noticed. Movement near to her caught her attention as she was heavily focused on the three in the club's doorway. A man dressed in black stepped towards the club, raised his arm and fired.

With her hand already on her pistol in the bag, she flicked it so it pointed at the back of the gunman. She was positioned behind him and in no immediate danger. Her finger moved to the trigger.

If he swung the gun towards her, she would fire through her bag. The bouncers dived for cover. Young women screamed and ran, but Fatema remained calm. Alex had reacted the quickest and had dived out of sight behind a concrete pillar. Ibrahem had grabbed Shani's hand and they'd darted in the opposite direction to Alex and away from Fatema.

Shivers ran through her, but with no opportunity to shoot Ibrahem, she kept her hand tensed on her pistol as the scene unfolded. The gunman, with his face covered, fired several shots towards Ibrahem and Alex. He then leaped in the open door of the black car which screeched away.

Deep in thought, Fatema surveyed the scene. As the first police car screeched to a halt outside the club, she yanked her hijab tight down on her head and hurried towards the tube station, her mind filled with a turmoil of theories and questions. Having left the scene unnoticed, she didn't relax until she perched on a seat in the tube train. Staring at the floor, her mind constantly replayed the scene she had witnessed. A doubt sprang to her mind, but she wasn't sure what caused it.

59

Alex lay still as the early morning light squeezed through the crack in the curtains in the unfamiliar room. Her body shivered. It had been a desperate measure to phone Vincent the day after the attempted shooting outside the club but she had relented. Having someone to talk through the incident had seemed a good idea at the time. Although she liked Vincent, who was a good guy, charming, witty and brill company, she hadn't wanted to finish up in bed with him. Having a man in her life was not part of her plan. It would complicate everything.

According to a news broadcast, Shani and Ibrahem had been uninjured in the gun attack.

The press had reported a gangland feud in which innocent bystanders were caught up. How they had escaped remained a mystery, as did the identity of the gunman. Alex couldn't go to the police computer to find the status of the enquiry as she wasn't allocated to the case and her activities could be traced. Sergeant Johnson had been off duty yesterday, so the opportunity of accessing the computer systems hadn't presented itself.

Disobeying Inspector Craddock, she had agreed to meet Shani and Ibrahem. Would she be discovered? The bouncers on the door would remember her, especially the one who winked. Had they dismissed her as an innocent bystander? She didn't speak to Shani or Ibrahem as they left, so unless they'd been seen together at the table in the corner, no one would assume them to be associated, although the closed-circuit cameras would reveal the truth if they investigated. The distinctive figure running hard would have caught many witnesses' attention, but she'd jumped onto the bus, which would be an excuse for rushing so some witnesses would not consider her relevant and perhaps neither would the police.

The cold morning light crept into the room and her nakedness made her shiver. The addresses passed on by Shani at the club were no longer her concern. At the earliest opportunity the following morning she'd emailed them to inspector Craddock but had to lie and invent a plausible excuse for them being passed into her possession. She had become involved deeper and deeper, and it wasn't what she wanted.

It would be unlikely that anybody at the Embassy would admit to passing the information, but she created a character who she had chatted to on the security staff who had asked her out for a date. It seemed plausible to Inspector Craddock who had accepted the email without raising questions. The addresses were passed into the system.

While she had a great desire to tackle Abdul Kadir again it required some serious consideration. What approach would extract the most information from him? He posed a serious threat. Danger surrounded him. Mustafa would be another person with information, but he wouldn't involve her. She had contacted Vincent and met him but not told him the truth. He insisted on taking her out for the evening. He kept conversations to general matters such as life in London and New York and had been witty, making her laugh. She had behaved like a slut jumping into bed on the first date, but she had become desperate for answers. The mystery of the interlocking crescents consumed her, filling her waking thoughts and many sleepless nights. Would he reveal information to her if she became closer to him?

Wrapping a sheet around her, she wandered to the studio kitchen to make coffee. 'It's too early,' pleaded the sleepy voice from the bed.

'No, it's not, I must leave soon as I'm on duty today.' She carried two mugs of coffee and perched at the bottom of the bed, out of his reach. With a groan, he pushed himself up and lay back against the headboard.

'You are uptight this morning! What's happened? We had a perfect meal last night with a bottle of wine and you were content and relaxed.'

'Yes, I enjoyed the evening but as soon as I woke this morning my worries surfaced. My friends are being threatened; it can't go on.' She'd been vague about the details and had only mentioned they were Egyptian. He moved down the bed, but she backed away and he picked up the message. 'They are frightened; I need to support them.'

'Don't fret, we'll make the crucial links.'

'No, Vincent that takes time, they are innocent people that the police won't protect, so my best option is to live with them.' Mustafa and Fatima would be pleased to have her to stay. 'I might deal with anyone unwanted who arrives unexpectedly.'

'Get real, Alex. You'll be unarmed. I don't doubt your martial arts skills, but against a gun they are useless and you may not carry one when not on duty.'

'I'll take that chance as my friends have no way of defending themselves and I will not let them down.'

He grunted and took a sip of coffee. 'I joke around with women, but you could become special to me Alex and I want our relationship to develop.'

She looked away to gather her thoughts. His request came as a surprise. Could she deal with her current problems and begin a relationship with him when her life had settled.

Alex's mind flicked back to the relaxed atmosphere and banter between Jane and Vincent. Was it an old relationship where they'd stayed friends? He cradled the coffee cup in his hands and went silent. Alex didn't speak. Would he reveal something to help her?

'Unofficially, I can give you a bit of information that will help.'

A wave of gratefulness brought a smile to her lips. 'If it will protect my friends, that's all I want.'

'You know from your insights into the Embassy that Shani and her father have been thrown out.'

'Yes, the Inspector told me.'

'As far as we can work out, they've been stitched up but we're not sure by whom.'

'That's not relevant to me and it's not helping protect my friends.'

For the first time that morning his face relaxed, 'Calm down. Let me finish. It will become clear in a minute. Did they tell you about a character called Abdul Kadir, who runs a large business?'

Just the mention of his name sent an icy shiver through Alex, 'Yes, I've heard of Abdul Kadir. Is he significant?'

'We let him in despite his past. In his youth he led the militants, attacked the government and would attack British targets and British people. Intimidation and protection rackets were his style, and he was one founder of a gangland group in Egypt.'

Alex jumped up, scowled and banged her coffee down on the bedside table, 'I don't want a bloody history lesson on thuggery in Egypt, I need to know how to protect my friends. Arresting the attackers is piecemeal, others will replace them. If Kadir is the planner, hit him hard, arrest his guys and kick him out of the country.'

'All right, all right, calm down. Abdul Kadir was the leader before it split into two factions. There has been a resurgence of the fighting and it has spilled to this country. The current generations are trying to resurrect both the rivalry and the actions they believe their parents' generation didn't take in terms of the taking down of the Egyptian government and targeting its friends, including big business which means in this country. Youngsters want to show their strength and therefore are prepared to use any means to intimidate and kill.'

'Is Abdul Kadir one group?'

'No, you are wrong, Alex. He is a significant businessman now and has a lot of money. Why get involved again? We let him into this country on the hope that he can deal with the young dissidents that he knows. From the government's point of view, we would much rather ship them all back to Egypt and let them sort it out. But many of them are genuine residents in this country.'

'So, they are sleepers!'

'No, nothing as dramatic as that. They have become irritated in this country with the lack of opportunities and have resurrected the past struggles.'

Alex, still clutching the sheet, wandered over to the window and yanked back the curtains, flooding the room with light. 'Do you know who they are?'

'No, that's the problem. We hoped by tracking Kadir he would lead us to the cells that are providing the hits.'

Alex's heart sank. Did they know she'd been to see him? Either the lookout hadn't been attentive, or she hadn't been recognised. The stakeout would take pictures and with no progress someone would be tasked with re-visiting the photos and she might be identified. Vincent would recognise her. They could spot Mustafa. Then it would only take a brief time before her involvement became widespread knowledge. It would bring her career to an end. She gulped, still no progress. Would she be dismissed from the police?

'What did the stakeout reveal?' She tried to hold the tremor in her voice.

'There are connections with the past.' Would they work out that Mustafa had been one of Abdu's gang in Cairo? 'We have bits and pieces, but we haven't joined them together yet. We have pictures of the previous generation and some insurgents in Egypt, but they are old grainy photographs and everybody's moved on thirty years. Abdul runs a legitimate business that operates twenty-four hours a day, so there were hundreds of comings and goings.' Would she be lost in the mass of pictures? The lack of recognition would be temporary. 'The new guard as it comes in is trying to resurrect everything unpleasant but spread it wider than Egypt.'

'Who's running the other faction?'

'It is too complicated to work out. We accept that

apart from some of their hitmen they are clever and far more sophisticated than the previous generation who were protection racket thugs and easy to identify. This new group are subtle with an anonymous chain of command.'

'Can you guess?'

'No.'

Alex downed the rest of her lukewarm coffee, 'Is it always this bad, there's a lot of information which the police and intelligence services are working on and coming to no conclusion.'

Vincent finished his coffee and laughed, 'Welcome to the real world of international espionage. It's never simple.'

'Are interlocking crescents a symbol of the original organisation?' Alex struggled to keep the tension out of her voice.

'Why do you ask?'

Alex forced her shoulders to relax and pursed her lips, 'You are being evasive, if you have some information why won't you tell me?'

The smile dropped from his face and his eyes narrowed, 'You must have a reason to ask, so tell me.'

Vincent's attitude had changed during the conversation and he had become intense. She remained desperate for information, but there was no way she would tell him about her secret quest. Some general information would have to suffice. Animosity and anger with the situation would get her nowhere, so making a conscious effort she allowed a broad grin to sweep across her features. 'On the attack in Brighton, the motorcyclist who escaped had interlocking crescents on his baseball cap.'

'For Christ's sake, Alex, get real.' He pinched the bridge of his nose and squeezed his eyes shut, assuming a gesture of impatience. 'If it is a significant symbol, they are hardly likely to display it on a baseball cap.'

60

Fatema's plan had not come together overnight. She had tried to act normally on her return home but Mustafa suspected that she had returned to her Cairo days. The argument between them had not lasted long as she refused to answer his questions. While not having a coherent plan, she did not have sufficient resources to mount a distraction, but she knew of a man who could supply her with the equipment.

She slipped out of the back gate early in the morning. Always up an hour before Mustafa, she wouldn't be missed. Relief had come with an early phone call to Doha. How could Alex collaborate with Ibrahem? It made no sense and she would not have believed it if she hadn't seen it with her own eyes. From conversations with Mustafa she was aware that Alex worked protecting diplomats, which is why she might relate to the Egyptian Embassy. Shaking her head, it didn't explain why she accompanied them to a run-down nightclub and had been near them when the shooting started.

Fatema shielded her eyes from the early sunshine. A customer in the restaurant, who Mustafa didn't like, ran his own business, which had a local reputation for stolen or illegal goods. His shops sold many genuine articles, but those that he kept in the locked storeroom interested Fatema. Wearing a full length black dress with a long coat and her hijab wound tightly around her head, she crossed the Edgware Road for the short walk to Paddington in the early chilling mist. She wrinkled her nose up at the stench from rush hour traffic. She scurried along the back streets as she wanted to return to the restaurant before Mustafa rose from his sleep and required his breakfast.

The dilapidated shop in the backstreets of Paddington was busy with Arab women picking up early morning deals. Could she trust the owner? No, but she would agree business with him. She reached the front of the queue 'Good morning, Fatema, what can I do for you today.'

Opening her purse, she rustled twenty pound notes which caught his attention. 'The goods I require are not displayed in the shop.'

His face showed no change in expression, but he gave a slight nod. 'Come this way.' He unlocked the door behind the counter. Without a word being spoken, his wife moved behind the till to carry on serving. Closing the door, he flicked on lights in a room covered floor to ceiling with cupboards. A lone bare wooden table stood in the middle of the room without chairs.

Fatema opened her purse and showed him a roll of twenty pound notes. 'I might not have every item you require.'

Fatema nodded, 'I want tear gas and a mask.'

With no acknowledgement, he moved to a cupboard and unlocked the door. He removed a wooden box and placed on the table. Fatema open the lid. Two tear gas canisters lay in the bottom with a mask still in its original wrapping.

'Both canisters?'

'Yes. Smoke bombs, please.'

'How many?'

'Three.'

Flicking open another cupboard door, he placed three on the table. Her eyes flicked across his face. 'Two hundred pounds.'

Fatema curled her lip but peeled ten twenty-pound notes from the roll in her purse.

With no further words spoken, she returned to the shop and purchased vegetables to hide the other contents in her bag. Leaving the shop, she hurried to reach the restaurant before Mustafa awakened. She had guns along with gas and smoke for a distraction attack, but she still had no straightforward plan.

61

Checking the time as she left Vincent's studio flat, Alex walked to Scotland Yard intending to be friendly to Sandy Johnson so she could search for further information. The people controlling the power in the Egyptian groups remained unclear. Only the hit men had been captured. The three from the kidnap attempt at Brighton remained in custody. What should she do?

With several narrow escapes in her plotting and planning, she would be caught before long. Then dismissal from the police would come and she might finish in jail, which would be disastrous for her cause. Who could she trust? Her sister? Shaking her head; Tanya would urge her to give up. She was on her own.

Walking through Trafalgar Square, she stepped around a pavement cleaner whizzing through the space. A sudden noise from a crate falling off the back of an early delivery lorry made her jump. The sharpness of the sound and the echo from the tall buildings of the Square gave the momentary impression of a gunshot. The terror outside the Harlequin Club flashed into her mind. Why hadn't she been traced at the club when she'd met Shani and Ibrahem?

Closed circuit cameras? Police checking the cameras

would circulate the pictures and someone would recognise her. A shudder ran through her body and walking became difficult as the realisation hit her.

She slumped onto a bench, placed her elbows on her knees and head in her hands. If she had stayed and identified herself to the police, she would have been reprimanded for meeting Shani, but now she would be given instant dismissal. Had she been set up?

Had they missed her at the club? If they hadn't, the only reason she wouldn't be on the carpet is if they ignored her activities. Why had MI6 missed her entering Abdul Kadir's business premises? They wouldn't, but had they again chosen to ignore her presence? After the Brighton incident, why had her list of misdemeanors concerning police procedures been ignored? The Sergeant and Inspector had threatened disciplinary action, but it had never materialised. The authorities would wait their moment and with the list of her misdemeanors they would choose a time to bring pressure to bear on her.

What did they expect of her? No clear answer presented itself. But being manipulated like a puppet didn't appeal. What could she do about it?

Turning towards Scotland Yard she saw Inspector Craddock arriving for work in jeans, trainers and a heavy anorak with her hair loosely tied in a bunch. As she closed on her, the pale face indicated no makeup. She followed her to the changing room, intending to deal with the problems she faced. She would not be a puppet. Checking they were alone, 'Can I have a word?'

'Is it urgent? I have an early morning meeting.'

'Yes.'

'What do you want to say?' The Inspector hung her

anorak in a locker. Alex ignored the offer of a seat and stood in the middle of the space.

'I've broken your rules and lied to you, ma'am.'

She stared hard as she took off her jeans, 'You better explain, Alex, as I do not understand what you are talking about.'

'I met Shani despite your directive.'

The Inspector nodded, 'I'd guessed you had, but given you obtained the addresses to accompany the names, I turned a blind eye. A new date from the Embassy staff is not your style.' Panic twisted her stomach into a hard knot at another example of the Inspector guessing the truth but choosing to ignore it.

The Inspector tugged her old sweatshirt over her head and stood braless, focusing on Alex's face.

Gritting her teeth, she willed herself to reveal the truth. 'It gets worse. I met her at the Walworth club. She and her boyfriend seemed to be the target.'

'That's more serious. You are at a major incident with gunfire, but you left the scene.' Her expression darkened with an unreadable emotion and a shadow of anger touched her face. 'Explain!' Despite wearing only knickers she moved close to Alex making her feel uncomfortable at the close presence.

Alex gulped as the words caught in her throat, 'Shani rang, requested a meeting and suggested the club. As we left, a gunman jumped from a car. I fled. The shots were too close for comfort.'

'Not good, Alex. Was anyone else nearby?'

She had been so intent on escaping that she hadn't surveyed the area. A black mark in police procedure. 'No, not that I noticed.'

The Inspector turned back to her locker and moved to the mirror with her make-up bag. 'Have you been setup?'

She took a deep breath. They were manipulating her like a puppet. But the Inspector didn't mean that.

'Set up?' Her mind raced with possibilities.

'There are two scenarios.' The Inspector leaned closer to the mirror to apply her eye liner and mascara.

'What are they?'

A small smile crossed the Inspector's face, out of character for her. 'Shani and Ibrahem could have been followed, a lookout summoned the gunman.'

'Yes, that's my conclusion.'

'Scenario two.'

'Yes.' Although she didn't want to hear the Inspector's train of thought.

'You have been set up.'

The words cut like a whip through her mind. 'Me!' Her voice rose, shaking a little, betraying her astonishment and concern.

'Yes, lured there by Shani and Ibrahem. Perhaps you know too much about them. When you left the club, did they escort you to the door to give the gunman his target?'

She gulped and with legs that didn't belong to her sank down onto the bench as being the target had never occurred to her. The silence stretched as she struggled to come to terms with the realisation that someone might have been shooting at her. 'Which is most likely, ma'am.'

'You are not thinking.' Finishing her make-up, she leaned over Alex, 'Think.' With no further words, she clipped on a bra and slipped into her uniform blouse and skirt with black tights. Ready to leave the changing room, the Inspector shot her a penetrating glare. 'From the description of the incident, given by the witnesses, there were three people outside the club, presumably you, Shani and Ibrahem, plus the two bouncers.'

'That sounds right from memory.'

'How far to the car?'

'Fifteen metres.'

'You are a trained officer in using firearms.' Alex didn't reply. 'Anyone, even an amateur, would hit at least one out of five from fifteen metres.' Inspector Craddock leaned over, 'No one had guns to reply. In the space of five seconds, think how many shots you might have fired. No one was shot, so work it out for yourself.'

'Scaring people.'

'You're right Alex, but whom and why?'

Alex's hands gripped the sides of the bench. Her head was spinning, making coherent thought impossible. 'I don't know.'

The Inspector straightened up and brushed down her uniform with her hand. 'You realise this is serious.' Her mouth thinned with displeasure. 'I shall report it up the tree of command.'

She had dug herself into a hole. Should she leave or keep talking? The Inspector had made her way to the door signalling the end of the conversation. But would she issue orders to Alex as she left?

She wouldn't be defeated and wanted more information, 'Why have none of the other disciplinary actions after Brighton been taken to a conclusion?'

The Inspector faced Alex; her eyes sparkled. 'I thought you might tell me; I have wondered whether you would ask.'

Alex grimaced and shook her head, 'I don't know.'

'Neither do I.' She hissed between almost sealed lips, 'I would have suspended you but have been prevented from doing so.'

Alex's mind raced. Actions were happening without her knowledge or understanding. Someone was manipulating her and it made her uneasy. 'Was it your idea to introduce me to Vincent?'

A swift shadow of anger swept across the Inspector's face, 'You saw us when we met, what did you think.'

She shuddered and failed to control the sudden tremor in her voice, 'He's not your boyfriend, is he?' The Inspector didn't answer, but Alex stiffened under the look of withering contempt from her narrowed eyes.

She had no words or questions left. Her voice failed her as she stammered, 'What happens next?'

'I've no idea, Alex?' Gripping the door handle, her lips curved into something between a sneer and a smirk. 'The powers that be have decided you are untouchable, so I can't suspend you. My current judgement would be to sack you from the police service.'

Alex gulped and swallowed the sob that rose in her throat, 'What shall I do?'

'Your duties the same as normal but be careful as I dislike my officers to be shot on duty or in their private life.' The cold-hearted, chilling words gripped Alex. They held no sympathy. 'If we were in my office, my words might be different, but two aspects strike me about you.' Alex didn't want to ask. 'Either you are using your charms,' she scrutinised Alex up and down, 'with a senior person.'

Alex shook her head.

'Or you know something or have become involved in a matter of national security that makes you indispensable.'

Alex shook her head again. 'Be careful Alex, the Egyptians might want to kill you, but if you become out of control, people do the dirty work for the British Government.'

62

Mustafa had problems as he scurried from Paddington tube station, muttering and swearing as he went against the flow of the arrivals wanting to leave the station for the London Underground. Trusting Abdul as he had always done, he hadn't come up with a solution. Not even the first inkling of one. He shuddered as the memory of Fatema's face returned. The expression had scared him as he had not seen those piercing eyes since Cairo. A loose cannon in those days, she saved them many times, but this was London in the twenty-first century. How can she deal with a Khan and not be arrested, then what would happen to his family and his daughter? Their background, all those years ago, would be investigated. He held his head in shame. Such an inquiry by the police would implicate Abdul. No, it couldn't be allowed to happen.

Lifting his head as he topped the escalator into the main concourse, the noise from London commuters arriving to transfer to their jobs deafened him. He stepped to one side and put his hand over his ears. He was never happier than when alone in his kitchen preparing meals. The solitude of his existence during the preparation he liked but accepted the gentle noise and bustle as business commenced in his restaurant and customers arrived. Blissful times.

But this noise and commotion added to the threats to his family. Only Abdul, outside of his immediate family, could have coaxed him out today.

Limping badly because it seemed he had to rush everywhere, he surveyed the scene in front of him. Bustling commuters came from every direction. Abdul wanted to meet near the entrance from the taxi rank which was located along platform one.

Mustafa took a deep breath. He had to concentrate. Perhaps his friend had found crucial information. He crossed the concourse but collided with people late for their jobs.

Grateful that the train which had recently arrived from Plymouth had emptied, he turned into the vestibule where the continual stream of taxis deposited their incumbents outside. He secluded himself into the corner as in the small area the noise from the main station dissipated. Glancing at his watch, the time of the meeting approached. Despite the chaotic nature of the early morning station, he found solitude as he tucked into the corner.

Doha must be protected but would Alex, unarmed, be able to defend her against Khan assassins. He was drawn from his thoughts, which had not organised themselves, as a taxi pulled up but it captured his attention as Ali stepped out first and surveyed the area with a grim but focused expression, only then did Abdul leave the taxi, followed by Malik.

With no acknowledgement between them, Abdul moved next to Mustafa. With their backs to the wall, Ali and Malik stationed themselves in front, watching the crowds. Mustafa's voice cracked, 'I fear for Fatema's sanity. She goes out for long periods but refuses to divulge her activities to me when she returns home. She is planning action.'

Abdul rubbed his chin, his eyes examining the entrance foyer for any unusual movement. 'Shani's father, Youssef Zaher, is in disgrace. The Ambassador told me he cannot afford to be tainted by association, so he has asked Youssef, Shani and Ibrahem Khan to leave the Embassy.'

Mustafa's sharp eyes never left the crowd. He scratched his head, 'This is bad news for us.'

Abdul glanced at him, 'It is my friend, as I'm convinced that Ibrahem Khan will blame us, so be prepared for action within days.'

63

Alex rode her motorbike up the hill to Bagshot Heath and drove into a spacious lay-by on a nondescript road, texted her location, then rolled her bike out of view behind an overflowing waste bin. It would be hidden from passing traffic. She sat on a wall in the drizzle carefully checking that she could not be seen by the cars as they roared past creating spray that swirled in the air.

Never had life overwhelmed her. Success she'd assumed would be hers, until the critical events of that fatal night had formed her dedicated campaign. But then she had control in pursuing her quest, but others had manipulated her. The control and her private mission had been undermined as she had been turned into a puppet. Her life had no value. She dreaded the arrival of the person she had texted.

She had failed the only person in the world she trusted but would she understand? Alex had become desperate. Seek help and talk to the doctors. But no doctor would solve her mental anguish. A car pulled into the empty lay-by; she lifted her hand in welcome but only made an empty gesture. She managed a halfhearted wave at her sister who beckoned her towards the car, but she didn't move from the rock where she sat.

Tanya climbed from the car and marched over, 'Why the hell did we have to meet in the middle of nowhere when it's sleeting. Come to the car.'

'No, we need to sit here.'

Tanya's eyes widened and she tilted her head up towards the sky. 'O Christ! What's happened, Alex?'

'Get your coat.'

Tanya snatched a wax jacket and flat cap from the back seat and dropped onto the rock.

'I'm in a mess, sis.'

'I can see.' Tanya pulled her cap down tighter and flicked up the collar of her jacket against the swirling sleet. 'Do you want to tell me?'

'It will take time; I need you to understand.'

'God, they will sack me at work for walking out and I must sit in the middle of a heath in the rain listening to a long story.'

'Hush, sis.'

Tanya flicked her sister's hand. 'I'm here and listening.'

Alex agonised how to tell her, 'Two groups want to kill me.'

Tanya's eyes flicked over Alex and she grimaced. 'You're being too melodramatic; the situation can't be that bad. This results from you carrying a gun and becoming involved with low life.' Alex shook her head, but then stayed silent. 'Who wants to kill you?'

'An unknown group of Egyptians.'

Tanya's shoulders slumped, 'The same group as in Brighton?'

'I can't be sure, but yes, it's connected with them.'

'This is out of my league, Alex. How the hell do you expect me to say anything? Who's the second.'

'The British Government.'

'Alex! Get real!' Her voice rose, 'They don't go around killing people.'

'They do.'

'And why you?'

'With our background they think I might have infiltrated the police force.'

'Our mother?'

'Yes and her Arab relations.'

Tanya raised her hands to cover her face. She rubbed the cold sleet across her cheeks, took her hands down and gave a loud groan. 'Carry on. Let's hear it all.'

Alex closed her eyes as she tried to steady the waves of fear that filled her body. 'I've been so foolish thinking it was possible to achieve the results on my own, but I am in deep and they won't let me out.'

Wiping the rain away from her face, 'Be rational. I don't want to know the details, but why not explain your concerns to Inspector Craddock?'

'She is the one who outlined the threats against me. I've made bad mistakes, sis, and brought danger to the ones I love.'

'Alex! Stop talking in riddles. What danger? We will have to deal with it.'

'Doha.'

'She is staying with mum and dad as Doha's parents need to redecorate the restaurant and our home would be more peaceful for her to finish her studies.' Tanya paused and studied Alex through narrowed eyes. 'I have just realised that it's not as simple as that.' Tanya shivered.

'Doha's parents have a gun to defend themselves. The poor girl may be a target.'

'What do you mean target? Target for who?'

'It goes back to gang warfare in Egypt. In his youth Mustafa was involved in the gangs in Cairo. The descendants of those gangs are killing people to gain supremacy and target the Egyptian government and large businesses.'

Tanya stood and marched away. She leaned against a tree with her hands shoved into the pockets of her jacket and her head bowed. Finally, she returned to stand in front of her. 'Alex, you must tell me the truth. You have always had a fanciful imagination. When you were a kid, you invented weird stories which none of us understood. Has the pressure been too much? You must have misunderstood and you're letting your mind distort the facts.'

'I've met the woman who was the subject of the attack in Brighton.'

'I knew you were involved and not just the chase.'

'I took on the gunman to save her.'

'Oh my God,' Tanya stared at the ground, 'Why did you meet again, part of your duties?'

'No, we are the same age. Now she's fallen into disgrace but wanted to meet, so we met in a club at the Elephant and Castle.'

Tanya snapped, 'Why go to such a disreputable area?'

Alex ignored her sister's interruption, 'Someone shot at us!'

'You think whoever it is will be on the loose and prepared to try again and snatch Doha.'

'Yes, but neither the police nor the Intelligence Services are any closer to a solution and are letting matters drift. The Intelligence Services think it's an internal Egyptian matter, but it's not.' Alex's voice cracked with emotion and she couldn't control the spasmodic trembling which wracked her body.

'How would you know what the Intelligence Services are thinking?' Alex didn't reply, Tanya leaped up again. 'Look at me.' Alex lifted her head, 'Is it a man?' She remained motionless, but Tanya nodded, 'You don't have to answer, I can see it written in your face. When you were in your late teens, you'd jump into bed with any man.' Alex shook her head. 'Don't deny it. We hoped with Matthew you had settled down and stopped putting yourself about. I understand now.'

'He's from MI6.'

'I know how your mind works. You've gone to bed with him to extract information, but what you've found out isn't what you expected.' Alex didn't have to answer.

'If I go home, it would be difficult to protect mum, dad and Doha. If they come, they will be armed.' Little prickles of panic crept up and down her back. 'It will make matters worse because they might be after me, not her, but they won't leave witnesses.'

'Are you sure your Inspector can't help?'

'She told me, I'm on my own and would have sacked me, but her hands are tied by the seniors. She was told to introduce me to Vincent at MI6 but doesn't know why.'

'Do you believe her?'

'I don't know who to believe. I can trust you, but I hate to burden you with my mess. But I've no answers and no one else to turn to.'

'Your situation is straightforward as you should have been sacked but have been given a free hand.'

'Yes, and even if I succeed,' Alex's brow wrinkled. 'I

am still expendable.'

Tanya steadied her breathing, tightened her shoulders and stared ahead. 'Is there anything else you want to tell me, Alex? You might as well tell all.'

'I think you've already guessed.' Her shoulders slumped and she lowered her head.

'I've had my suspicions for a while and they've gradually increased but I want to hear you explain it.'

Alex took a deep breath, 'I joined the police with the sole intention of finding out who killed Matthew and Mariam.'

'How can you place your life on the line when you can't bring them back? Someone will kill you. I don't want you seeking revenge as I want my sister with me.'

'I don't know what to do.'

Tanya sat up straight. 'You're becoming muddled and emotional which is not like you so we must think. Doha is a target. It will make matters worse if you are at home because they might come searching for you. If you are the target those at home are safe providing you are not there.'

'Yes, but there is no solution.'

'Yes, there is.' Tanya stared ahead rubbing her hands together then flicked more icy rain from her face. 'Stay away from home. Ring Mum and Dad to tell them you're busy at work and can't come home for a while. Stay in a hotel.'

'But what about Doha?'

'I will stay at home with mum and dad.'

Alex shook her head, 'You can't do anything to protect her, if they come after her, they will be well armed.' Tanya touched Alex on the shoulder, making her turn to look at her. Tanya had the slightest of grins. 'When we get through this mess, it will cost you, sis, and I shall make you pay big time.'

'I don't understand.' But an expression of clarity flooded her sister's face, as though she had solved the problem.

'I've met Malcolm through pentathlon events. He is always asking me out, but I don't particularly like him, so I refuse, but he keeps trying. When we are finished here, I shall ring him and say it's his lucky day. He is ex-Special Forces. I don't know what he has done, but I've been on shooting days with him at Bisley. He handles guns well.'

Alex shook her head, 'He won't have pistols, people can't carry those.'

'No, but he's keen on game shooting and is a farmer so has several shotguns. I can invite him to our home for a few days and ask him to bring his guns so we can have some practice and suggest some time away on a shooting holiday.'

'Will he cooperate?'

'He will do anything for me if he thinks he can get me into bed.'

Alex's eyes opened wide, 'Sis!'

'Can you think of a better way? You've already compromised yourself.' Alex looked down at the ground. Tanya understood her so well. 'I never believed my sister would force me into a position that I have to go to bed with a man I don't like. But it might solve our problem.' Alex hugged her sister and a hollowness formed in the pit of her stomach. 'You need more protection.'

'Any suggestions?' Alex's voice shook with emotion.

'Yes, you need to disappear.'

'I can't, as they would come after me. Both the police and the Intelligence Services could easily trace me.'

'You are entitled to a holiday, but it's important you carry on normally.' Tanya put a reassuring arm around Alex's shoulder. 'Try to get mundane tasks such as paperwork.'

'Why?'

'So, they do not become suspicious.'

'Act normally, book a holiday, tell everyone where you are going which will be somewhere in the EU. When you arrive disappear from there and cross several countries.'

'I see what you mean, they will have a hard job tracing me if I drive across Europe.'

'The alternative is to get yourself sacked by the seniors.'

'How? They are resisting doing it.'

'Try punching the Superintendent on the nose.' Alex chuckled at the scenario which flashed through her mind. 'At least you will be in jail and safe until matters resolve themselves.'

64

Mustafa had lost control of what would happen next. The news of Ibrahem Khan's dismissal from the Egyptian Embassy had added to his concerns. Abdul had no answer but had arranged to meet the Ambassador who Mustafa regarded as a weak man who would go with the best bidder. Mustafa's mind jolted back. Was Hamada part of the Ahmed family? Weak and cowardly, they changed sides frequently. He could not be trusted.

Mustafa pointed towards the round figure of the Ambassador hurrying along the pavement accompanied by two muscular men, 'Here he comes.' Abdul nodded.

Puffing from his brisk walk and with his face clouded with uneasiness, he halted in front of them. Hamada hugged Abdul and Mustafa, while their eyes constantly scanned the pavement along the Thames Embankment. Taking a step back, his face was grim and solemn, 'I fear for your lives, my friends.' His words sent a chill of fear through Mustafa, leaving him trembling and frightened. His peaceful life was spiralling downhill. Every day brought another problem to face. Big Ben struck eight. The streets full of early rush hour traffic created noise, so they had to raise their voices. Ali and Malik waited out of earshot along with security personnel from the Egyptian Embassy.

Mustafa gulped and tried to swallow the sudden bile that had risen in his throat while he stared at the grey swirling water of the Thames. Hamada leaned forward with an air of conspiracy and his brow creased with worry, 'I had to tell you as early as possible and it is better to meet here as the walls of the Embassy have ears.'

'What have you heard?' snapped Abdul, 'Tell me.'

'Following the dismissal of Youssef Zaher from his Cabinet Post, I was forced by my Government to tell him, Shani and Ibrahem to leave the Embassy.'

'Have they gone?' A sneer curled its way across Abdul's lips.

'Yes, but in doing so they have sworn vengeance and I overheard your names being mentioned.'

Mustafa rubbed a weary hand across his face, 'Have they left the country?'

'I don't know, the leaving became acrimonious as Youssef and Ibrahem were on the verge of attacking me and accused me of siding with you.'

They waited for a group of runners to pass by and then shuffled with their escorts along the Embankment towards Charing Cross. Mustafa's face was drawn and tense, 'Can you obtain more information about their destination?'

'No, they have diplomatic privileges until midnight, so I suspect they will make the most of their time but leave before the deadline.'

'Thank you, Hamada,' Abdul shook his hand, 'At least I know I can hide until they leave the country.'

'Yes, my friend, but I have further bad news.'

'What is it?' The trio came to an abrupt halt and Mustafa drew in a quick, painful gasp as he waited for Hamada to speak.

'Youssef and Shani are distant relatives to Ibrahem.'

'So,' Abdul paused, and his mouth straightened into a hard line, 'they are also Khans.'

'Yes.'

As Mustafa absorbed this latest information, a prickle of fear touched him. They hugged Hamada who then hurried away accompanied by his two security guards. Mustafa and Abdul lost in their own deliberations stood silently side by side gazing over the choppy water.

65

As Alex drew her motorbike into the kerb, she expected it to be her last escort duty. After meeting Tanya, matters had moved quickly. Malcolm complete with shotguns had been installed at her parents' house by the evening. Inspector Craddock had spoken to senior officers immediately after her meeting in the changing room at Scotland Yard and tomorrow Alex would be in front of the Superintendent on disciplinary charges.

Before leaving for her escort duty, Inspector Craddock had informed her she'd overstepped the line too many times and serious consequences were on the cards but wouldn't pre-empt what the Superintendent might say. Sergeant Johnson, already briefed, had given her an encouraging smile as he allocated a simple escort duty, which she had almost completed. An Ambassador wished to visit his old college at Cambridge. The elderly man was escorted safely into the building. The Embassy car pulled away; her job had been accomplished.

The police radio remained quiet and as she was a fair distance from London, she didn't expect a call to another job. A small giggle surfaced at Tanya's suggestion she should punch the Superintendent. That method wouldn't save her as she would be dismissed from the police. The trouble was self-inflicted and impacted on her friends and her family so she would have no grounds for complaint if Tanya ignored her.

Alex drifted her police motorbike through Cambridge towards the M11 to return to London. A private call buzzed through but because of the traffic she was denied the chance to glance at the screen so she ignored it. Her mind became set on what actions to take. The police would dispense with her, so the other obvious conclusion would be to disassociate herself from MI6. It might come because of the police action, but she would have preferred her relationship with Vincent on normal terms of no background between them.

The phone buzzed again. She flicked the buttons and answered. 'It's Vincent, this is urgent, don't hang up on me.'

'What is it?'

'Where are you?' She didn't like the tone of his voice, normally calm and in control. He sounded agitated and gabbled out his words. 'Are you on duty on your bike?'

'Yes, coming down the M11, returning to London.'

'Come through to your home.'

Alex shivered, why ask her to go to the house as he'd never been there. How did he know her parent's address? She had been circumspect about mentioning her family and hadn't told him where she lived, although he could easily find out. Was he there?

'What's happened?' Her pulse raced as tension gripped her.

'I'll tell you when you arrive, it might be nothing serious, but it's too much of a coincidence for my liking. Come as quickly as you can. Don't go to the house, I've stopped in a pull-in near the garden nursery.'

'I'm on my way.' Alex closed the call, flicked on the siren and blue lights, then sped at over a hundred miles an hour down the outside lane. She radioed in, 'Diplomat requested a change of route, so I am following his instructions. Will report in when I have reached the destination.' Control would monitor her. They would note that while on diplomatic duty, with no emergency, she travelled at high speed. They would query her actions, so she flicked off her radio.

Deliberately losing contact with the control centre would be another procedural failure on her behalf, but with the amount of disciplinary matters stacking up against her it would be viewed as a trivial issue. Leaving the motorway, she sped through the A roads. As the miles flew past, she focused on her driving rather than speculating about what would greet her at the end of the journey. A tremor of unease gripped her. A few miles from the nursery she left the blue lights flashing but switched off the siren. Turning onto a side lane, she spotted Vincent leaning on his car in the pull-in.

Snatching off her helmet, she rushed towards him, 'Tell me what is happening! What are you doing here?'

Vincent ignored the question, 'Do you live down the road in the white painted house set far back with the in and out drive?'

'Yes, that's my parents' house. Why are you here?'

'I have been tailing a guy. Intelligence has come through that something significant might happen today, so we picked up people on our list to follow hoping they would take us to the leaders. I'm after one guy on the list that you handed over. He's in a white van further down the lane. Others might be with him, but I couldn't get close enough without causing suspicion. I remembered you came from Essex, so I searched for your address. I drove past the van, but there are no signs of life.'

'Where is he parked?'

'There's a rickety gate that leads to a track.'

'My God! That track sweeps round to the back of my parents' house.'

'We don't know he has gone there.'

'The lane is a dead-end. He must have gone to my house. She twisted away from him. I'm going there.'

66

Mustafa quivering with fear for his daughter and wife but with no knowledge of what to do pushed back the blinds covering the front windows of the shop and stuck the paper in his hand onto the windows, 'Restaurant closed–until further notice–family illness.' Replacing the blinds, he ensured there were no small gaps. With shaking shoulders, he spun around, 'I demand to know what you are doing and where you are going.' He crashed his fist down on the nearest table.

Fatema tilted her head on one side as she sat at the usual table for folding serviettes, but today there were none in front of her. She remained calm and untroubled by her husband's shouting. 'Judging by your increased nervousness, Mustafa, I assume Abdul has passed on bad news.' Slumping into a chair, he banged his fist on the table in frustration. 'Ibrahem Khan has been thrown out of the Embassy and blames us.'

Fatema nodded, 'It is time to fetch Doha and leave.'

His eyes fiercely focused on her, 'Leave? Where to? Where are we going? This is our home.'

'We cannot mount an attack on Ibrahem, it is too difficult, and Abdul will not use his men.'

Mustafa sighed, 'No more violence, please.'

Fatema sneered, 'Matters are out of our control and Doha is in danger.'

Mustafa leaped from his chair, 'I demand you tell me what you know.'

Taking her time to reply, she crossed her arms while her expression stilled and became serious, 'I do not understand what is happening. The other night I trailed Ibrahem and his girlfriend, Shani.'

Mustafa gulped and beads of cold sweat formed on his forehead. What had she hoped to achieve by stalking them? 'Where did they go?'

'To a poor night club where they met Alex.'

He sunk into his seat, 'Alex,' apprehension tightened the muscles in his face and his voice dropped to a whisper, 'but she is protecting Doha.'

'We can trust no one, so we will take Doha and leave London.'

'Where will we go?' Unease rolled through him like a chilled dark wave and his throat contracted with emotion. Was running away the only solution?

'Birmingham.' Fatima didn't seem to notice his nervousness. Her voice remained calm and determined. 'It's the best place as we can blend in with the local population and become anonymous. We have savings to help us through a few months.' Leaving Mustafa open mouthed, she passed into the storeroom and returned with the holdall, 'I have the pistol in my bag.'

Mustafa nodded while a shadow of alarm crossed his face, 'It is a desperate situation. Is this the best solution?' Fatema ignored his words. She already had her coat on and with a hardened expression, she checked the pistol in her bag.

67

Alex's mind reeled at the possibilities. They, whoever they were, had come to get her and Doha. She leaped forward.

Vincent grabbed her arm, 'We'll use our training and confirm there is an issue before we call for support.'

She shook her head, as the situation didn't need blue flashing lights and sirens.

'Don't call for support, they are killers who will shoot whoever is inside.' Alex stripped off her leathers and threw them in the back of Vincent's car. She re-fixed her holster as Vincent checked his gun. They ran down the lane, crouching low and keeping close to the hedges. Alex held out her hand to stop Vincent, 'It's around the next bend, I'll go over the fence here and come from the field to the van.' He screwed his eyes, studying the lane. 'The lane is exposed.'

Vincent pointed, 'There's a ditch down the far side, I'll go along there under the hedgerow. Three minutes and we approach the van from both sides.' Alex nipped over the fence and tucked herself into the field side of the hedgerow. Keeping low, she skirted along the edge of the field but slowed as she approached the van tucked into the gateway. With no obvious movement from inside, gun at the ready, she nipped through between the gate post and hedge. Vincent waved and they sprinted the last few yards with guns pointed at the van. The driver's door opened at the first pull, but the van was empty.

He wasn't waiting for his friends, although they might have laid a trap after calling support, but the empty van indicated he had gone to the house. 'This field isn't visible from the house.' She jumped over the gate. Sprinting across it, they climbed the next gate, which took them into a small coppice. 'We are about a hundred metres from the house. There are stables which will shield our approach.'

Skirting the coppice, they crossed to the stables. Two horses, tied to the building, had been saddled. Had Tanya been trying to act normal and hadn't explained to Malcolm the reason for inviting him? Alex peered around the corner to the front of the house.

Vincent whispered, 'Who's in the house?'

'Dad's away. Mum's car is there so she will be in with Doha. Tanya's car and another I don't recognise, but it could be Malcolm's.'

Alex led him away from the barn, then squeezed through a hedge and sidled along the edge of the wall. They stopped at the trees. 'The kitchen is on the left, but there's movement in the lounge, it's Tanya.'

'We need a plan?' Vincent rubbed his forehead, 'but we need to know whether there is anyone in the house with your family.'

'I can see shadows moving, yes that's Tanya my sister. I'll ring her.' She drew the phone from her pocket and dialled the house number. They waited. No one answered. 'There! There!' She pointed.

A dark-clad figure moved across the lounge. 'Time to

go for support.' Vincent caught her arm.

Her stomach twisted and turned, but no better way sprang to mind, 'We don't want sirens blaring.'

'No, I agree. Let's return to the front of the house and I'll call from there.' She hated having to trust the Intelligence Services, but they were more likely to deal with the situation rather than the local police, as a mistake on their approach could be easily made. They retraced their route and stayed out of sight behind the barn.

She kept watch. As she waited a tendril of panic seized her chest and her heart thudded louder and louder. Vincent would explain the circumstances. 'Wait, the front door has opened.' A masked figure dragged Doha onto the driveway. She gasped as her mum, Tanya and Malcolm were led out with their hands tied behind their back. A black van roared into the drive. Alex froze at the horror of the scene that was being enacted before her eyes. An icy chill crept up her back. 'They will take them away.'

68

Jane was winning, she sensed it. The Brighton incident had been resolved. She relaxed with a small sigh, while no accolades for her, understandable under the circumstances, she had detected no criticism of her in the report. The blame fixed on the Sergeant and gung-ho constable. A good way out of the crisis in her department, but she had to deal with Sandy Johnson and Alex Drummond as they were too unpredictable to be in her unit.

Getting rid of Alex would remove the fascination from Vincent. He had not been true to her and the matter needed resolving. A good lover, wonderful and funny company, she wanted him. He would turn a blind eye to her other nocturnal habits if he ever found out.

Jane laughed and relaxed back in a comfortable chair in the Superintendent's office. His eyes drifted to her legs whenever he expected her not to notice. She flashed a small, tight smile; he hadn't made a play for her yet, but she had little doubt it wouldn't be long. Her plan would come together as he would move the Sergeant to another division and sack Alex. She wouldn't have a rival with Vincent and she could tag along with the Superintendent to help with her career. The world was looking good.

She frowned at the knock on the door. He called, 'Come in.'

Sergeant Johnson thrust open the door and strode in. She removed the smirk from her face too late. Johnson had noticed the relaxed attitude and curled his lip.

The Superintendent moved to the chair behind his desk, 'What is it, Johnson?'

'Several important incidents, sir.' Jane moved to the edge of her seat. 'An MI6 operative has called out anti-terrorist units to an address in Essex.' The Sergeant straightened his back. 'The address is where Alex Drummond lives.'

'Where's Alex?'

'Scheduled to return from Cambridge at the end of an escort duty.'

'Where is she?' snapped the Superintendent.

'Radio contact lost,' the Sergeant checked his watch, 'over forty-five minutes ago.'

'Tracker?'

'High speed down the motorway, now located close to her home, but not moving.'

'Jane,' the Superintendent frowned, 'Sergeant, draw arms and get yourselves there. Keep me informed, I'll advise the Anti-Terrorist group you are on your way.'

The Superintendent rose stiffly from his chair and fixed Sergeant Johnson with a stare, 'Who's with Drummond?'

He stared at the floor, 'Inspector Craddock instructed me to put her on light duty. An Ambassador requested an informal escort to visit his old college, so Alex is on her own.'

The Superintendent wiped his face, 'This could be

an embarrassing mess.' His mouth took on an unpleasant twist. 'I need you two to make sure we do not finish up with egg on our faces.'

69

Alex's stomach tensed. Her mother cried out and appeared near collapse as the van backed up to the front of the house. She agonised whether to break her cover, but Vincent's arm restrained her. Twenty metres away from the front of the house, she lay side by side with Vincent on the ground, peering around either side of a pile of timbers used for fencing. Alarm and anger rippled through her. 'Only fire if necessary,' whispered Vincent. 'Support will negotiate, but we must keep them in sight.'

Opening the back doors, the masked men pushed Doha into the van. Alex waited; her finger poised on the trigger. It would be too dangerous to shoot as she might hit a captive. Alex counted, fighting to keep control, the driver and two men at the van. Two more who covered the three tied adults with their guns. Five, all armed.

Would they leave without the captives, then she would only have to worry about Doha? But the gunmen pushed the three towards the van. The driver shouted in Arabic, 'Kill them.' Alex's mother screamed from behind the tape. The man raised his gun and took aim from ten metres.

Without hesitation, Alex fired. The bullet hit him in the head. He crumpled into a heap. The driver leaped into the van. One man dived into the open door. The other raised his gun toward Alex.

Vincent fired and Alex hit the man as he twisted to the floor. The van accelerated away in a cloud of dust with Doha on board. Alex couldn't shoot for the worry of hitting the young woman.

Alex rushed across to her mother while Vincent kept low, watching in case they returned. She caught her mother as her knees buckled, removed the gag and freed her wrist, then held her tight as she sobbed in her arms. Tanya's wide eyes were a picture of sorrow and fear while Malcom's expression held a mixture of confusion and horror.

Alex snapped, 'Help mum, Tanya. Malcolm, do you have your guns?'

'Yes, in the car,'

'Take mum and Tanya into the house. Threaten anyone who comes near.'

'What about these?' He gestured towards the two unmoving bodies on the ground.

'They are dead, leave them for support when they arrive.'

Tanya reached out and grabbed Alex by the arm, 'Please don't go.'

Alex shook her head, 'We must go after Doha.'

Vincent had disappeared down the lane. Alex sprinted after him, attempting to catch him as he neared the nursery. 'I'll call support,' shouted Vincent. She snatched her helmet and flicked the switch for radio communication. She jumped on her bike and roared down the lane.

When she reached the road, the traffic was stationary. Leaping off her bike, she ran to a lorry driver whose vehicle blocked the exit from the lane.

'Has a black van left the lane.' His eyes widened as he glanced at the gun.

'No, I've been here for fifteen minutes, the traffic is at a standstill.'

She radioed in, 'Where have you been?' The voice was sharp.

Alex ignored it, 'What has caused the local traffic problem.'

The controller repeated, 'Where have you been?'

Anger surfaced and Alex snarled, 'Answer the bloody question.'

The controller taken aback, 'Articulated lorry jack-knifed at the roundabout a mile west, the traffic is in gridlock.' She cut the call and accelerated her bike back to Vincent, who still spoke with support.

'Correction Constable Drummond is not in pursuit. I'll confirm details shortly.'

'The main road is blocked; the van definitely didn't leave the end of the lane.'

'What about the side lanes?'

'They are dead ends. A farm and three cottages. Support will struggle as the roads are gridlocked and we do not want a helicopter.'

Vincent nodded, 'We'll take the farm first.'

'I can call them as I know them well.' Alex pressed the number in her phone, 'Hi, Judy its Alex Drummond, have you noticed any strangers?' Alex shook her head to Vincent and ended the call. 'All normal, they have seen nothing suspicious and they are working with several people next to the farm buildings.'

'Okay, it must be one of the cottages.'

'Two are neighbours, the third is unoccupied. There

is a footpath parallel to the lane behind the hedge, so we won't be.' They checked their guns as they climbed the stile.

70

Why had Sandy Johnson allowed Alex free rein outside of Scotland Yard? Did the man have no sense. Light duties meant sorting out the filing system in the office where even Alex could not manage her maverick approach. Being with an MI6 operative made her suspicious and added a dimension she didn't like. She would make her views clear to all when the incident had been resolved.

Jane Craddock raced the police Jaguar through the streets of East London at a speed that terrified Sandy Johnson as he held onto the grab rails. She drove at traffic and pedestrians, assuming they would move out of her route. She screeched into the radio without taking her eyes from the road, 'Urgent update required, who raised the call for the anti-terrorist group.'

'Not known, ma'am, labelled restricted information.'

'Look out,' shouted the Sergeant.

'Bloody secret spies playing at games,' moaned Jane as she sped around a bemused pensioner standing in the middle of the road. Driving one handed, she stabbed at her phone in the hands free and jabbered meaningless phrases into the phone after it was answered.

'Control Desk, how may I help, Inspector.'

She gabbled, 'Who raised the call for the attendance of the anti-terrorist unit at Ongar?'

'Vincent Marshall.'

A pang of jealousy assailed her, 'What the bloody hell is he doing with Alex?'

71

Keeping low behind the hedge, Alex peered through a gate and pointed. 'There are the two cottages. The women from each cottage are talking as they hang out washing.'

Vincent touched her elbow and inclined his head towards a distant rooftop, 'Let's move on.'

Crouching down, they moved forward in silence. A shudder rippled through Alex and her grip on the gun tightened. What awaited them at the last cottage? Would they be able to rescue Doha unharmed? The path narrowed as the house at the end of the lane came into view.

Vincent parted a hedge to peer through, 'Perfect setting. Holding her there until a ransom is paid would be easy.'

'I'm not convinced they want a ransom.' Her voice trembled as the words left her lips.

Vincent ignored her comment, 'I'll ring support to give the location and advise them to have a helicopter ready.' He ducked behind the hedge and spoke in a low voice into his phone.

Creeping back, he dropped beside her, 'Ring your sister and tell them that a police Land Rover with an armed unit on board is coming over the fields, but with no sirens or lights.'

Taking out her phone, she pressed Tanya's number.

'Where the hell are you, Alex, we need you back here.'

'We've followed the van to their hiding place but will wait for backup before making a move to save Doha.'

'Where are you?'

'The Ramsay's old house, but I need to tell you a police vehicle will come over the fields to you.' Vincent signalled with a flick of his wrist it was time to move on, 'Love you, see you soon.'

Vincent had been peering through the bushes. 'The woods will provide good cover. They can't be anywhere else, but there is no van or cars parked outside.'

Alex inclined her head towards a large stone building set back from the cottage, 'The barn near the woods is large enough to hold vehicles.'

Acknowledging the information with a brief nod, 'Let's check.'

They crossed a field on the other side of a rise in the ground, ensuring they remained hidden from the house. Vincent climbed the fence to reach the back of the barn. Despite his size, he pulled himself up the wall to peer through a ventilation air brick positioned above head height. He silently dropped back to the ground and re-joined Alex.

'The black van is there, along with several other cars.'

The muscles in her stomach clenched nervously as she absorbed this information. 'I've been watching the house, but there is no movement.'

'My guess is they are settling in for a long stay. They would have expected us to follow them to the main road, but they may not know about the chaos. A silent message flashed through on Vincent's phone. 'The traffic is now flowing, so support will reach us. They never intended going to the main road. They will have used this house to monitor your home. Being close by reduces the risk of identification while travelling. If they kept their nerve, they would have stopped at the bottom of the lane to check no one followed.'

They took up observation positions. She covered the back of the house and the lane. Expecting a long wait for support, she settled on a tree stump, though the gun in her hand remained ready for action and all her senses were on high alert.

The purr of an expensive car engine broke the silence on the lane. Almost holding her breath, she listened with rising dismay as it came nearer and a wave of apprehension surged through her. Vincent joined her and whispered in her ear, 'This must be the leader.' A solitary man stepped from the driver's seat, scanned the area and flexed his shoulders.

Shock flew through her as she stared at him. Her eyes widened in alarm, 'It's Abdul Kadir.' Her voice trembled as she uttered his name.

'You know him?' The accusing tone of Vincent's voice sliced through her.

'I've met him,' she spluttered in response. Confusion swept through her. He was Mustafa's friend. What was he doing here? He wouldn't have kidnapped Doha.

'You never mentioned it.'

She ignored him, 'It makes little sense to me.'

'Why doesn't it.' His voice was low pitched and cold. 'He has a background of violence when he was a war lord in Egypt and has returned to his old ways and is orchestrating the new regime. But this time, it's international.'

'No.' When she'd met him, he had refused to be drawn towards a violent conclusion. 'I don't accept that.'

'Let's face it Alex, we know more than you.'

'No, you don't. I've met the man.' Vincent's face flushed with annoyance. 'Use your eyes. Abdul is on his own. He's worried, that's not the attitude of a warlord, as he always goes everywhere with bodyguards. Why would he come to a remote cottage on his own with no heavies, his presence makes little sense?' In silence they waited as Abdul took his time to approach the cottage. 'Doha the young girl they are holding is the daughter of one of Abdul's best friends.'

'Do you know his best friend?'

'Yes, it's Mustafa and the same as I know Doha.' She gave time for the information to register with Vincent. 'Doha's sister was killed in the terrorist attack with my husband.'

Vincent's eyes opened wide and he raked a hand through his hair, 'Oh Christ, this is a complicated mess.'

'Abdul would never harm Doha. Will it be a stakeout?'

'We will take time, it's the best way. The longer the siege lasts, the better chance of success and freeing the young girl. It will be a stealth operation.'

'It's the wrong approach.' Her voice cracked into a sob.

'Alex,' he patted her arm, 'we have experienced teams.'

His patronising manner brought a surge of irritation, 'I don't give a damn. Think of the attack at Brighton. Two more dead today. Can't you see they are martyrs. If they have explosives, they will wait for our team to get close and then blow the lot sky high. Why am I dealing with such amateurs?' she hissed and glared at Vincent through narrowed eyes.

Abdul Kadir made his way slowly along the path. His body posture was rigid. His knuckles white from tightly clenched fists. The door opened and he disappeared inside.

'The leader.' Vincent smirked.

'Crap, he was expected because they informed him, they had kidnapped Doha. What do we do now?'

'You're such a bloody smart arse, you tell me.' Alex scowled at the harshness in his voice. 'The best approach for the support team is via the woods and the garage.'

With a brief nod of approval, they both edged silently towards the back of the cottage but sank into the undergrowth as a door opened. A man emerged. The strap of an automatic weapon nestled on his shoulder. In an unhurried manner he lit a cigarette and dragging deeply leant against the doorframe. They lay motionless in the long grass; she did her best to ignore the wasp crawling down her face. It seemed to last an eternity. Finishing his cigarette, he flicked the remnants to the path and his eyes scanned the area before he twisted away and re-entered the house.

The closed curtains prevented them from detecting any movement inside. Using the protection of the hedge, they returned to the wood behind the barn. Vincent glanced at his phone. Another silent message must have come through. 'Support require photos, you take the back and I'll do the front.'

72

Jane concentrated on her high speed driving. The police radio blasted into life, 'All units approaching the incident at Ongar in Essex are not, repeat not, to use sirens or lights.'

'Bloody hell,' muttered Jane as she swung the car along the main road and flicked off the siren and blue lights but did not reduce her speed. 'It's a major operation, I hope Alex comes out of it okay.' A fleeting smile flashed across her lips, and she snapped into the radio, 'Status update required.'

Johnson held on tight as the speedometer topped one hundred and twenty. 'Come on, we're getting close, we need to know.' The radio controller's voice reverberated, 'Information quality low, contact has been lost due to no mobile signal. PC Drummond's radio is not responding.'

'Come on, Alex, where are you.'

'Crucial information coming through. The first Essex police arriving near the house are holding position along the track. Two dead bodies can be seen on the drive to the house. Roadblocks not yet in place.'

'Why so bloody slow?' shouted Sergeant Johnson.

The radio operator kept a calm voice, 'Heavy traffic following an accident has restricted access and movement.

Kidnap victim believed to be at a farm approximately one mile from the house involved in the initial incident.'

'We'll go to Alex's home and divert from there.' Jane headed along the lane and sped past the garden nursery, 'That's Alex's bike.'

The radio crackled into life, 'Stealth operation at the farm, repeat stealth operation do not approach.'

73

Alex slithered under the fence surrounding the property and crept to the rear to snap pictures with her phone. Her concentration stayed on the house, but it remained quiet. Vincent had set off in the opposite direction and had disappeared. With the photos taken, she sneaked back to the woods pausing every few steps to check all was quiet.

A loud groan halted her movements. Holding her breath, she crouched low and waited. Vincent staggered and his knees buckled as a man with a heavy lump of wood attacked him. Alex drew her gun as a second man jumped around the corner and pointed a gun at her. If she fired, he would as well and she'd be hit. The cold steel of another gun rested on her neck. 'Drop the gun.' Alex had no option.

Two other men, both armed and waving their guns, joined them. Then with her arms twisted in an agonizing grip up her back, they forced her and a groggy Vincent into the house. With considerable aggression they were shoved into the old dining room and forced to lie on the floor. Two men watched over them with automatic weapons. Vincent groaned. He was only semi-conscious. The men would be trigger-happy. No means of escape presented itself, so she lay motionless on the floor. Her mind whirled. How were they going to get out of this alive?

Movement and voices echoed from elsewhere in the house, but she struggled to work out what they were discussing. Although she tried focusing on Arabic and then English, the words were too indistinct. Pain shot through her as a boot kicked her in the ribs. A man tied her hands with cable ties and then moved across to Vincent who received the same treatment.

Alex's whole body trembled, and she tried to think of a way to escape, but her options were limited. Would she be killed? Fear rattled through her. In Arabic she said to the man who stood guard over them, 'Can I speak with Doha?' He didn't respond and left the room. The level of voices in the house rose but were unintelligible. Speaking with Doha would help to keep the young girl calm.

The door of the dining room flew open, Doha was catapulted in. She sobbed and squealed behind the tape that had been strapped over her mouth. Tripping over Vincent, she crashed on top of Alex. 'Doha, my darling.' The wide eyes showed terror. The door slammed shut. Her wrists remained securely bound, but by twisting round her fingers were able to grasp the tape across Doha's mouth and inch by inch she eased it away. Rolling around she faced Doha, who was pale and tearful.

'I'm so frightened, Alex.'

'We all are darling, but we must keep calm and wait for an opportunity to escape.' She had said the words but didn't believe them.

'How are you, Vincent?'

'Okay.' But his glazed and vacant eyes told a different story. He struggled into a sitting position and propped himself against the wall. The cut on his head had bled badly. Doha gasped at the blood covering his face.

'It's not bad, head wounds give a lot of blood. He's concussed and needs treatment, but we must escape first.'

74

Fatema's hand slid into her bag and she let her fingers run over the cold metal of the gun, 'When we reach the Drummonds drive slowly, we do not want to arouse suspicions. Then we leave with Doha. If anyone tries to stop us, I will show them the gun.'

Mustafa's eyes opened wide as he drove past the garden nursery.

Fatema curled her lip, 'You stay in the car with the engine running. I will grab Doha, shoot in the air and drop the tear gas.'

'Tear gas?' Mustafa's voice trembled.

'Do as I say then we will escape with her.' Fatema's fingers caressed the gun in her bag and prayed for a peaceful exit with her daughter.

Mustafa slowed the car, took a deep breath and swung it into the drive at the Drummond's home. Taken by surprise at the scene, he slammed on the brakes. A man sprinted towards their car and raised his shotgun at the windscreen. 'Get out of the car slowly.'

Mustafa lifted his hands into the air, but Fatema's hand slid into her bag as she stared at the bodies on the ground. The two police cars with armed officers fifty metres away confused the situation for her. What had happened?

'Get out or I will shoot!'

Marwa Drummond rushed across the gravel drive from the house, waving her hands in the air in an agitated manner. 'Do not shoot, Malcolm, they are Doha's parents.' She grabbed the door handle and yanked the door open, her voice hysterical as she jabbered in Arabic, 'Evil men have taken Doha, Alex shot these two and has gone after Doha and the others.'

'Let's go,' shouted Malcolm, 'Bring the guns.'

'Do not leave me,' wailed Marwa.

'We will help Alex.'

Fatema slid from the car, still clutching her precious bag to her chest, and was enveloped by a sobbing Marwa. Fear trickled like ice water through her veins as the garbled words hit her. Doha had gone. Dead bodies lay on the drive. A ball of worry and foreboding twisted in her stomach as Marwa clutched onto her in a bear like grip.

'The horses will be quickest,' Fatema raised her head as Tanya, already carrying her gun pointed towards the back of the house.

She and Malcolm sprinted to the stables. A few minutes later they galloped into the drive. A police car stopped twenty metres from Fatema, 'Put down weapons and all lay on the floor.'

'Go,' shouted Tanya. The horses raced across the gravel.

Another police car screeched into the drive. Jane Craddock and Sandy Johnson leapt from the car and pointed guns at Fatema and Mustafa. Fatema gave vent to a long, loud, hysterical wail. The first officers shouted again, 'Armed police all lay on the floor.'

The horses darted forward past the parked car and leaped the front bushes onto the verge in the lane. Sergeant Johnson rushed into the lane, but as he lifted his gun, the horses entered a track opposite and jumped the five-bar gate.

Fatema sank to her knees, opened her mouth and screamed. Where was Doha? What was happening? Her hand instinctively reached into her bag and touched the cold barrel of the gun. She would fight. She would kill to get Doha back.

75

Alex held her breath as the door slowly opened. Abdul Kadir entered the dining room and closed the door. His hands weren't tied. Squinting, he opened the curtains and light flooded into the room. He moved towards Doha, 'How are you? Have they hurt you?'

'No.' The exchange confirmed the friendship between Mustafa and Abdul. Doha had met him before. At least it would be another face she recognised. Abdul dropped to the floor next to her. Vincent coming back to consciousness struggled to his knees, attempting to edge towards him.

'Calm, Vincent. There is no danger in this room.' Abdul sneered at Vincent through narrowed eyes filled with loathing.

'I've come for Doha's sake.' Abdul's voice sounded strained, 'I've done my best to prevent this, but I've lost control.'

'Who runs this group?' snapped Vincent.

'That's been the problem from the time I've arrived in England, I don't know.'

'Have you seen the leaders?' Vincent pushed himself up onto his knees.

'No. Only the thugs.'

'Any guesses?'

'No, not that it will matter, you realise that.'

Alex nodded toward Doha, 'Don't give up on her.'

'I won't.'

Movement in the house increased. The door flew open and Ibrahem prowled into the room carrying a pistol with a hard and resentful expression.

Alex, standing near the window, gulped as he levelled a brutal and unfriendly stare in her direction. 'You!' Her quiet voice held a tremor.

Abdul dropped his head, 'I should have known the Khan family would cause these problems.'

Ibrahem waved his gun, 'You will pay for the difficulties you caused us, Alex.' His voice had a savage edge and his cold eyes seemed to stare right into her soul. 'Abdul. It's payback time.' He pointed at Doha, his lips twisted into a cynical cruel expression, 'We knew the bait would work.'

The merest hint of uncertainty flashed through Abdul's brown eyes and sweat beaded his forehead, 'We can work something out between us, Ibrahem.'

'You tried to kidnap Shani but failed, we took Doha.'

'They weren't my men; I didn't give the orders.'

'Can't control your own troops, you're losing it, Abdul.' A sneer of contempt and ridicule gathered on Ibrahem's harsh features. 'It won't matter as it will be a successful day with you and Alex dead. Then I will be in charge to run the operations my way.' Alarm and anger rippled along Alex's spine as he uttered his chilling pronouncement of imminent death.

'Well said, darling.' Shani dressed all in black stood in the doorway. Her eyes glowed with a savage inner fire as she crossed the room to Alex, Doha whimpered. 'You were so brilliant in saving me at Brighton and I hoped you would become a useful contact for us in the British Police, but why did you have to ask questions about the interlocking crescents? Once I knew you pursued that symbol, you wanted to unearth the past and we couldn't allow that to happen.'

Alex shivered, and a wave of apprehension swept through her. Had she found the people she wanted?

'Your husband was killed in the Leicester Square attack,' Shani's lips twisted into a bitter sneer, 'but that wasn't us.' Confusion at this pronouncement swept through Alex and she searched Shani's face to find out whether she was telling the truth, but her expression gave nothing away.

Ibrahem snapped, 'You're talking too much, she will have called her friends, we need to leave before they arrive. We'll think of you when we are back in Egypt. Disgraced as we are, we'll have no problem getting through the airports, the British want us out of the country.'

The unmistakable and rhythmic sound of a helicopter filled the room.

Alex let out a long breath, Vincent had said no helicopters, it must be one for Ibrahem and Shani. 'Our guys will cover us and then make their own escape.' Ibrahem waved his gun, 'Your security forces will be in for a surprise.'

'Come on, Shani, the guys will finish them.'

'Goodbye Alex,' a shadowy ironic sneer hovered on Shani's lips, 'it was good to know you.' With hands tied behind her back and being covered by guns, she remained rooted to the spot. Her breathing stalled. Her eyes remained fixed on the finger which hovered close to the trigger as Ibrahem stood by a window pointing his gun at Alex. The light shone on his slick black hair and moisture beaded his forehead. His narrowed eyes remained icy and dark. Full of evil and hatred.

The helicopter noise increased. Through the window, the swirls of dust and debris showed it had landed in the field behind the house.

'You'll never get away,' Vincent growled and pulled at his bound wrists, 'they know we are here and are coming for us.'

'But they will be too late!' snarled Ibrahem, 'and you will never be able to tell them.' Silence filled the room as Ibrahem raised his gun. Alex squeezed her eyes shut and waited. Would it be quick, or would death come slowly and painfully? She held her breath. Each second seemed like a lifetime.

76

Alex's eyes flew open as a blast blew out the window, throwing Ibrahem back across the room. Broken glass sprayed across the floor. Doha screamed. Two shots sounded from outside. Another loud blast. Alex crouched on the floor next to Doha and glanced at Vincent, who shook his head, as another shotgun blast sounded close by.

Shani dropped onto the floor near Ibrahem, who writhed in agony, blood pouring from multiple wounds. Alex saw her opportunity. She rushed at Shani before she picked up Ibrahem's gun. Doha slithered across the floor and kicked the gun further away. Crashing into Shani, Alex aimed her head at Shani's chin. She yelped in pain as the sharpness of bone dug into her scalp, Shani twisted and hit the wall with the side of her head and slithered down into a heap.

Abdul had leaped up, grabbed a knife from the writhing Ibrahem's belt and slashed through the ties as Alex turned her back. Shouts and scrambling in the corridor alerted them. Abdul positioned himself behind the door and crashed it into a gunman as he entered, then punched him hard in the gut and the gun clattered to the floor.

Vincent staggered to his feet and picked up the gun.

'Let's go!' Alex dragged Doha to her feet. On unsteady legs, Vincent led them into the hall. Another blast of the shotgun took out the hall window. Several shots sounded outside. Abdul crept to the front door and opened it. A gunman outside fired, hitting him and he crumpled into the corner. Vincent spun around and using the wall as a prop fired towards the gunman. Alex dragged Doha through to the kitchen. She opened the back door, glanced and ran with Doha, across the garden towards the woods.

Halfway across the garden, a loud piercing voice filled the air, 'Stop,' screamed Shani. Looking over her shoulder, Shani stood with a gun in her hand. No alternative presented itself, so she halted and pushed Doha behind her. Then she faced Shani, who levelled the gun towards Alex's head with her finger poised on the trigger. An evil smile stretched across her thin lips, 'I wanted to see the whites of your eyes before I killed you.' A noise behind Shani made her spin, Vincent staggered out of the house. Shani fired and Vincent crumpled into a heap.

Alex twisted around ready to run, Shani screeched, 'Stand!' She raised the gun once again towards Alex. A blast juddered through the air and blew Shani from her feet. Alex spun around; Tanya had the shotgun at her shoulder. Dragging Doha with her, she raced towards her. Shouting came as Abdul staggered out of the kitchen door. Shouts in Arabic followed him. A gunman appeared and took aim as Abdul limped across the grass. Alex took the shotgun from Tanya and in a sweeping movement blasted the gunman back into the kitchen.

Instinctively Tanya took cartridges from her pocket and handed them to Alex, who broke the gun and reloaded. Two shotgun blasts echoed from the house. Tanya shouted, 'It's Malcolm.' Alex moved across the lawn as he appeared around the side of the house, 'I think they are all dead, but we'll make sure.' The helicopter swept up into the air and twisted away.

Alex passed Doha to Tanya. Malcolm and Alex checked their shotguns had been re-loaded and crept towards the house, checking that Shani was dead on the way. Alex checked Vincent. He breathed rapidly with blood pouring from his shoulder and groaned semi-consciously. She would return and try to stem the flow of blood. Abdul slumped and gazed at Alex with vacant eyes. He held his hand over his bleeding arm.

Alex with cover from Malcolm nipped into the kitchen. The shot gun blast had killed the gunman. Systematically they covered the house. Ibrahem was dead. Two gunmen were alive, but unconscious. She removed their weapons and they dragged them to the back garden. The silence broke as a megaphone shouted, 'Armed police lay down your weapons.' She and Malcolm glanced at each other as they broke their shot guns and placed them on the floor.

The police officers pointed automatic weapons at them, 'All lay on the grass.'

'That won't be necessary.' Jane Craddock jumped from her car, 'They are Constable Drummond and Agent Vincent Marshall, but I don't know the other man.' She raised her gun at Malcolm.

'Lieutenant-Commander Grayson, Special Forces.' He added with a grin, 'Retired.'

77

Alex wended her way along the Edgware Road. The slow traffic created a smog of pollution, which she tried to clear with a shake of her head, but the heavy fumes infiltrated her breathing. Stopping to cross the road, a new restaurant caught her eye. Workmen admired a sign they had installed. Alex gulped. Mariam's–Authentic Egyptian Restaurant.

Alex caught her breath, crossed the road and pushed open the door. Two decorators nodded but carried on their conversation about football. She weaved her way through the unpacked furniture. Stopping to appraise the space, she calculated it would hold three times more diners than the Nile Restaurant.

Opening the door to the kitchen, Mustafa directed workmen installing the cookers. 'My dearest, Alex.' He enveloped her and with a kiss on each cheek stepped back while catching her hands. 'Come, come! My wife and Doha are upstairs.' He led her two steps at a time up the newly decorated hallway with its lush carpet and embossed wallpaper. 'Look, who's here.'

Fatema hugged her and began crying. 'It is a joyous occasion.' The corners of Mustafa's eyes crinkled, and he slowly shook his head. Fatema sobbed, 'I never believed this day would happen. It's God's blessing that he has spared you.'

Over Fatema's shoulder, Doha appeared in the doorway with a gentle grin. 'Doha wishes to speak with you and as it is a sunny day, sit on the balcony with her, while I prepare food.' Alex's pleas of not to bother would be dismissed, so she anticipated a good lunch with the Mohameds.

'A good name for your new restaurant.'

Mustafa nodded and a broad smile stretched across his lips, 'I anticipated you would like it.

It is larger and a better location than the Nile and I owe it all to Abdul.'

Alex wasn't surprised after seeing the friendship between him and Mustafa.

Mustafa lowered his voice, 'He never expected to come out of the troubles with his life. He is adamant he will support those who stayed loyal to him, I tried hard to insist I needed no monetary favours only his continued friendship. I owe him as he tried to save Doha's life. But he insisted and paid cash for the building and the extensive refurbishment.'

Alex, conscious that Doha waited for her, went to move away, but Mustafa caught her hand. 'Abdul wants to meet with you.'

'We have nothing in common.'

'His lips are sealed about what happened at that cottage, he would not tell me.'

'It is for the best.'

'Abdul has a lot to say to you as you saved his life. He is desperate to meet you.'

'Tell him I am grateful for the offer, but I will decline

to meet him.'

Alex gave Doha a hug, 'Come, let's chat.' The balcony, bathed in sunshine, overlooked the backyards and alleyways behind the shops of the main road. 'How are you?'

'I'm good.'

'Have you finished with the hospital?'

'Yes, they kept me for one day.' Her eyes sparkled as bright as Alex had ever seen. She had no nervousness and stretched on a reclined chair in the sunshine.

'Have you told your parents what happened? I am sure they asked.'

'I asked the doctor at the hospital for his advice.'

Alex opened her eyes wide at the maturity of the young woman.

'He said that if I felt comfortable keeping the information to myself and it didn't cause nightmares or nervousness, then I should if I wished. I have told no one apart from the police. But...'

Alex held up her hand, 'It's in the past, a bad experience for both of us, but we move on. We would not enjoy talking about it and a conversation might bring back bad memories.'

'I agree.'

Doha stared over the rooftops but gave a little shake of her head and turned with a broad smile for Alex, who was relieved she had returned to her usual self as such an experience could have been so devastating for the poor girl.

'While you are here, can we talk about my going to University? I need advice.'

Would she follow in Mariam's footsteps and develop

her undoubted language skills? 'Fire away, I'll help if I can.'

'What's the best degree?'

'It depends on what career you want afterwards.'

'After University, I shall join the police force.'

Alex froze in her chair. 'Haven't your experiences put you off?'

'No, they have confirmed it's the job I wish to do. Criminals are evil who want to disrupt the lives of normal people, so I want to stop them by joining the police. I've not told my parents for obvious reasons. Dad wants me to take a year off before I go to Uni, but I haven't made a final decision on that yet, as I want to join the police force as soon as possible.'

78

Late afternoon arrived before Alex left the Mohameds and drove to Chelmsford. A difficult task beckoned. Eventually finding a car parking space, she strolled through the hospital corridors. What words could she say? It would be a difficult conversation. Tapping on the private room door. A strong voice answered, 'Come in.'

Crossing to the bed, 'Hello Vincent, how are you?' She kissed him on the forehead. 'The bullet fractured the bone in my arm, but the surgeon said it will heal.'

'That's great news.'

'You haven't been before.' His voice held a hint of reproach and he lowered his head.

'No, I guessed it better to leave what I wanted to say until you had recovered.'

'I can take it.' He made a mock face. 'It's over between us isn't it, Alex.'

'Yes.'

'Your heart was never in the relationship, which is a pity because I have fallen in love with you.' The flamboyance and flirting had gone. He had avoided eye contact as he spoke.

Her stomach twisted. A good guy, but not for her.

'You're only saying that to make me feel rotten. It is difficult, Vincent, you are a good man and, in the past, I would have welcomed you into my life but what has happened has forced me to withdraw into my shell.'

'I can help you, but you are too harsh a character to feel rotten about dumping me.'

'That's not kind.'

'But you and I know it to be the truth.' Alex shook her head. But the words had hit home. 'It was love at first sight when I met you.'

'Don't tease, Vincent, this is hard for me.'

'It's even harder for me as I dumped my girlfriend, Jane, to go out with you.'

'Jane?' She didn't want her expectations confirmed.

'Jane Craddock. I'm sorry Alex, but it will be difficult for you at work, if you intend staying in the police.'

'I'll stay if they will have me, but I doubt it after what I have done.'

'Shall we let the future months settle and then can I call you?' Alex hesitated. 'If we haven't anyone else in our lives, could we give it a go again?'

It wasn't what Alex wanted to hear. Even though a good guy, he didn't appear to regard their relationship as easy sex and seemed to be interested in the long term.

'Please, it's no big deal. We can meet and chat in a few months and then decide once the recent stresses and strains have disappeared into the past.'

Alex lowered her head and took a deep breath, 'Not before three months.'

'It's a deal,' he caught her hand and kissed it.

79

Alex waited. In her full uniform, she stood and stared at the door. The meeting would determine her future. The door opened with a flourish by the Superintendent's secretary, 'Come in Constable Drummond.' Alex moved in front of the desk, with a dead-pan face and standing to attention, she focused straight ahead at the wall decorated with a picture of the Queen.

'Constable, I have asked Inspector Craddock and Sergeant Johnson to be with me for this meeting.' Both sat stony faced staring at Alex. 'Do you realise why you have been brought before me?'

'Yes, sir.'

'As well as the number of disciplinary matters that have occurred, we would wish to discuss your record in the police before deciding what action to take. Is that approach acceptable to you?'

'Yes, sir.'

'We have documented the number of times when you have not fulfilled your obligation to the police service and its procedures. You have been given the list before this meeting. Before we proceed, I must ask you if you wish to contest any matters on that sheet.'

'I do not, sir, and accept the statements.'

'Some are relatively minor but are still breaches of discipline; many would normally have been dealt with by your Sergeant or Inspector, but they have accumulated rapidly.' Alex tensed; the list had been endless but thorough. Apart from a few minor points, they read as a poor indictment of her behavior.

The Superintendent waited for Alex to make eye contact. The steady glare of Inspector Craddock and Sergeant Johnson rested on her. 'In an off-duty moment at the Walworth club you did not behave as I would expect an officer in my command to react. Normally an off-duty officer running away from the scene where weapons were discharged might be viewed as cowardice. And I do not use the word lightly. Take cover to escape the initial incident, but then return to assist colleagues in the investigation. I would normally suggest to an officer who ran away that a career in the police service is not for them. No one doubts your bravery in the face of life-threatening events. I can accept the need to safeguard yourself, but to leave the scene entirely is poor policing.'

Her Inspector's eyes fixed on Alex. There would be no support from her. She had taken her boyfriend from her and then dumped him. Vincent's words rang through her. 'Each time you transgress our rules and procedures there appears to be a mitigation. Despite being warned to follow the rules, later that morning on your way down the motorway you deliberately turned off your radio to take a cross country route. You could have informed control, called Essex police and kept in contact. As the call originated from a member of the Intelligence Services, we would expect compliance. Our colleagues from those services often shortcut the rules, but in the police we do not.'

Alex drew in a deep breath, ready to speak, but the Superintendent held up his hand. 'You will have your chance in a minute. To take your case for persistent breaking of the rules to a disciplinary panel would cause a lengthy investigation for the accumulation of the events, and it is our belief that the result of such a panel could not be predicted.'

Would they sack her? Hardly daring to breathe, she waited. While words rattled in her head, she had little genuine defence. 'Your Inspector has requested you are removed from her team. The Sergeant initially requested the removal but has reconsidered his position on the matter.' Jane Craddock stared at her Sergeant.

Alex waited for the conclusion which would come soon. 'You appear from your behaviour to be a maverick, determined to pursue matters in your own way.' He straightened his papers and leaned forward.

'Constable Drummond in the short time you have been in the police force you have shown outstanding bravery during incidents that many officers never meet once in their whole careers. This meeting has caused me and my senior officers a great deal of concern. This morning I arrived for work early and sat at my desk studying two pieces of paper. Do you know what they were?'

'No, sir.'

'One the list of disciplinary matters I have outlined. The other, a list of equal length of citations and recommendations for bravery and policing awards.'

'I do not wish to receive any form of acknowledgement, sir.'

The Superintendent shook his head. 'I will ask you

directly, Constable, do you wish to remain in the police force?'

Alex had no hesitation, 'Yes, sir.'

'You have so much to offer the police force so I will not accept the recommendations put to me but make my own decision. I wish you to undergo retraining. Is that acceptable to you?'

'Yes, sir.'

'I will leave these two sheets of paper on file but be warned this is your last chance.'

80

Alex couldn't believe the result of the meeting as she slumped onto a chair in the open plan office.

'Still a copper,' asked one guy as he passed.

A chorus came from the others, 'We hope so.'

'She's the one who I want at my side when we enter trouble,' added another one.

Appreciating the spontaneous show of affection, 'Yes, still a copper,' she smirked and settled in her chair to let the information sink in.

An administrative assistant strolled into the area, 'Alex, there is a man in reception who refuses to leave until you've spoken to him, but he won't divulge his name.'

'Haven't reception thrown him out?'

'No, as they are worried that he might be one of your informers, although he doesn't have the appearance of one.'

'What's he like?'

She grinned, 'Too old for me, but he is handsome and dresses like a film star.'

Perhaps a past friend of her husband, but why wouldn't he give his name. Taking the lift to reception with the assistant they entered a small room to peer through the two-way mirror.

'Do you know him?' asked the constable, 'or shall I throw him out?'

'I know him and will speak with him.'

'Looks like a dressed-up villain to me.'

Alex grinned, 'That's because he is.' Leaving the surprised constable, she made her way into the reception area, 'Abdul, here I am.'

A deep furrow tangled his brow. His eyes travelled up and down her uniform. 'A police constable's uniform, nothing unusual.'

'Are you free to walk outside, as I want to speak with you, but this place gives me the creeps.'

A grin flashed briefly across her lips. Alex led the way to the door and held it for him as his arm was still in a sling. They exited onto the Embankment. She narrowed her eyes and scanned the area, 'Aren't your guys with you?'

'I don't need them anymore.'

Alex's eyes travelled across his face searching for clues, 'Is that because you've renounced violence or have resumed the top spot again with no rivals.'

'You're a harsh woman,' he laughed. 'I'm the same as our mutual friend Mustafa, we left violence in our youth.'

'Was it your men that attacked Shani? You can answer truthfully, I am not wired up or trying to trick you.'

'No, it came as a surprise to me and still gives me concern. Ibrahem and Shani had targeted me from the old days. They must have traced Mustafa and wanted revenge, much like the times in Cairo, when Ibrahem's father was killed.'

Alex had arrived at the same worrying conclusion but couldn't be sure of Abdul. They walked to the wall overlooking the Thames. 'Why did you want to meet?'

Abdul gave a harsh chuckle, 'You saved my life and wonder why I want to meet you. I have set up Mustafa, a true friend from past days, with a fine restaurant.'

'The restaurant is perfect, I visited there yesterday.'

'I'm a rich man so name your reward and it shall be yours.'

'Abdul, I'm a rich woman.'

He laughed. 'You English have such a wonderful sense of humour. You are a lowly police constable, albeit a very brave one, and I earn more in a week than you do in a year so you cannot be rich by my standards.'

'I do not joke. I come from a rich family and my former husband, a successful film star, left me a fortune when he died.' Abdul received the information with a raising of his bushy eyebrows but made no comment.

They meandered further; the pleasure craft drifted on the Thames.

Abdul kept glancing at her. 'Why work as a lowly constable?'

'It is my wish.'

'In that case, as I cannot give you anything, will you give my family the honour of visiting us in Egypt?' The invitation hadn't been expected. Alex would have to decide. 'I can understand why you hesitate but do any checks on me you like both in this country and in Egypt. You will find many dubious activities in my youth which will give you displeasure, but nothing apart from being a reputable businessman for the past thirty years.' A small ferry full of tourists meandered up the Thames. 'To encourage you further, I will invite Mustafa, Fatema and Doha. And may I assure you my opinion of you hasn't changed since we first met?'

'What opinion?'

'I still believe that if I did anything wrong to you or your friends, you would have no hesitation in killing me. After the experience we shared, my view is confirmed. I will never cross you purely for my safety.'

Alex chuckled at his words, 'Thank you, Abdul, I will accept your invitation, but now I must return to my duties.'

'I will be in touch, Alex,' his tight expression relaxed as he left.

She strolled back along the embankment. The interlocking crescents still focused her, although the tantalising private tattoo of Shani had turned out to be a temporary transfer that had been removed before her death. A trip to Egypt to meet Abdul could be combined with more investigation into the death of her husband and Mariam. Perhaps when she was better acquainted with Abdul, he might explain about the significance of the interlocking crescents and why he was so reluctant to discuss them.

81

'Would you like an ice cream, constable.'

Alex spun round, 'Tanya, my darling.' They hugged. Tanya stepped back and gulped, holding out her hands.

Alex caught them, 'What is it?'

'It's when I see you in full uniform.' Tanya shuddered.

'Come on, you promised me an ice cream.'

'Are you allowed to eat them in uniform?'

'We are.'

She stopped to have her picture taken by Japanese tourists. The warm overcast sky made the uniform uncomfortable, but Alex wouldn't complain.

She caught Tanya's hand. 'How are you coping, sis?' A shiver from Tanya ran through her hand. 'We could not get together as you've taken care of mum.'

'And you've been involved in the debrief or whatever it's called. Life will never be the same.'

She stroked her sister's hand, 'Life moves on, many events happen that are unpleasant and unwelcome but we can't dwell on the past. Magnum choc ice for me.'

The vendor broke into an open and friendly smile, 'No charge for a police officer.'

Tanya grinned tolerantly and paid for hers. They

found a place on the grass by the mime artists in front of the London Eye. Alex understood her sister; she wouldn't be able to let go of the terrifying events. Tanya had been there to listen when she needed her. It was her turn. 'We are here together, no one else, talk to me.'

Tanya furiously licked her ice cream, 'It might melt.' Alex waited. 'Can I ask you a question?'

'Tanya, darling, don't go there, wherever it is, I can tell.'

'No, I need to be clear.' Alex didn't want her to continue, but Tanya had decided so she had no option. 'I won't shy away from it.'

'Trauma counselling helps many in the police.'

Tanya licked her ice cream, 'You don't expect me to see a bunch of looney doctors, do you?' She grinned at Alex with ice cream spread over her lips.

'No, I don't.'

'Stop being so damned evasive and answer my question.'

Alex nudged Tanya, 'You're going dippy, you haven't asked me a question.'

Tanya gripped Alex's hand, crushing her ice cream. 'How many people have you killed?'

'Tanya?' her eyes pleaded with her sister. 'I keep my operational duties from you, mum and dad because it causes distress.'

Tanya turned, 'That bloody ice cream is going over your head, posh uniform or not, unless you answer the question.'

'Two in the shootout. It's not a figure I ever want to increase.'

'What about the rapist in the park?'

'That was self-defence.' Tanya's eyes told Alex she hadn't been believed. She finished licking her ice cream and gave it to Alex. She didn't like the wafer, and since they had been kids, she'd always handed it to her.

'Christ, you are so bloody annoying.'

'What have I done now?' Alex smoothed her uniform.

'It's your fault, I can't think of the right question to ask.'

'Calm yourself, sis. It's better you ask, but you might not like the answer.'

'Little sisters are so bloody annoying.' She gripped Alex's hand. 'I've got it.'

'The question?'

'Yes.'

She shivered, Tanya's face indicated the one question she wouldn't want to answer.

'All right sis.'

Tanya nodded, 'Bloody memories are frightening.'

She soothed the back of her hand, 'Question?' raising her eyebrows.

'Remember, I've been there and saw it unfold.'

'It's not…'

Tanya held up her hand with an expression of superiority, 'How many would you have killed if you had the opportunity.' Alex moved her shoulders. 'No, Alex. You did the same as a kid and then you lied or let your vivid imagination run away with you. How many? Tell me.'

'No clear shot in most cases or the opportunity. Four in Brighton but they were firing near the innocent public.'

'Tell me about the cottage.'

'That's easy.'

'Is it?' Tanya's eyes opened wide.

'Yes, Vincent and I were there but didn't intend attacking for obvious reasons. Once the chaos broke out, I would have killed anyone who pointed a gun at me or an innocent person.'

'If you had the opportunity, you would have killed them all.'

'If they didn't surrender and attacked, yes, all of them.'

'Including Shani?'

'Yes.'

Tanya didn't reply and glanced away, cocking her head on one side, observing a mime artist. Alex waited. The silence carried on as Tanya's head responded to the artist. Alex did not understand what passed through her mind. The artist finished his performance, Tanya clapped. She didn't take her eyes from her sister as she walked forward to pop a pound coin in the bowl.

Tanya dropped back down to the grass, and Alex caught her hand, 'Talk to me, sis.'

'For the first time I can see why you do your job, I hate it, but from now on I can understand. I'll do my best to get mum and dad to accept it.' She became lost for words and hugged Tanya. They broke their grasp on each other. 'Killing someone and living with it is difficult, but I'll cope. Strange I should say this, but because the police is now your chosen career, I hope they haven't kicked you out.'

'No, only retrained.'

'Does that come as a surprise.'

'Yes, I expected dismissal, but my Sergeant and the Superintendent wanted me to stay.'

'What about Inspector Craddock?'

'She recommended I was sacked.' Tanya burst out

laughing. 'What's so funny, it was a serious disciplinary meeting.'

'Men wanting you to stay and the woman wants you out, doesn't that tell you anything?'

'I've hardly met the Superintendent.'

'But he knows all about you, what about the Sergeant? You don't have to answer your face tells all.' She gave her sister a playful shove.

'An evening out would be good.'

'I'm on enforced recovery leave but I need to change, I can't see a night out on the town dressed like this would be in favour with the seniors.'

Tanya giggled, she relaxed.

'Malcolm will be here soon.'

She didn't want to ask after Tanya's initial comments about him but had to find out. 'How's life with him?'

'He's brilliant, what a man!'

She caught her sister by the shoulder and grinned, 'What did you just say? If I remember correctly, you dreaded going to bed with him.' A pang of unease surfaced as Vincent's face flashed through her mind. Tanya's relaxing and smiling face provided relief to Alex.

'Whenever I'd met him before at the pentathlon events, he seemed cold and aloof, but I've discovered that he gives that impression because he's nervous. He's a brilliant lover, the best I've ever had.'

Alex raised her eyebrows and giggled, 'Tell me more!'

'Definitely not.' Her expression stalled and grew serious.

'What is it?'

'That ghastly day keeps coming back.' She caught her hand. Tears welled up in Tanya's eyes, but she blinked them away as they headed towards the Golden Jubilee Bridge. 'Mum loves him to bits, dad has had several rounds of golf with him and I've spent many long hours talking to Malcolm. Having come face to face with the evil you have been chasing, I can understand what drives you. I don't like it but can accept it.'

'Here comes Malcolm.'

With unabashed enthusiasm he enveloped Tanya in a hug, 'Hello, darling.' The joy spread over Tanya's face.

She'd only briefly met Malcolm occasionally but there had been other people present. He stepped back, 'Hello, Alex.' His nervousness gave him a serious expression.

Alex stepped forward, hugged him and kissed him on the cheek. 'Hello, Malcolm. Will you walk me back to Scotland Yard?'

They crossed the bridge with the London Eye inching its way on its circular route. Tanya and Malcolm chatted, but she stayed quiet. Her desire to stay in the police force had been granted. The meeting with Abdul jumped into her mind. She rolled her shoulders as they arrived at the entrance to Scotland Yard.

Tanya caught her hand, 'You're serious, sis, what's the matter?'

'If I ask you a question, will you think before you answer?'

'Yes, okay.'

'Abdul Kadir has invited me to spend time with his family in Egypt.' Tanya stared at her. 'Will you and Malcolm come with me?'

Her sharp eyes focused on Alex's face. 'Why would you want to visit a country...' Her voice tailed away? 'You haven't given up your mission, have you?'

'No, I never will.'

THE END

Enjoy this book? Please leave an honest review.

You can make a big difference to my writing and stories. Honest reviews are the most powerful tools in my arsenal for attracting attention to my books. If you've enjoyed this book, I would be very grateful if you could spend a few minutes leaving a review (it can be as short as you like) on the book's Amazon page.

Receive my monthly newsletter containing information about future publications and a few anecdotal comments about the writing process.

No spam from me guaranteed.

Free e-Books
Visit the website for free e-books.
Web address: www.tmgoble.com
Follow me on Facebook.

Please feel free to contact me: theauthor@tmgoble.com

My Fiction Books
Alexandra Drummond Thriller Series

Alexandra Drummond's blissful life is ripped apart on a deadly night in Leicester Square. The gunmen killed two. Escape came under the cover of smoke bombs and panic. She battles the nightmares of the devastating evening. Watching and waiting, she expects arrests, but they never come. The future looks bleak. Peace will never be hers. Above all, she craves justice. She must have closure to salvage her life.

Book One – Retribution (326 pages)
Book Two – Coercion (306 pages)
Book Three – Pursuit (256 pages)
Book Four – Vengeance (307 pages)

The Reluctant Detective Series

Josh Anderson is reluctant to return to Blackford, the town of his youth, after his promotion to Detective Sergeant. The new post is a surprise as he doubts whether his appointment is justified. On several cases, luck was in his favour, but that is not a policing policy for promotion. Expectations are thrust on him in his new role, but will he be able to succeed? His confidence sags at the thought.

Book One – Gambling to Kill (295 pages)
Book Two – Rocky Death (333 pages)
Book Three – Threats of Death (332 pages)

The Sheaf Psychological Collection

Lies, fear and the unjust intensify lives and lead to chilling issues. Decisions must be made, but if they are wrong or incomplete, the desperation will nag at their minds. The first hints of unsettled lives appear. The cracks become wider. Who will draw the short straw?

A sheaf is a collection of harvested straws. The River Sheaf gives its name to the industrial city of Sheffield, which is the location for these standalone thrillers.

Fake (308 pages)
Guilty (354 pages)
Captive (479 pages)

The Braxton Collection

Envy, bewilderment and anger enter the lives of some Braxton women. The high hills market town in northern England has had varying fortunes over the years. Some women arrive seeking hope while others leave. Finding their piece of solace may come after the striving or reality may impinge and set its own outcome of love, marriage and friends.

Forever Friends (359 pages)
Picking up the Pieces (370 pages)
Past Glories (383 pages)
Chasing a Star (305 pages)

Historical Fiction Collection - Before they were famous

Fictional accounts of real people in history. Their trials and tribulations as they attempt to establish themselves in worlds of poverty and danger. Against the odds they must rise above mediocracy to climb the ladder of acclaim.

Ben - Words for the King (254 pages)
Anna - Seeking Betrothal (320 pages)
Niccolo - Power and Glory (310 pages)

Countryside Moods Collection
Seasonal Recipes

(All books are in full colour and approximately 120 pages)

Two great interests of mine are walking and cooking. So why not combine the two? I live and walk in the Peak District National Park in the United Kingdom. The fresh country air in the hills builds an appetite. I have put together my homemade recipes that are my favourites at the different times of the year along with the photos of the countryside that inspired them. The books are seasonal so you would expect Spring, Summer, Autumn and Winter but at any time of year the grey gloom can descend, so I have added a book for Grey.

Book One - Spring
Book Two - Summer
Book Three - Autumn
Book Four - Winter
Book Five - Grey

Heritage Literature
Peak District Writing
(All books are in full colour and approximately 100 pages)

For availability, please check the website www. tmgoble.com

Series Description
With a love of walking and reading, the Peak District in England appealed to me as I discovered references to famous books which set me exploring. My fascination was piqued when I made several discoveries of well-known

authors. I plotted them on a map. Gradually a pattern emerged as I focused on the oldest books through to the mid-twentieth century. Then came a walk to join them together. The result is 130 authors, spread over fourteen books with walks for each book. Each novel or non-fiction work is accompanied by the background to the author.

Book One - Rural Bliss
Ellastone, Snelston, Mayfield
George Eliot, Jean Jacques Rousseau
 Book Two - Poor Writers
Ashbourne
Alexandre Dumas, Samuel Johnson, Catherine Booth

Book Three - Happy Valley
Ilam & Dovedale
William Congreve, Samuel Johnson, Isaak Walton

Book Four - Down Under
White Peak Villages
Daniel Defoe - D H Lawrence

Book Five - Caves and Time
Matlock Bath and Dethick
Nathaniel Hawthorne, Mary Shelley, Alison Uttley

Book Six - Boys and Water
Darley Dale & Villages
Robert Louis Stevenson, Richmal Crompton

Book Seven - Elope
Haddon Hall

John Manners, Ann Radcliffe

Book Eight - Satanic Mills
Bakewell & Monsal Dale
Jane Austen, John Ruskin

Book Nine - Families
Chatsworth & Baslow
William Wordsworth, John F Kennedy

Book Ten - Pursuing a Sage
Millthorpe
E M Forster, George Bernard Shaw

Book Eleven - The Plague
Stoney Middleton & Eyam
Mary Howitt, Anna Seward

Book Twelve - Heroes
Hathersage & the Derwent Valley
Charlotte Bronte, Sir Walter Scott

Book Thirteen - Love in Hell
Castleton
Lord Byron, Ben Jonson

Book Fourteen - Wild Moors
Mam Tor & Kinderscout
Conan Doyle, Agatha Christie

Printed in Great Britain
by Amazon